In The Shadow of a Broken Spire

Also by Edward J. Flora

Ropes in the Attic

The Triangle Forest

In The Shadow of a Broken Spire

Praise for 'In The Shadow of a Broken Spire'

"Flora gives hometown pride a hellish spin with In The Shadow Of A Broken Spire, a demonic double helix of Thomas Olde Heuvelt's Hex and Stephen King's Salem's Lot. They always say you can never go home again, and with Broken Spire, well, you may never want to..."

— Clay McLeod Chapman, author of Wake Up and Open Your Eyes

"In *In the Shadow of a Broken Spire*, a brutal murder, a witchy urban legend, and an eclipse combine to plunge the small town of Blair into a fear-fueled Fall Fest for the ages. Attend at your own risk and, whatever you do, avoid blood pacts and making friends with ominous, all-knowing goats."-

— Angela Sylvaine, Bram Stoker nominated author of Frost Bite

"Did you wish *Stranger Things* took a more folk horror turn? If so, check out *In The Shadow of a Broken Spire*. Flora does exciting small town big cast horror in the vein of early Stephen King. There's nostalgia, there's teenage joy, and there's so much darkness...but also, goats! Don't miss this one!"

— Corey Farrenkopf, author of Living in Cemeteries and Haunted Ecologies

"In the Shadow of a Broken Spire is a modern day *Salem's Lot,* a blood-soaked ride into darkness that goes straight for the throat and doesn't let go."

— Vaughn A. Jackson, author of *Southern Cross*

In The Shadow of a Broken Spire

Edward J. Flora

Cover design by Alejandro Colucci

ISBN: 978-1-7327414-8-5 (trade paperback)

First edition, 2025

Gravesend Books / gravesendbooks.com

*Remembering
Carol Pierce Filmanski*

In the Shadow of a Broken Spire

Edward J. Flora

Chapter 1
Blair, New York, 1793

It was the sight of the flower that made Nathaniel Fischer believe he could protect his home from the mysterious disease known as consumption.

The northern village of Blair, New York, sat isolated, away from the horrors taking place over in New England. However, it was only a matter of time before the stories began to trickle in from across Lake Champlain. Accounts of sickness, death, and what took place after. The way Nathaniel's neighbors in New England treated their dead. The rituals, the cleansings. It filled him with fear and repulsion. It was unlike anything he or his neighbors had ever heard of. The fevers that plagued neighboring settlements seemed to have been conjured up from Hell. A prolonged, unbreakable cough progressed until the ill-stricken began to spit up blood. People losing their appetite, losing weight and withering away, almost as if an outside force, or entity, were draining them of all nourishment, of their very souls.

The separation between Blair and this novel sickness was shrinking. Eventually, consumption would spread to their own doorsteps, bringing death and misery.

That could not happen. Nathaniel could not bear to see his neighbors, his family, fall ill. He knew that having to bury his wife or children was a pain he could not endure.

And so, Nathaniel Fischer became obsessed with finding a way to protect his village. He vowed to assure Blair would remain safe—he would keep it safe by any means necessary. It nested in his mind like an unscratchable itch. It continued to burn, even when he was engaged in unsavory behaviors—while he spent evenings with a woman who was not his wife. A stranger, in fact. The woman who lived on the outskirts of the village was an outsider to Blair, not yet a part of the community. And yet, Nathaniel was drawn to her.

Her name was Grace, and that was all most of the village knew about her. Nathaniel, however, was learning her well.

He understood that Grace had come from someplace far away. He learned she was a specialist in the field of botany and natural medicine, bringing with her this new type of flower. He also learned her touch as he felt her fingers clawing at the flesh of his back.

His hands slipped as he gripped her wrists, pressing them into the wrinkled sheets as they both moved. The last glimpse of sunlight faded, darkening the single room of her isolated cabin.

Grace closed her eyes tight, her breathing intensifying as Nathaniel's grip on her wrists tightened. Wisps of air grazed Nathaniel's ear; a tingle rolled down his spine. Shame masquerading as pleasure.

All the while, Nathaniel stared ahead, focused on one thing. The flower on her mantel.

This plant, not native to the northeastern corridor of New York, caught his eye when Grace first arrived in Blair. It sat casually on her mantel, as if it were a common sight, its stem erecting out of the vase and splitting off into branches. A smooth purple flower, so dark it was almost black, marked the edge of the stem. Its petals shimmered in the twilight, unlike anything Nathaniel had ever seen before. He was captivated by it, and the closer he got to this woman, the closer he got to the flower. He needed to know more about it, about her. Desperately needed a way to protect his home.

A final warm breath hit Nathaniel's face, and he rolled over, wiping his brow. He stood from the too-small bed and uttered, "I have to go."

Grace sat up in bed, covering herself with the sheets. She watched Nathaniel get dressed without taking his eyes off of the mantel. The look in his eyes frightened her. This hungry passion of wanting. It was the look he'd given her when she first arrived in Blair. It was the look she was afraid to say no to. Especially to a man like Nathaniel Fischer, a member of the recently established House of Representatives. His influence was wide-reaching. If he spoke, people listened.

"Tell me why you come here," Grace breathed. She held the sheet close to her body, as if it would protect her.

Nathaniel turned, locked eyes with her for what felt like the first time. "What is this flower?" he asked. "I have to know."

Grace sighed. "It is called the Devil's Spiral. It belongs to the nightshade family of flowers and is also known as thornapple or jimsonweed. It gets its name from its twisting shape and its dark shade of purple."

"It really is beautiful," Nathaniel said, approaching it.

"Careful," she said. "It's very delicate. And very rare."

When Nathaniel turned around, she felt dread in her heart. She knew the conclusions people conjured up about women like her. What they *did* to women like her. A woman's place was as a family's matriarch, subordinate to her husband. But Grace sought out knowledge about science and medicine. Her fear grew as he approached, but her instinct to protect the flower exceeded it by the smallest margin.

"Rare," he said. "You have a garden in your yard, no?"

"I do, but this flower is special," she said. "An original. It is native to my homeland and has not yet acclimated to this climate."

"Where are you from?"

Grace only looked at him. Her red hair was as vibrant and mysterious as the sky during sunset.

"Not important," Nathaniel said. "Tell me then, why is this flower so special?"

"It is said that the Devil's Spiral has healing properties. If used correctly, I believe it has the ability to ward off the harshest of disease. Additionally, it has numbing properties, for minor ailments such as toothaches."

"Fascinating," Nathaniel said as he inched closer to the flower. He reached out to graze its petals when—

"Please," Grace said, almost a whisper. "Please...it's very delicate."

"Why are you so insistent? I want to try it." Nathaniel looked out the window. The view of the Winooski River was beautiful. He could see Halfmoon Cave in the distance, a patch of plotted dirt leading up the embankment. He had seen Grace planting more of this "rare" flower. There was certainly more.

"If you don't let me touch its beauty, I will expose you for who you really are. A witch. A whore."

She gasped at this. "Calling me a whore when you're the one with a wife and family?"

"Don't," Nathaniel said. "Don't have me correct you. I will have you burned." He turned back toward the flower. "I must try it."

"Are you ill?"

"No," he said. "But I need to see for myself. I need to feel it."

"I don't think that's advisable. I am still learning this plant. I don't know what effect it might have on a healthy person—its effects on the sick have been questionable, even frightening. I saw one person seize up, shake so badly you'd swear they were possessed. I am not a doctor, and I believe this flower should only be consumed under the supervision of one. Besides, Mr. Fischer, you have a family at home. What if something were to happen to you? Please, think about them."

"Do you want me to tell the town that you are practicing witchcraft?" Nathaniel spat. "I said I want you to show me what this plant can do. I *need* to know. It's only a matter of time before consumption spreads to our town. I must be able to protect Blair from the pain and suffering of the virus. Either you help me and be remembered as a hero or stand against me and be remembered as a witch—someone who allowed evil into our small community. The choice is yours."

Chapter 2
Stuart Reinhart

They had been so bad to that boy.

This notion lingered like a black cloud in Stuart Reinhart's mind. One of his students had gone missing, and it was haunting his every step.

Martin Welch was one of the brightest seniors in his Gothic Literature class, and Stu desperately hoped the boy would turn up unharmed. But it had been nearly two days. While there was no reason to think he couldn't still be found, it felt like the window of opportunity was closing.

The Blair High School senior class of 2024 were finalizing their college applications. Stu recalled that Martin was planning to apply to the earth science program at Johns Hopkins University in Baltimore, close to eight hours south of where they lived in Blair, New York.

If only he could have gotten away from this place.

Martin was fascinated by what made the natural world function, a quality Stu was impressed by. The student wanted a deeper understanding of the phenomena of our existence—his own existence—the improbability of which was a beautifully terrifying gift. The idea that Martin may have lost that singular gift was tragic.

He couldn't stop thinking about how hard junior year had been for Martin. It all seemed to start when a boy by the name of Tomas Fischer moved to Blair—or at least, moved *back* to Blair, as the story went. As a new student, Tomas had a chip on his shoulder, meaning to assert his dominance on all who crossed his path.

They had been so bad to him.

The image was burned into Stu's memory: Martin on the stage of the school's theater, head down, covered in garbage that had been dumped on him from above, like Carrie White at prom.

The regret of not doing more to stop it chased Stu on his early morning run. It was a morning ritual for he and his German shepherd, Paula, to traverse the streets of Blair just before sunrise. They took Holy Cross Road (aptly named after the town church), which stretched from Mr. Reinhart's home before merging onto Colchester Point Road, and passed by Owl's Head Park on the west end of town before looping back home. The pair had run this path routinely for the last six years, since Paula was a puppy. Not once had the well-trained German shepherd ever veered off course—not until this brisk September morning. It was the same morning Johns Hopkins had set as their application deadline. Time was up.

Paula took off, barking and darting into a patch of trees that lined Owl's Head Park. Stu chased after her but stopped short after the dog bore down on her defenses. She was barking anxiously and juking from side to side, as if trying to alert Stu to impending danger.

He knelt down next to her. "What is it, girl?" She continued to bark at the baseball field at the far end of the park.

The morning fog had yet to lift as Stu slowly approached the gloomy wall of trees that surrounded the edge of the baseball diamond. He felt his Under Armour cling to his body as cold sweat dripped down his back—not a result of his jogging, but of the creeping unease he felt in his gut. It was like the mist hovering over the trees:

gray and oppressive, weighing Stu down. It felt as if his body were about to confirm his worst fear about Martin Welch. Because sooner or later, the good times had to end. They always did. Fleeting and fragile, like a bubble in the moments before it pops and disappears forever. No more neighborly hellos, no more pleasantries. It felt as if he were staring directly into the downward spiral of the small town's doom.

Stu could feel the damp twigs bending under his running sneakers as he approached the crest of trees. He ordered Paula to stay as he proceeded to investigate; he could hear her panting nervously as he approached. Something dreadful bubbled up in his stomach, and for a moment he thought he should just turn back. He could take Paula and the two of them would go home, have breakfast, and start their day. They could leave uncovering the inevitable to some other poor soul. The thought lingered, even as his feet took him closer. Then he saw it.

Chemistry is cool!

The world began to spin as Stu caught a glimpse of the colorful *Chemistry is cool!* patch on the mangled backpack. The same patch that had made the boy a target for bullies prior to his untimely death.

They had been so bad to him.

Stu gagged at the horrific sight. The undulating tone ringing out in his ears drowned out Paula's barking as his mind began to register what he was looking at. The manner in which the body was lying, facedown in the foliage, a mangled, bloodied mess. Even those who feared the worst had not fathomed *this*. He could see Martin's backpack, torn to shreds, spilling its contents onto the ground. Dried blood and loose dirt smattered the boy's clothes and skin. There had been a struggle. A quick and violent one, Stu could only assume, and he felt his stomach drop.

He began to see spots, his vision blurring. As he fumbled for his phone to dial 911, he saw Martin Welch in English class. Blurry memories of the boy eagerly raising his hand, participating with enthusiasm. The place the boy had thrived the most—and then the image of...

Head down, covered in trash and holding back tears. If he cried, it would be worse.

If only he could get away from this place.

The police arrived shortly after, and then Stu broke down. He did his best to explain what happened through his own tears for the tragic death of one of his students. The boy had an infinitely bright future ahead of him...all he had to do was make it out of Blair High School.

Then the poor boy's parents entered his mind, and Stuart became sick.

The humming sound of a single school bus driving past the scene was barely audible in the growing commotion near Owl's Head Park. On its way to pick up the students of BHS, unknowing what the day was going to bring them. Unknowing that the good times had come to an end. Stuart wondered how he could possibly face his colleagues, the student body. He questioned if he had the strength to explain that one of their own had been murdered, and that all hope was gone.

* * *

Despite the urge to stay home, Stu got himself ready. Hand shaking, he took an electric shaver to his face, running it up and down the contour of his chin. His shuddering breath fogged up his bathroom mirror.

It would have made sense to stay home, take a sick day, curl into a ball on his couch with Paula and mourn. But what happened to Martin didn't make sense. The way the boy's body had been ripped apart and left in the dirt like a piece of trash. Who could do such—

"Shit." Stu flinched, grabbing his throat. He had nicked himself with his shaver, a droplet of blood forming over the cut. He grew agitated. He needed to get out of the house, get away from the deafening silence of his own thoughts.

He cleaned himself up, threw on a pair of dark-wash jeans and a blazer that covered his wrinkled button-down shirt. His black hair was messy, hints of gray edging its way around his sideburns, covering the arms of his black-rimmed glasses. Stu had convinced himself he needed routine but couldn't help feeling like routine was ending here. In the mirror he looked disheveled, but it was nothing compared to how he felt. Stu always joked that the school needed him, how he brought some much needed culture and awareness to BHS. But the reality was, he needed them. He needed to be around people, around anyone who would allow him to cling to normal for just a little while longer. Because he knew deep down that normal was ending. Everything after this would be unprecedented.

Stu's greatest passion in life was teaching English Literature at Blair High School. He adored the classics, from Mary Shelley's *Frankenstein* to Bram Stoker's *Dracula*, two essentials which the school board had no qualms including in the curriculum. Then there were the works of H.P. Lovecraft, whom Stuart found particularly fascinating despite the author's gross bigotry. However, the works were so unique and engrossing, Stuart felt they were the perfect subjects to dissect. He felt he would be depriving the class of important discussion if he didn't include, at the very least, a reading of *The Call of Cthulhu* and *At the Mountains of Madness*. Then there was the bibliography of the great Edgar Allan Poe, the only American writer with a flawless body of work, at least in Stu's opinion.

The discussions that blossomed from these classic works gave Stu something to look forward to, particularly the opinions some of his students held regarding these all-time greats. Some of his students genuinely impressed him with their keen insights. Some, however, found the "old-timey" writing hard to digest. Even Stephen King fell into this category. There was a disconnect between the new generation of horror readers and King's style, which could include a hundred pages of character backstory before the action got going. While it was a subjective opinion, Stu thought it was sacrilege. Each school year, the number of students who fell into this category seemed to multiply. The preference for more modern takes on the genre increased, their books overflowing with beautifully written gore. Stu was torn on this. At least his students were reading, and that was the most important thing.

Some didn't even care to read, which was the most heartbreaking revelation. It was true, the paperback was old news, and this generation was much more likely to watch a movie or TV show than pick up a novel. Sometimes, even sitting through a feature film was too tall a task. The most palatable scares these days came packaged in short-form viral videos with a jump scare at the end.

However, it was these curious minds, spawning engaging conversations no matter the form of media, that moved Stu toward school this morning. Students like Martin were bright and eager to absorb information, to have a dialogue. That was why Stu showed up. The students deserved to know that he had their back. He needed to be there for them, as did every other member of the faculty.

Stu knew it was going to be a hard day. The foreseeable future was going to be difficult. The student body would soon be hit with a bombshell. But if they stuck together, they would pull through and become closer as a result of this tragedy. At least, he hoped they would.

Chapter 3
Jaycie Brogdon

Chatter filled the air as the students of Blair High School filed into the cafeteria, as was routine every morning before homeroom. Jaycie Brogdon hauled her books to a table in the back right corner. The air smelled like fresh toast, fried potatoes, and coffee. Masking it all, however, was the oppressive aroma of maple syrup, which several students made sure to douse their entire breakfasts in no matter what was on the menu.

Jaycie put her books down and took her usual seat. Her friends had arrived before her and already picked up their breakfast. Rose, who was working on a breakfast burrito, smiled in her offhanded way as Jaycie sat down. Her layered blonde hair reached her shoulders. Rose had what they endearingly referred to as "resting bitch face," so Jaycie returned the expression.

Mabel had a paper cup with black coffee (her breakfast of choice) in one hand. In her other hand was a menu highlighting the day's lunch specials. When Jaycie turned to her, her smile softened.

"Buffalo chicken wraps and pizza burritos," Mabel read unenthusiastically. "If you can roll a food into a cylinder, this school will put it on the menu."

Jaycie laughed faintly. She always enjoyed when Mabel aimed her dry humor at the school's food offerings, but today there wasn't much humor behind her laugh.

Mabel lowered the menu. "How are you holding up?"

The truth was, something felt wrong. Jaycie had a strong intuition that something bad was going to happen...or *had* happened. The girls knew Jaycie was worried about Martin Welch, who had been missing for almost two days, but this morning the worry was drawn soundly on her face. Jaycie knew she wouldn't be able to eat anything for breakfast this morning; her stomach couldn't handle it. She felt a presence, as if a black cloud had sucked itself down in size to fit into the cafeteria and dominate the goings-on of a typical high school morning. She felt better knowing her friends cared about how she felt, and being around Mabel never failed to lift her spirits.

Jaycie exhaled and slouched forward. "I'm worried something happened to Martin; this is so unlike him. On top of that..." She resigned her brown paper lunch bag into the middle of the table. It was heavily crumpled and even torn in a few places. "I was attempting to defend my lunch's honor, but Hector got away with my tuna sandwich. He said he needed it *for more important things*, but at least I have my apple," she said sarcastically, turning the bag upside down and letting the lone apple roll onto the table. "I hate him."

"He's an asshole," Mabel said, and she took a sip of her coffee. "You can use my lunch credit today if you're hungry. I don't think the *pizza burrito* will be that appetizing to me."

"And I wouldn't worry about Martin," Rose added. "I'm sure he's fine. This is Blair we're talking about; nothing ever happens here."

Jaycie disregarded Rose's attempt to lighten the situation and smiled at Mabel instead. "Thanks, girl, but I don't think I'm going to have much of an appetite today either."

"Attention students and faculty: Today's morning homeroom will be canceled. Instead, please go to the gymnasium for a school assembly. Once again, today's morning homeroom is canceled. Please report to the gymnasium for an important school-wide meeting. Thank you."

The announcement hit Jaycie's ears like a jolt from an electrical outlet. The more she thought about Martin, the more every little thing seemed to indicate trouble. She looked at her friends across the table, and they both seemed unfazed. Was she the only one with a bad feeling? Was she overthinking?

Several students followed the cue from the loudspeaker and began to file out of the cafeteria early. But the girls remained seated. Mabel took another sip of her coffee and then leaned forward.

"Did you hear about the party at the Fischer House this weekend?" she said discreetly. "We should all go. We're graduating this year, and *you* haven't been to a single party since our freshman winter formal." She judgingly pointed in Jaycie's direction.

"So what?" Jaycie's cheeks flushed with warmth. Of course she *wanted* to go to a party with Mabel, but the Fischer House scared her. She also wanted to play it cool.

"You can't go your entire high school career without going to a party," Mabel scoffed.

"I don't see why not," Jaycie said.

Mabel sighed. "Because we never do anything *fun*—not together, anyway. We're supposed to be best friends, but we only ever see you at this table before homeroom and during free periods. Rose and I are starting to wonder if you even actually like us."

Jaycie turned bright red. Of course she liked them. In fact, she had recently realized that she maybe *really* liked Mabel. At first, Jaycie thought she was being weird, because for the past three years, she'd had no interest in boys the way other girls at school did. She chalked it up to her interests leaning more academic than social. There was nothing wrong with loving literature and science, after all.

"That's not true," Jaycie said. "We used to have sleepovers all the time."

"Again, not since freshman year," Mabel corrected, her blue eyes now making a compelling case toward going to the Fischer House.

The truth was, Mabel made Jaycie feel different. Mabel was smart, and enjoyed the same subjects Jaycie did, but there was something more to her. Something stood out. Maybe it was the rebellious streak of purple she kept hidden under her jet-black hair like a secret. Maybe it was her icy blue eyes, which contrasted so sharply with her hair and other dark features. Jaycie wouldn't have cared if Mabel were a boy or a girl—anyone with those features would have captivated her. More than anything, Jaycie admired how Mabel pulled her out of her shell and allowed Jaycie to just be Jaycie.

The first month of freshman year, she'd sat alone in the cafeteria, reading whatever she could get her hands on. She wouldn't even sit with her twin brother; he had his own friends. In fact, some people hadn't even realized Jaycie and Jax were related, let alone twins, until about halfway through freshman year.

But now Jaycie had friends too. Real friends, who she loved spending time with.

"Earth to Jaycie!" Rose waved a hand in the air. "Are you with us? Or are you staring at the weird new kid again?"

"He's not weird," Jaycie said. "Did you forget that I used to sit alone and read during lunch too? That is, until you interrupted me."

"Yeah, and it was *weird*," Mabel laughed.

Jaycie turned to look at the mostly empty table occupied by the new kid, Calvin Roberts. Calvin was a senior who'd moved to Blair from New York City over the summer to start his senior year in a new school. The handful of times Jaycie had seen him, his face was buried in a book. In fact, while he ate with one hand, his other held a paperback.

"I think it's cool," Jaycie said.

"So why don't you go hang out with him?" Rose said, pushing her half-eaten breakfast burrito aside.

"Because I don't know him." Jaycie shrugged. "Besides, you two are my best friends...I don't know. What's wrong with reading in the cafeteria?"

"Look, Jaycie," Mabel said. "You've busted your ass for four years and gotten enough A's to secure your spot at the top of our graduating class. Nobody else is even close. You owe it to yourself to loosen up and have a little fun with us."

"Fine," Jaycie conceded. "But is this party really at the Fischer House?"

"Yeah, why?" Rose asked.

"Well," Jaycie said, "I just..."

"We know, you're weirded out by Tomas," Rose said. "But he's honestly fine. Your brother hangs out with him all the time. You can't go your whole life not associating with people because of a hunch or whatever. Besides, he's kind of cute. Plus, I heard his dad has a lot of money...that house must be so cool on the inside. An old house like that? I bet you there's a bookshelf that leads to a secret hallway or something."

Jaycie's skin crawled when Rose called Tomas Fischer "cute." And she had more than a hunch. Jaycie knew those boys were trouble despite the fact that Jax hung out with them. Tomas, Hector, and Gabe, the three of them seemed to... She couldn't explain it. They brought a black cloud with them. And despite the hearsay of Tomas's dad having a lot of money, no one had ever seen or heard from him. It was weird. Blair was a small town, and parents always turned up at one time or another. But Jaycie felt sure Tomas was in that big house on Overlake Drive alone.

Besides, Hector had stolen her tuna sandwich just this morning, and she was expected to go to a party at Tomas Fischer's house, where Hector would certainly be, and act like everything was fine? Jaycie was skeptical.

"Just come," Rose said. "Jax will be there, and we'll be there, so you know it will be fine."

"Okay," Mabel said. "I am making this executive decision as your best friend: You're coming with us to this party. I will not allow your entire high school career to go by without attending a single social event. That kind of blunder will follow you into college and through the rest of your life. People can smell it on you, you know. It's a fact.

You *think* college will be a fresh start, but it won't be. They'll *know* you didn't party in high school. They'll say, *There's Jaycie, she was a nerd in high school and didn't have any friends*, and then before you know it, four years of college will go by and you won't have any fun there either. Then you'll graduate, get some office job somewhere, I don't know. Soon you'll be thirty and wonder why nobody at the office ever invites you anywhere, and eventually they'll pass you up for promotions because you're the weirdo who doesn't attend anything. It all starts here, Jaycie. We're nipping this in the bud right now. What is your future going to look like?"

"Fine." Jaycie smiled. "This is why I love you."

"Ditto." Mabel turned to Rose. "Do you think your dad will let you borrow the car?"

Rose nodded. "Definitely."

"See?" Mabel said. "Everything will be perfect."

Chapter 4
Jax Brogdon

Is he smirking at me? Jackson Brogdon sat with his hands folded. He couldn't help but fidget with his thumbs as he watched Alan Marcus, his guidance counselor, skim through his high school transcript. He could have sworn the edges of Mr. Marcus's mouth curled up ever so slightly as he analyzed Jackson's record of the last three years.

Jax could hear Mr. Marcus's chair creak under the man's weight. The sound deadened inside the chasm that was Mr. Marcus's basement office. The room made Jax uncomfortable—a sentiment shared by all seniors who were assigned Mr. Marcus as their college advisor. There was something unsettling about going down to the school's basement. The dim lighting and lack of windows made students feel like they were in trouble, even if they weren't. For anyone working with Mr. Marcus, this made the college selection process an unpleasant one.

The walls of the office were dressed with hard brown paneling, which made the already dark room even more uninviting. The walls and furniture had been out of date since the 1980s (about as long as Mr. Marcus himself had been out of date). The archaic disposition of the room clashed with the brand-new MacBook on the desk, a contrast which, quite frankly, gave Jax a headache.

No matter. He would be out of here soon enough.

Mr. Marcus cleared his throat with a loud, wet rasp. He was an intimidating man. Not in the traditional sense; no, he wasn't the type of person who commanded respect. He was imperious, similar to how a bully can command out of fear rather than any reasonable rationale. He usually wore a not-quite-denim blue button-down shirt that looked like it was from a cheap sporting goods store. His belly bloated the shirt outward, making the buttons work overtime. The shirt was as much in need of retirement as the man. His salt-and-pepper hair was combed in a way that concealed the worst of his balding. His face was perpetually stuck in a stern—trying too hard to look strict—face. Jax imagined it must have been exhausting to hold that face for eight hours a day.

Yet, he imagined it must be exhausting to become a guidance counselor in the same place you went to high school yourself. Alan Marcus never left Blair, New York. He attended Blair High School, went off to college to get his degree and then came right back to start his stagnant career. For brief moments, Jax recognized the human element of how a person could be so bitter. But those moments were brief, because when Mr. Marcus began to speak, Jax returned to his loathing hatred for the man.

"Mr. Jackson Brogdon," Mr. Marcus began. "Only a few more months, is that right?" His smirk slowly blossomed into a smile, getting under Jax's skin. He hated how he called him *Jackson*. It was like he was reading the boy's mind, like he knew he was provoking the troubled senior with scalpel-like accuracy.

"Yes, sir, that's right." Jax took a deep breath. He did his best to push down a reactive, sarcasm-filled reply of his own. He knew having an attitude at this stage would not benefit anyone. He had gotten many warnings from the school's faculty about his "attitude," especially when hanging around his friends.

"I see here you're applying for the art program at Tufts University. Boston, nice," Mr. Marcus commented. "Tell me, what about this program intrigues you?"

"I want to study art history," Jax explained. "I think Tufts is a viable option for me while staying kind of close to Blair. Plus, they offer a study abroad program after the first year, and I would really like to study in the Netherlands." Jax shifted in his chair, which was arranged too close to Mr. Marcus's desk to be comfortable. A desk lamp twisted in Jax's direction, which made him feel like he was being interrogated instead of guided. The lamp cast a yellowish glow onto the walls and highlighted Jax's bleached blonde hair—a point of contention the school's dean had a few choice words about. Mr. Marcus himself had stated it was against school dress code to show up with hair dye of any kind. Regardless, Jax continued to push his overgrown, altered hair behind his ears, sporting an under shave inspired by the guitarist from his favorite death metal band—another gem of a detail which the school board had issue with. However, it was none of their business what Jax listened to on his own time. His lean frame was hidden beneath a black denim jacket with a gray hood peeking out from underneath.

Alan Marcus nodded. Jax noted something in the man's eyes. A subtle inclination of pleasure?

"Mr. Brogdon, you realize that your grades are not likely to get you into a school like Tufts. Their arts program is extremely competitive. They don't play games there. And you also must realize that the first year of the program isn't all about art? You have to take core classes, which, quite frankly, you have not excelled at here. History, math...in order for you to qualify for their study abroad program, you need to excel, not coast by."

"I realize that, but I'm ready to put in the work." Jax felt heat rising up in his face. "This is what I want."

Mr. Marcus shook his head. "I'm sorry to say it, but I just don't see how, at this stage, you'll be able to make up enough credits to get into Tufts."

"Can you help me fill out the application, at least?" Jax asked. "I've been working on my letter of intent, which I think—"

"Mr. Brogdon, I'm sorry, but it's just not going to happen. I believe you'll be better suited for something a little more traditional, if you know what I mean." Mr. Marcus pulled out a brochure and handed it to Jax. "Trade school. You'll get to work with your hands—which is kind of like art anyway. There's nothing wrong with learning a good trade."

"Mr. Marcus, I want to apply to Tufts."

Alan Marcus leaned forward, his chair creaking beneath him once again. Jax could see the lines in his forehead squeeze together. "I will not put my neck on the line for you, Mr. Brogdon. No. You've had the last three years to think about your future. You've sat in this office numerous times and ignored my advice. I told you to shape up, and you didn't. You skipped classes, coasted by with a C average. Do you think they send C-average students abroad? No. They send the best and brightest, not students who've been caught smoking cigarettes in the parking lot—students who can't follow dress code. You've taken *none* of the advice you've been given. It gives me no pleasure to say this, but it's too little, too late."

The words *gives me no pleasure to say this* rang in Jax's ears like the tolling of a bell. Something about Mr. Marcus's tone made Jax doubt that statement very much. In fact, Jax believed it *did* bring Mr. Marcus pleasure to say those words. Everything Mr. Marcus had said to him over the past three years, every oppressive reprimand over nonsense...there had been a sanctimonious tone in his voice since the beginning. Jax had felt *judged*, not guided, ever since he stepped foot in this school. Alan Marcus wasn't there to help students; he was there to break their spirits. Alan Marcus was there to groom identical little clones who had no originality or creative drive. Alan Marcus proudly *shunned* originality and self-expression. To shut down that organic stage in a kid's life gave people like Alan Marcus a thrill. He was there to breed the next generation of Blair High School teachers who would never leave this town.

Sure, Jax hadn't taken well to most of the basic high school curriculum. The only class Jax ever had any interest in was Mr. Reinhart's Gothic Lit class. Even then, it wasn't the subject manner that captivated Jax so much as it was Mr. Reinhart's approach. He allowed his students to speak their minds and formulate their own conclusions. When a student had the floor, Stuart Reinhart gave them the opportunity to let their ideas develop. It was good practice for other areas of importance, such as debate. Besides, Mr. Reinhart seemed to genuinely care about what the students thought. He said things like, "This is how we *all* learn, by hearing each other out." No other teacher made students feel like he could learn from them as much as they could learn from him. Jax didn't feel like Mr. Reinhart was out to get him.

Jax looked at Mr. Marcus, whose chair creaked again. Mr. Marcus certainly knew that Jax was seething, but he didn't care. He had put Jax in his place. On his face was a look of triumph. He got to show another punk kid who was in charge. The look on his face said, *Judge me now, because one day it will be you sitting in this creaking chair with your own beer belly and receding hairline. Misery breeds misery, son.*

This sweaty fuck and his cheap denim shirt. His pit stains are probably older than I am.

Too little, too late...

Jax ran his fingers through his blonde hair as the heat in his face swelled. He knew his cheeks had gone red and that Mr. Marcus was probably reveling in the moment. He had to get out of this musty old office before he said something he would regret.

"Fine," Jax said and stood up to leave. "Thanks anyway."

Chapter 5
Calvin Roberts

The cafeteria chatter deflated to a wordless murmur. The automated way in which voices siphoned out of the room put Calvin in a weird place. The mindless shuffling of feet and the echoes of plastic lunch trays being dropped off became the dominant sound in the cafeteria. The last-minute cancellation of morning homeroom was jarring. It reminded him of the story his mother told him about being a high school student in NYC during the September 11th attacks. Specifically the ominous announcement over the loudspeaker, followed by an early dismissal.

Calvin's heart sank.

He wondered if anyone else felt a wave of anxiety rush over them in this moment of abrupt schedule change. Then he locked eyes with Jaycie Brogdon, who was walking by with her friends. She was desperately close to Mabel, almost touching, clutching a book to her chest like a security blanket. Calvin pursed his lips as Jaycie's brown eyes filled with worry, with fear. He wasn't alone. There *was* something wrong. This informal call for a student assembly was not normal.

Calvin tucked his book under his arm and stood, joining the rest of the student body. The efficiency in which they fell in line was eerie. Everyone formed two lines in the hallway like helpless animals being led toward slaughter.

There were scattered whispers, speculations rising about what this could be. It seemed like nobody knew for sure, but Calvin's stomach ached in anticipation. There was something gangrenous in the air. Even the voice from the loudspeaker's tone reeked of bereavement. Calvin wished he had someone to talk to. Loneliness crept in. It seemed like everyone had someone to lean on except for him.

A cynical *mooo* came from the back of the line, and Calvin felt even more uncomfortable. He lowered his head and focused on regulating his breathing. Nothing like imitation animal noises to truly make him feel like herded cattle.

The line began to move, finally, and they filed into the gymnasium. Several faculty members were already lining up near a microphone at the midcourt line in the middle of the room. They moved slowly, somberly, like they were in a funeral procession. The bleachers quickly filled up as groups of friends claimed the most ideal seats.

Calvin found a seat in a gap in the front row and looked up at the teachers and faculty lined up before him. The gravity on their faces was heavy, and Calvin knew this was going to be bad.

Chapter 6
Blair High School

Jaycie took a seat on the bleachers in between Mabel and Rose. There was a shroud-like sense of unease in the room as she peered around. Of course, there were a few exceptions.

On the far right back row of bleachers, Jaycie could spot her brother, Jax. He sat with the group of boys she had spent the last year trying to avoid: Hector Stroud and Gabe Coleman, the most opaque, uninspired excuses for high school boys she could have conjured up. She was still angry—unsurprised, but angry—at Hector for stealing her lunch. Jaycie was sure those two aimless cases had never had a single original thought in their lives. Until last year, when they began to follow around the one person at BHS who scared her the most: Tomas Fischer.

Tomas was from out of town, but his family, from what she heard, had ties to Blair. He moved into the historical Fischer House on Overlake Drive last year and enrolled at BHS, joining their junior class.

Now Tomas was a senior like her, but he seemed older. It was the way he never reacted to anything, as if he didn't have a heart. Even now, as looks of worry covered the faces of everyone in the room, Tomas sat there stone-faced, pale. He had his hood pulled up, covering the top of his face, as if he were too good to be bothered with trivial matters like school assemblies. He and his lackeys seemed exempt from the feelings of dread shared by the rest of BHS, and that lack of basic empathy scared Jaycie most of all.

Those boys continued to rudely banter among themselves, unfazed by the obvious gravity of the situation. Jaycie's secondhand embarrassment grew knowing her brother was up there, keeping that kind of company. She didn't understand it. The way her brother fell in line with those other boys was uncharacteristic of him. It was as if he had no control over the effect Tomas had on him. It was like some kind of divine ability to suppress who Jax was at heart.

Calvin Roberts, the new kid from New York City, abruptly slapped the back of his own neck. The sudden movement from the front row of the bleachers caught Jaycie's attention. Just like in the cafeteria, Calvin was by himself and off to the side. He was, however, in direct line of the group Jax was sitting with. Calvin slapped his neck again. Then Jaycie noticed the small white gob sailing through the air in Calvin's direction.

Spitballs.

Jaycie grew furious. Not only were they being disrespectful during an important school meeting, but they were straight up bullying the new kid. Bullying the only Black kid.

Jaycie watched as her brother looked in her direction for a brief moment. A common myth about twins was that one could tell what the other was feeling by some sort of telepathic anomaly. Jaycie used to be able to feel this too, like during one family vacation in Lake Placid. Jax had fallen from his bike and scraped his elbow, and Jaycie could feel her brother's pain before she even had the chance to turn around and find him picking himself back up. However, since Jax began hanging around the likes of Tomas Fischer, that ability seemed to have turned off. It was like a Bluetooth device: in range but unable to connect.

Her eyebrows furrowed, and her cheeks turned red with embarrassment. Jax was a different person entirely when he was with those boys. She made eye contact with him from the opposite end of the bleachers, but his detached expression made him feel like a stranger. She wanted to shake him.

Calvin leaned forward and pulled the hood of his sweatshirt up to shield the back of his neck from projectiles. One of the teachers lined up in the center of the gymnasium gave the boy a distrustful glance. Jaycie wanted to shout at them.

A sharp pitch of feedback echoed through the speakers as the school's principal, Joyce Holden, tapped on the microphone.

"Good morning, everyone," she began. "I know it's early, and this meeting is unexpected, but we all felt it was the right thing to do." She motioned toward the faculty lined up next to her. "We felt it would be irresponsible to withhold information from you, so we called together this assembly right away. This is without a doubt the most difficult announcement I've ever had to make as principal, but just this morning, Martin Welch was found..." Her voice trailed off.

She took a necessary pause. It was clear that simply talking about Martin was a daunting task under the circumstances. There was a synchronized gasp among some of the students at the unfinished but unmistakably bad news.

"Unfortunately," Principal Holden continued, "Martin Welch is no longer with us." The student body waited for more information, but it seemed like the principal had exhausted her own words. She had nothing left. It was like all the air had been sucked out of the room, and all that remained was the black cloud which only Jaycie could see.

Jaycie felt the air go out of her lungs. She buried her face in her hands as tears silently streamed down her face. Her intuition, no matter how precise, could not have prepared her for this crushing blow. Her friend, sweet and innocent Martin, was dead?

No more joining each other on family vacations. No more watching Martin and Jax try to fish in Lake Champlain. No more study groups or lab partners. All of her memories with Martin seemed insufficient now, like they would never be enough, and all of their future plans had crumbled in an instant.

Most of the students sat in silent shock as they absorbed the news, but there were audible sobs scattered about the room. The existential reality proved difficult to grasp. How could someone their age be dead? How could this be real? For some students, this was the first look at their own mortality—an unwanted magnifying glass on the fragility of their lives.

It felt like an eternity before anybody spoke, but finally, Mr. Alberts, the school's music director, approached the mic stand. The students remained silent. The music director cleared his throat before speaking, but his voice still broke as he started. It was a jarring departure from his usual baritone.

"We know this is a difficult situation, and many of you were close to Martin," he said. "All faculty are making themselves available to talk to any students who want to talk. We've never experienced anything like this before, so we've agreed it's best to navigate it together. If anybody needs anything, we're here."

More silence from the student body.

"That said," Mr. Alberts continued, "we're going to allow those of you who feel like you need to leave to go home early and be with your families. The faculty will be here until three p.m., but classes are effectively canceled for the rest of the day."

Among the silence, Jaycie could hear a whispered but celebratory *yes*. The blatant disrespect was vile, but she had a feeling she knew where it came from.

Jaycie remained in her seat, still finding it hard to accept reality. She looked up at Mr. Reinhart, who was standing among the other teachers in the center of the gymnasium. While the other teachers began to talk among themselves, Mr. Reinhart had a far-off look in his eye, almost as if he, like Jaycie, could see the metaphorical black cloud. Almost as if he had seen something else.

Jaycie had to talk to him.

She felt a hand on her shoulder. "Do you want to go home?" Mabel asked.

Jaycie shrugged. "I don't know," she said. "I think I want to try and talk to Mr. Reinhart."

Mabel nodded. "I'm so sorry, Jace. Martin was a good kid."

Chapter 7
Jaycie

Jaycie found Mr. Reinhart in the parking lot, going home, while the rest of the teachers stayed behind as promised.

"Mr. Reinhart, wait!"

He turned around, looking even more restless and disheveled up close. It was like he'd thrown himself together haphazardly.

"Jaycie," he started, "I don't know what to say except this is terrible. I'm sorry." He shook his head. He was nervously clutching onto the sling bag that rested across his shoulder. He looked tired, and his attention seemed scattered, almost paranoid.

He knows something.

"Mr. Reinhart," she said. "What happened to Martin?"

Stu's breath caught in his throat. He took a step away, almost in a panic, as if her question had triggered him. This wasn't the eloquent, confident teacher she knew. The man standing before her looked deeply troubled. It scared her. What had he seen?

"Go home, Jaycie," he said. "Go home and be with your family." He gave a pitiful nod as he backed away and approached his car.

Jaycie stood for a moment, confused. Mr. Reinhart must have

seen something to make him have such a reaction to her question. He didn't look quite himself earlier, in the gymnasium, and he certainly was not himself just now. All she'd wanted to know was what happened to her friend, but now a very real fear spawned at the notion of possibilities.

What *did* happen to Martin?

She turned to head home herself when she saw the silhouette of a figure in a second-floor window of the school. Had someone been watching her interaction with Mr. Reinhart?

Chapter 8
Jax

By late afternoon, the halls of BHS had descended into a dead quiet. There was a subtle rustling sound coming from the science department, but no one was around to hear it.

After a summer spent planning the perfect senior prank, they had it figured out. It was Hector who had conceived the idea to target the new kid, Calvin Roberts. It was a nasty little scheme which, when presented to Tomas Fischer, had caused a sadistic grin to break out across his face.

Four boys stayed behind to seize the rare chance of the entire school being vacant—now they could begin phase one of their operation. The tragic death of Martin Welch and the decision to send everyone home early was the perfect setup, so they had to strike today. It was now or never.

Tomas, Hector, Gabe, and Jax spent most of the time after dismissal staked out in the library. They claimed a table, set several books in front of them, and pretended to study. Despite the fact that none of the boys' grades reflected any attempt to actually study, it worked. They spent hours pretending to read while the rest of the school dealt with the Martin news in their own ways. The enthusiasm oozing from Tomas was palpable, as if he expelled an energy that prevented any of the other boys from backing out of the plan, even if they wanted to. He held them in a sort of stranglehold. Tomas intended to make Blair his own, and this was the beginning of that endeavor.

When three o'clock hit, they abandoned their post in the library.

Gabe was pivotal in their strategy. His mother, Mrs. Coleman, was the biology teacher at BHS, and she had keys to the science lab—access was essential for what they had planned. Several days earlier, Gabe had snuck the set of keys off of his mother's desk and made copies at the hardware store. He wasn't exactly sure which key was *the* key they needed, the key that would grant access to the science department's supply closet, but he'd made copies of everything, just in case.

The four boys made their way over to the science department with white, nondescript masks slipped over their faces. In the off chance they'd run into another student or a teacher, this would all be for nothing if they were caught. The science department supply closet was off-limits to unsupervised students.

There wouldn't be another opportunity like this. It was the perfect day to pull off such an operation. The only day they wouldn't be questioned for being the only students in the building, because this day was uniquely different from the rest.

Jax followed the group from behind. Apprehension bubbled in his stomach like the first time he'd inhaled cigarette smoke, thinking it would do permanent damage to his lungs on first contact. He'd tried to contend that stealing was wrong, but, like with that first cigarette, he caved to the pressure. There was a grip in Tomas Fischer's tone—in his glare—which made Jax shut up and comply. Tomas's words were authoritative in a way Jax could not explain; he had an enigmatic way of convincing those around him that he knew best. His tone implied there would be consequences for going against him.

"You got the keys, right?" Tomas asked as they navigated the dim hallways of the high school. He moved through the darkness like he belonged to it. Painfully sure of himself, of their plan. It made Jax feel weak for having any sort of doubt to begin with.

"I got it," Gabe said confidently. "I made copies of everything my mom had, so it's definitely here."

"It better be," Tomas said, "or I'll make sure you end up like Martin Welch." His grin was sharp and threatening.

Gabe swallowed hard. "Not cool, man." He produced the set of keys from his pocket as they approached the door to the supply closet.

Jax was looking all around, convinced someone was going to find them. His breath behind his mask was hollow. He didn't want to be here, but he didn't think he had a choice. It was either this or find out what happens to those who say no to Tomas.

They watched as Gabe tried the first key. It didn't fit. Jax could feel Tomas's eyes bore into the back of Gabe's head as he tried the next key. This one slid into the keyhole but did not turn. Gabe's hand began to tremble as he tried a third key. This one went in and turned. The door clicked as it unlocked.

"I told you I had the right key."

Tomas didn't say anything. He just shoved his way into the supply closet, with Hector following like his shadow. Jax stayed back near the doorway, looking into the long and narrow closet. The shelves were lined with beakers of various sizes, petri dishes, and flasks, rows of test tubes and cylinders underneath. There was a shelf dedicated to safety equipment, such as goggles and gloves and chemical solutions.

The liquids had their own row on the bottom shelf, which included rubbing alcohol, food coloring, and baking soda, as well as salts, sugars, and starches. There was also a large tub of hydrogen peroxide. Finally, Jax spotted what they'd come for: chloroform.

Chloroform was stocked specifically for the advanced biology class project, which was a frog dissection. The possibilities of pranks they could pull with any of the supplies in this closet were endless. Jax imagined mixing the baking soda with vinegar and dish soap to unleash a tsunami of suds down the hallway that housed the freshman lockers. A giant mess, yet ultimately harmless. However, once Tomas heard Hector's chloroform plan, there was no talking him out of it.

Jax thought a prank involving chloroform didn't seem much like a prank at all. It felt serious. It felt like a place he didn't want to go. Yet Tomas had a convincing pull on the boys, especially when they were around him. Jax couldn't speak for Hector or Gabe, but he often felt an uncanny influence from Tomas.

"We're going to show a certain newcomer that he doesn't belong in Blair," Tomas declared.

As they made their way out of the science department, navigating the empty halls toward the exit, they heard a sound in the distance. Coming from the music hall, the faint sound of drumming.

Chapter 9
Calvin

Calvin Roberts stayed behind after most of the student body had gone home. He wasn't planning on speaking to one of the counselors or teachers about Martin Welch's death. He had other plans.

Unlike most of the BHS students, who had gotten to know each other as freshman (some even coming from the same middle school), Calvin never knew Martin. It wasn't his fault. He was the new kid. He did feel empathy for those affected by Martin's passing, though—he couldn't even imagine. The kid was *his* age.

The sound of Calvin practicing drums echoed through the empty hallways of the music department. Twice a week, Calvin would stay after school, renting out one of the practice rooms to do what he loved most. Today, when the rest of the school took advantage of the early dismissal, Calvin opted to stay behind and get extra time behind the kit.

The drums were his favorite instrument. He had already come a long way from the set of foam practice pads he'd had to settle for when he and his mom lived in their NYC apartment. They didn't have room for a full drum set in the city. The most enticing factor in moving to Blair was having a basement at home. A dedicated space for his drum set once he saved up enough money to buy one. He had his heart set on a beautiful Pearl kit on display at the local shop in Plattsburg.

Calvin was also appreciative that BHS's music director, Mr. Alberts, allowed him to use the practice space twice a week. That generosity allowed Calvin time behind the kit before he could buy his own. Additionally, Mr. Alberts had encouraged Calvin to participate in tryouts for the school's jazz band next week. His technique was already on par after years of practice on the foam pads. Being invited to try out by the school's music director was a boost of confidence Calvin needed. Maybe life in Blair wasn't going to be *all* bad.

He found playing drums to be a sort of therapeutic workout. Calvin wasn't drawn to sports. He wasn't in a rush to join football or track to get his sweat on. He would prefer to stick to the drums.

The pounding beats drowned out any noise coming from outside the soundproofed room except for a direct knock on the reinforced door—the door's window would show any visitors' faces.

Calvin hit the snare, and its snap echoed in the small space. The booming bass he could feel in his stomach—one of the other reasons he loved this instrument was how he could *feel* the vibration of the sound waves bouncing about the room.

His T-shirt grew heavy with sweat as he practiced varying beats on the kit. His thigh and calf muscles worked to propel the bass pedal along to the driving beat. The booming sound thundered inside the room, accompanied by the snap of the snare drum twice every measure.

Something odd happened after a few repeated measures. The *bom-bom-bom-bap-bom-bom-bom-bap* played over several times, but Calvin could have sworn something was off.

It wasn't the first time he'd felt he could hear something from outside the practice room. One time when he'd stayed late to practice, he swore he could hear movement from the hallways. He'd stopped playing and checked, and, sure enough, volunteers were moving around tables and chairs for a parent-teacher conference later that night. But they weren't disturbing him, and he wasn't disturbing them, so he went about his practice.

This time it felt different. The noise seemed calculated, almost in sync with his playing. It seemed as if his drum pattern had been memorized, and every time he hit the snare there was an accompanying knock at the door. Like someone was outside the room, matching his beat. Like someone was fucking with him.

The first time Calvin heard it, he ignored it and continued playing, focus unbroken. He concentrated on staying on beat, following the metronome. However, after a couple of measures, the occurrence turned into a distraction. The knock, which occurred once every measure during the second snare hit, was ever so slightly off beat, and it threw off his playing.

Calvin stopped and let his arms drop to his sides, giving his muscles a much-needed break. He looked up at the little window in the soundproofed door, and it was empty. Yet he could sense a presence behind it.

Someone was most certainly fucking with him, and he was losing patience. While he felt confident he would do well in the upcoming tryouts, he didn't need feckless distractions. This was *his* time. *His* personal space. He set the drumsticks on the snare and stood up, ready to shoo away the nuisance at the door.

The metal door handle clicked as he opened it slowly. He peered out into the hallway, but it was empty.

Pests, Calvin thought and rolled his eyes.

He let out a sigh, closed the door, and returned to his throne, picking up where he left off. *Bom-bom-bom-bap-bom-bom-bom-bap*, and by the time he made it to the second measure of the pattern, the knock had returned, playing just off tempo with the sound of his snare. This time, when he looked up at the window, a face filled the square opening, glaring down at Calvin.

Calvin stopped playing. Whatever coward was peering into the room, into Calvin's personal space, was wearing a mask. A ghastly white, expressionless mask that exposed only the eyes of whoever wore it. Inside those eyes, Calvin saw something he recognized easily.

Hatred.

The kind of hatred that bled through that smooth, white mask was universal. In any language, it was the hatred of that which was different. The racist, foolish hatred that Calvin was unfortunately all too familiar with. The lowlife behind this mask, like all cowards who foster such hate, didn't have the balls to confront what they hated face-to-face. Instead, they used cheap intimidation tactics like this one.

Calvin locked eyes with whoever this person was and raised a middle finger up above the crash cymbal. The idiot in the mask kicked the door hard before running off.

Figures.

Calvin shook his head and wiped his face with a towel. This practice session was effectively over. He stood up, wiped down the kit, and stretched his arms and legs. *Let them try it without a stupid mask, face-to-face.* Calvin wouldn't be intimidated by such vermin.

Chapter 10
Stu

By the time Stu got home, he felt a tension in his neck. About halfway through the day, he'd caught himself repeatedly looking over his shoulder. As the initial shock of finding Martin Welch wore off, Stu realized he was not only afraid for Blair—he feared for his own safety. Whatever had killed Martin like that, in cold blood, was still out there.

Stu let himself into his home, where he presumed he would break down, let it all out and cry. However—

Paula was not at the door to greet him. Instead, Stu found her cowering beside the couch, making herself as small as possible.

"I'm sorry, girl," he said, approaching his dog and gently caressing her head. He felt terrible. He'd been so concerned with filling his own day with distractions that he hadn't even stopped to think that Paula was home alone with her thoughts.

The German shepherd's ears pointed up, and she stood, wagging her tail in appreciation that Stu was finally home.

"It's been a hard day for all of us," Stu said. He grabbed a beer, plopped down on the couch, and let out a heavy sigh. Paula watched, wagging her tail. "You want to go out, don't you?" he said. Paula barked, her ears turning toward his voice like little satellites. Stu slouched. "How about we compromise? Does the backyard sound okay to you?"

Paula tilted her head.

"Alright, backyard it is." Stu got up. "I promise we'll go on a proper nighttime walk tomorrow."

He secretly hoped the dog wouldn't hold him to his promise. Despite wanting to push through and stick to his routine, he knew that was no longer an option.

For the first time in his life, he questioned the safety of Blair. He feared the violence perpetrated against Martin Welch was only the beginning. The air itself seemed to vibrate differently, the way some animals can sense an oncoming storm.

Stu got up and let Paula out into the yard. The hair on the back of his neck stood up as he watched his dog carefully edge her way into the yard, tail between her legs. Stu stepped outside with her, keeping an eye on her movements. Such trepidation was unlike her. Even when she was a scared, newly adopted pup, she never behaved this way. Especially in the yard, her territory.

The cool air of dusk felt nice on his face, but Stu was troubled by his dog's behavior. She still did her business, but her routine of circling the perimeter of the fence that surrounded the yard would not take place tonight. The dog would go no farther than a couple of feet away from the house.

Stu paused. It was hard to see the edge of the backyard in the twilight, and if it wasn't for Paula's strange behavior he would have thought he was going crazy, but he was certain he saw rustling in the tree branches hanging over his fence. Was something out there? Was Paula aware of a presence outside their house, or was she still spooked from the morning? Stu knew he was.

He squinted, leaning in to get a closer look. His legs felt like cement, refusing to carry him any farther into the yard, away from the safety of the house. Something caught in his throat.

"Paula, come on. Inside," he said, and the dog darted back into the house immediately. Stu's eyes remained fixed on the edge of his yard, though. There was no more movement in the leafy branches that covered the top of his fence, but he saw it—movement out of the corner of his eye. He felt the same sensation he felt earlier, a presence shrouded in the trees.

What if whatever killed Martin Welch had been lurking on the edge of Owl's Head Park when Stu discovered the body? What if that same something had followed Stu home?

He felt an icy chill, as now it seemed like the fence and trees were getting closer. The cloak in which this ominous presence hid was closing in, destroying one of the few safe places Stu had left. If he wasn't safe in his own yard, where was he safe?

The branches above Martin's body had rustled in the wind. But there was no wind. There was only stale, dead air, choking Stu with the stench of death. That same stench was approaching again. The branches rustling, as if a mysterious creature was lurking, hunting for its next meal.

"Alright, it's time for bed," Stu said, locking the door and drawing the curtains. A chill lingered on his flesh, reminding him of that which he wished to erase from his memory.

Chapter 11
Jaycie

Jaycie watched her mom plop a serving spoon into the casserole in the center of the table. Steam rose from the oval dish, and she thought how utterly unappealing dinner looked. Not because it was casserole night—she would have had distaste for any meal tonight. Her appetite was nonexistent. The news about Martin was soul crushing, and there was no way she could stomach making a dent in the metric ton of cheese and gravy that sat before her.

Jax, on the other hand, looked lethargic. He scooped a serving of casserole onto his plate and proceeded to slowly move it around with his fork. His head was lowered, and it was clear he, too, was thinking about Martin. Jaycie was confused, as Jax had seemed to lack any empathy or awareness at all while they were at school. It was like he was a different person around Tomas Fischer.

Speaking of school, Jaycie prayed her parents wouldn't bring it up. There was nothing to be said. At least, nothing that would help. But her parents' faces and body language were like smoke from a fuse. Unwanted conversation was coming like the inevitable bang of a firework.

Her father, for instance, was frowning slightly as he ate, glancing intermittently at Jax. Seth Brogdon never handled silence well, and when he made eye contact with Liz, he swallowed and put his fork down.

Oh, please don't tell us how sorry you are about Martin...

Jaycie slouched in her seat, watching her untouched casserole, avoiding her mom's eye. She just knew her mom was looking at her with a forlorn expression. Liz Brogdon just couldn't eat if her children weren't touching their meals.

Oh, please don't start talking about how important these family dinners are.

Jaycie knew her mom wanted to hang on to these moments for as long as she could. How having all four of them at the dinner table was a precious, fleeting moment, and she didn't know when the last time they'd all be together as a family.

Jaycie couldn't bear to sit through the awkward platitudes, the stating the obvious. None of which would bring Martin back, therefore none of which she wanted to hear.

Seth cleared his throat.

Here it comes. Jaycie could feel the silence breaking.

"Are you kids doing okay?" Seth asked. Jaycie could only shrug. Jax's shoulders seemed to slouch even more. Liz reached out her hand and touched Jaycie's.

Seth continued, "I can't imagine...that poor kid. Who would do such a thing?"

"I don't want to talk about it," Jaycie said with a little more attitude than she intended. No, she didn't want to talk about how she and Martin would no longer be lab partners. How they wouldn't get to volunteer at the library this year. How they wouldn't get to buddy-read that *Clown in a Cornfield* book—and try to convince Mr. Reinhart to add it to their class's reading list instead of that stuffy old Lovecraft again.

"You're going to have to talk about it at some point." Seth's voice was already more tempered from Jaycie's misinterpreted shortness.

"I'm sorry, but..." Jaycie pursed her lips. "This is really hard, and if I don't want to talk about something, I'm not going to." She pushed out her chair and got up from the table.

* * *

Later that night, a knock came at Jaycie's door. She pulled her headphones off, still focused on her game and said, "Come in."

Jax entered his sister's room and sat down next to her. "*Blood of the Innocent* on a weeknight?" he said. "That's a bold choice."

"Hey, I did all my homework. Therefore, I'm more than qualified to save the world from the undead before bedtime," she said confidently. "So, what's up?" She was happy to see him. Lately it felt like they'd been growing distant, with their own friends and priorities.

"Just wanted to check on you," Jax said. "I heard you were planning on going to Tomas's house this weekend."

Jaycie's room was packed to the brim with media. She had books filling bookshelves, books in piles next to her bed, books stacked on two floating shelves fastened to the wall. She collected different types of Japanese manga and graphic novels. Junji Ito was her favorite. Her TV was pushed to the far wall, and her feet were propped up on its stand.

"Correction—*forced* into going to Tomas's house," she said. "You know I don't care about parties, but the girls insisted."

"Right," Jax said. "How did they find out about it anyway? I didn't think they were inviting more people."

Jaycie shrugged, hitching up one shoulder as she pressed a series of buttons on her gaming controller. "Don't know. I assume they got the invite from one of your buddies." A monster's head exploded in a shower of gore as Jaycie's character performed a kill shot.

"Right," Jax said. "Anyway, I just wanted to say be careful. They're different over there. They kind of play by their own rules."

"Hey, don't be getting all big brother on me now," Jaycie said. "I should be the one telling you to be careful—you're the one who's hanging out with them all the time instead of going to class." She paused the game, freezing the screen on her character reloading her weapon.

"I don't even know why you hang out with those guys; they're bad news. You *know* they're bad news, and you *know* I don't like them."

When Tomas arrived last year, he was nothing but a bully. He specifically targeted the bookish type, the kids like Martin. It troubled her that Rose seemed to have a crush on Tomas. Sure, Tomas wasn't ugly, but he was mean. And aside from the rumor that his father had a lot of money, Jaycie didn't see any redeeming qualities. Which is why, when Jaycie heard how Jax was part of Tomas's little incident in the library last year, when he turned all the dust jackets of books in the history section inside out and wrote obscenities on them, she felt betrayed.

"I saw you guys during the assembly today, by the way. It was very disrespectful how you guys were acting when they announced what happened to Martin. He was my friend. He was *your* friend too, and it's like you didn't even care."

"I do care," Jax said. "It's just hard to think about. I've missed Martin since the ninth grade. I just haven't known how to deal with it."

"What do you mean?" Jaycie asked.

"Well, you know, we were separated into different classes after the first half of freshman year. You were too. You and Martin were put into the advanced courses because you guys were just *perfect*. Me, on the other hand, I was sorted in with Hector and Gabe and, well, what did you expect? You and Martin started having lunch at the smart kids' table, and I stayed with those guys. It's just normal high school shit, I guess, but it still sucks to see you guys go off knowing you're already on a better track than me. It's like I was already being left behind because I wasn't a straight-A student. I feel like my whole future has already been decided for me."

Jaycie never saw it that way, but her brother was right. It must have been hard for him to be taken away from her and Martin, who he was comfortable with, just because his grades weren't perfect. Like he was being punished for not being perfect. She couldn't imagine the blow to his confidence and motivation that must have been.

She watched as her brother pulled his shirt sleeves until they covered the scars on the palms of his hands—an injury from last year, one Jax still wouldn't tell her about.

"Of course I've missed hanging out with Martin. He was my best friend. But I always assumed we'd have a chance to catch up before we graduated. I didn't think that chance would be taken away from me." Tears welled up in Jax's eyes.

"I'm sorry," Jaycie said. "I had no idea you felt that way."

"And now I'm probably going to be stuck here in Blair while everyone goes off to college," Jax continued. "It's not fair. Just because I didn't put all my effort into one class doesn't mean I can't handle the advanced shit. I know about chemistry and advanced bio and all that. I felt like we were learning the same shit over and over again, and I'm the one who's punished for it."

"But Jax, pretending like you don't care is exactly why you were sorted into those classes in the first place," Jaycie said. She knew this was about more than just school. Jax had become different person since Tomas arrived. She wished he could break whatever grip that boy had on him.

"I wish I could make it up to him, or tell him that I care about him," Jax said.

"Well, you could start by telling the people you still have in your life that you care about them," Jaycie said. "It might be too late for Martin, but it isn't too late for you."

Jax smiled and hugged his sister. "I love you, Jace."

"Ditto," Jaycie said.

Jax looked back at the paused screen of *Blood of the Innocent*. "So, did you find all the secret—"

"Uh-uh! Stop," Jaycie said. "No spoilers, please!"

Jax laughed. "Remember when we used to stay up all night and I'd beat you in *Mario Kart* until you cried?"

"Excuse me? I think your brain must be broken," Jaycie said. "If I recall, we were fairly matched in *Mario Kart,* and *you* were the one who got all moody when you lost. Convenient to only remember your victories, dude."

"There's only one way to find out who's right, I guess," Jax said.

Jaycie smiled. "Oof, you are so dead." She switched off one console, switched over to the Nintendo system, and handed Jax a controller.

"I miss this," Jax said as he selected his character.

"You know, we're allowed to have different friend groups and still be cool with each other," Jaycie said. "I'm still your sister. You can always talk to me, that will never change."

"I know," Jax said. "Ditto."

Chapter 12
Liz and Seth Brogdon

"Hey, look," Seth said, turning toward Liz, who lay next to him in bed. "Just got a notification from the front door, but there's nothing out there." He showed her his phone.

They lay in bed with the lights turned low and *The Tonight Show* playing in the background. Liz read a book while Seth was playing on his phone until they both grew too tired to stay awake, as was their nightly routine. Usually they'd fall asleep with the TV on.

Seth's phone pinged with another notification from the Ring doorbell app. They had a small camera set up at their front door that enabled them to see any movement outside the house. It was helpful, especially when there were package deliveries. Theoretically, the camera was a deterrent, to keep trespassers away, but in the town of Blair, trespassers weren't high on the list of threats.

Seth held up his phone, their vacant porch bathed in darkness on the screen.

"Weird, right?"

"It's probably a small animal or something." Liz yawned. "Maybe a squirrel, I don't know." She closed her book and placed it on the nightstand.

"Yeah, I guess so." Seth drew the phone back and studied the screen.

Liz turned off the lights and the TV (one of the rare nights they remembered to before drifting off to sleep). Seth spent a few more moments studying his phone until Liz leaned over and kissed him goodnight.

"Get some rest," she said. "The front lawn will still be there in the morning."

Seth chuckled and put the phone away, and they fell asleep shortly thereafter.

Two hours later, they were jolted awake. A loud *ping* sounded in the dark room. "What was that?" Liz asked, rubbing her eyes. She checked the time on her watch—1:50 a.m. Annoyed, she turned over, adjusting her pillow.

"Something set off that damned Ring camera again." Seth checked his phone, only to find the vacant front lawn again. "I think I'll go downstairs and check," he said, climbing out of bed and sliding his feet into a pair of slippers. "There has to be something stuck out there, like a bag or a piece of debris. The wind is probably whipping it around, setting off the camera."

"If you don't see anything, just turn the app off," Liz suggested. "We can figure it out in the morning."

Seth nodded and headed downstairs. As he approached the front door, he had a strange feeling. The odd sensation of being watched, like he was the one with a camera pointed at him. The idea that someone could be out there in the dark—a stranger whom he could not see—got under his skin. His mouth went dry as he unlocked the front door and peered outside.

River Road was completely quiet. There was nothing outside but the stillness of the night. Not even enough of a breeze to carry debris across the lawn and trigger the camera.

Seth stepped outside to inspect the porch railing closely.

Nothing.

His breath shuddered at the absolute stillness.

From the porch, he took one last look around the front lawn and scratched his chin. *There's nothing out here.* He turned to inspect the camera itself, which was set on the door frame.

Everything seemed fine.

He headed back inside and locked the front door. Finally, he took out his phone and disabled the app. He would check back tomorrow, maybe call the support hotline to ask if there was some sort of bug in the system.

* * *

The next morning, Seth Brogdon filled his to-go coffee mug and slung his work bag over one shoulder. He pulled the front door closed, and something occurred to him that didn't usually cross his mind as he left for work:

He turned and locked the front door.

Locking the door at night was one thing, but in the town of Blair, it was normal to leave doors unlocked during the day. Seth, typically being the first one out the door, was always sure his wife or one of the kids would lock up on their way out, but even if they forgot, it generally didn't matter. Their town was safe. Yet this morning, he took an extra measure and made sure he locked the door behind him. He couldn't explain why, but thinking about last night made him uneasy.

Stu took a moment to scan River Road from the porch before descending the steps. He was walking along the front lawn and toward the car when he noticed a dark spot among the green.

Something was tangled within the well-maintained lawn. He knelt down, slowly reached out, and plucked it from the grass. A long, black strand of hair. Seth held it up to the sunlight and then quickly tossed it aside.

He stood up, wiping his hands on his jeans in disgust. There seemed to be more of this hair all around him. It looked as if a tuft of hair had been pulled out of someone's scalp and scattered about the front lawn.

Chapter 13
Calvin

A dvanced Biology was an elective class for fourteen BHS seniors who had excelled in all areas of science since freshman year. In order to qualify for one of the advanced science electives, a student must maintain a minimum B average in all science classes leading up to their senior year. If they successfully completed this prerequisite, they had the option to choose an additional science credit as a senior, which would carry over for those who planned on majoring in a science field for their undergraduate degree. There was a choice between Geology, Earth Science, or Advanced Biology (which was taught by Mrs. Coleman).

Advanced Biology was the most difficult elective, not only because of the thesis project, which included a frog dissection, but because of how hands-off Mrs. Coleman was as a teacher. She expected her students to be attentive and do the work themselves. There would be no hand-holding in Advanced Biology. This was a well-known and intimidating fact for some students. Others, like Calvin, respected it. At his last school, every class was like that. Coleman said all of the information you needed to succeed in her class was provided during lecture and in the reading materials. If you couldn't handle it, you shouldn't be taking Advanced Biology.

You aren't going to have your hand held when you get to college, so it's best to break that habit now.

Jaycie opted into two out of the three electives. Advanced Biology being one of them specifically because she and Martin had planned to be lab partners.

Mrs. Coleman was already setting up the smart board as her students began filing into the classroom. Not a moment of class time was to be wasted.

The desks were high-top tables with space for two students, meant to be shared by lab partners. Jaycie was now paired up with Calvin Roberts. Calvin was promptly the first student in the room, taking his seat before anybody else. He nodded hello to Jaycie as she arrived. She returned his greeting with a timid smile, dragged out the metal stool from under the desk, and took her seat.

Jaycie felt weird knowing so much about the new kid without ever having said a word to him. But she knew he and his mom had just moved to Blair from NYC, and it was just the two of them. It didn't seem fair to know so much about a person from word of mouth alone. She thought this might make it harder to actually strike up a conversation. But they would have to talk eventually, even if it was just about Advanced Biology.

Mrs. Coleman cleared her throat and began her lecture about the frog dissection project. She spoke about the importance of animal dissection and how it provided a deeper understanding of anatomy in general.

"You do have the ability to opt out of the dissection procedure at your own discretion," she explained. "However, in that case, you will be required to turn in a thesis paper instead. This paper will hold equal weight as the dissection on your final grade. I expect the paper to be properly cited and well-researched. It isn't uncommon for a well-written paper to take the majority of the semester to complete. I expect an outline to be turned in the week of dissection itself, and a first draft for approval before Thanksgiving break. The goal of either assignment is to prove the student's knowledge and ability to understand and perform the task."

Calvin wondered whether choosing the thesis paper over the dissection was even worth it. The dissection would be a one-and-done deal.

"It is my job to explain the reason behind this procedure," Mrs. Coleman explained. "There are many reasons, actually. Of course, the most basic is that this allows us to understand the body's organs on a deeper level. You can only learn the intricacies in such detail with dissection—you can't fully understand the body without knowing it inside and out. Besides, there very well could be the next great surgeon among you; it's possible."

Calvin wondered what the first person to perform a dissection had been thinking about. What would drive a person to do such a thing to another creature? Was it out of pure curiosity? Or had all previous avenues been exhausted, and dissection was an act of pure, barbaric desperation?

He was aware of the procedure's influence on the advancement of medicine, but still. To be the first one? There had to have been something extreme going on in that person's mind.

He glanced over and saw Jaycie taking notes.

"Now, before we get into the procedure next week, I want to go over some rules and information. The materials we'll be using will include a scalpel, forceps, scissors, dissection pins to hold your specimen in place, and probes. Also included in the materials will be a glass jar to house your specimen, as well as chloroform-soaked cotton balls, which will be distributed by me."

Calvin glanced at Jaycie, who had taken a deep, anxious breath.

"You okay?" he whispered. Mrs. Coleman continued to explain the intricacies of the procedure, ignoring the fact that several pairs of students had begun to whisper among themselves.

"I'm fine," Jaycie said. "I just feel bad for the frogs. The chloroform and all...seems like a rough day."

This made Calvin grin. "You're funny," he said.

"Doesn't the chloroform seem kind of barbaric?" she asked. "I've read that the frog is actually still alive at the beginning of the procedure. A thesis paper doesn't seem so bad now that I think about how cruel this seems."

"I wouldn't worry too much," Calvin said. "I don't think they actually make us do any of the frog-killing; that's an outdated method. At my last school, the senior class had a similar project, but the jar and chloroform were just for show."

"I'm not sure," Jaycie said. "Blair does hold on to a lot of outdated traditions, unfortunately. Kind of a weird thing to keep a jar and chloroform out on display if we're not going to use it."

Calvin just shrugged, as if to say, *Hey, I'm just the new kid, I don't make the rules.*

"I don't think we've been formally introduced, bee-tee-dubs," Jaycie said. "My name is Jaycie."

"I know who you are." Calvin smiled. "But it's nice to formally meet you, lab partner." He shook her hand. "I'm Calvin."

Chapter 14
Jaycie

Jaycie stood in front of her open locker, looking at the *Chemistry is cool!* sticker she had placed on the inside wall. Martin gave her the sticker because they were the two top-scoring students in New York's chemistry standardized testing. After the results came back, Martin approached Jaycie at her locker to congratulate her. He noticed the other stickers decorating the inside of her locker. Some bands he recognized, others he didn't, but he wanted to give her something to add to the mural. They had discussed the test earlier in the year, and it was safe to say they'd likely both score within the top five of the school. Maybe even place high in their home county results. But they had no idea they would be the top two students statewide. The top two students coming from the same school was almost unheard of. They had every reason to be proud.

Jaycie's eyes welled up. The corner of the sticker had begun to peel a little. She reached into her locker and held it in place for a moment. That's when she heard a frustrated groan a few lockers down.

She peered beyond her locker's door to see Calvin Roberts

wiping his own locker with a book. She raised an eyebrow, curious. Then she closed her locker and approached her lab partner.

"Hey, what's going on?" she asked, but she saw the answer caked onto Calvin's locker, clear as day.

"It's tuna," Calvin said furiously. "I hate tuna."

"I'd hate anything smashed into my locker like that," Jaycie said, trying to make light of the situation. "I'm sorry, dude. Here, let me help you." She took out the pack of wet wipes she kept in her bag and handed a few to Calvin. She took a few herself and began wiping the mess from the violated locker.

"Why are you helping me?" Calvin asked.

Jaycie shrugged. "It's the right thing to do. Besides, you seem like a decent guy." She was thinking of the previous day, when Hector had stolen her tuna sandwich. She couldn't help but speculate that the tuna used in this locker attack had once been her sandwich.

"It's been tough, you know? Coming here," Calvin said. "People treat me differently. I know why. I'm obviously different than the majority of Blair residents. It would be one thing if people *just* avoided me. But they don't have to go and do shit like this. It's like I'm not even welcome here."

"Well, you *are* welcome here," Jaycie said. "Blair just has a major asshole problem. Trust me, I'm not immune to it either, but this is certainly next level. I'm sorry. Besides, I think that tuna was once my sandwich. For that, I'm extra sorry."

Calvin laughed out loud. "Damn. I'd offer it back, but I doubt you'd want it in this condition."

When they removed the last remnants of tuna from the locker, Calvin wiped his hands together.

"But seriously? Tuna? Of all the sandwiches you could have brought for lunch. Tuna?" This made Jaycie laugh. "I appreciate you helping me out. And for telling me I'm welcome here. You're a good lab partner."

"I'm not helping you because you're my lab partner," Jaycie said. "But it helps, I suppose," she chuckled.

This made Calvin smile. Now, with his locker clean, he opened it, and Jaycie's eyes lit up.

"Woah, look at you," she said, pointing at the stickers on the inside of his locker door. "*Blood of the Innocent*, huh? I didn't think you had it in you."

"Great game," Calvin chuckled. "Although I can't get past the level where you have to sneak into the cemetery."

"Not cool," Jaycie joked. "You shouldn't flaunt a sticker for a game you haven't beaten yet."

"I'm *almost* at the end," Calvin defended.

Jaycie said, "I'll give you some tips on how to beat that level after we finish our lab assignment."

Chapter 15
Stu

The start of the new school year began, as it always had, with a staple of Gothic Lit: Bram Stoker's *Dracula*. Each year, Stu looked forward to discussing the book's themes, of which there were many, with the new lot of students taking his class. However, this year felt different. Stu felt a sort of forbidden nature to tackling a story like *Dracula*, given the gruesome discovery at Owl's Head Park. But, the school year had to go on, he supposed.

This time, he gave the class a set of expectations. "I've had previous classes bring up several consistent themes within the text. For example, the fear of female sexual awakening. During the Victorian era, men typically subjugated women into two categories. Either she was a wife, or a virgin. Right? What happens to Lucy after Dracula succeeds in turning her? The male characters no longer view her as pure; thus, her value is destroyed. Clearly not consistent with a woman's place in society by modern standards—although there are some more conservative factions of the population who would *still* base a woman's worth on her quote-on-quote purity.

"Another theme I've heard brought up is Dracula's acknowledgement of the fear of outsiders. An *otherness*, if you will. This is a major theme in *Frankenstein* as well, but I can see where connections can be made in *Dracula*. Because Dracula is so different, the fear of an 'infiltration' on English culture is at the forefront. What else? Does anyone have anything they'd like to add? What do you think we can pull from *Dracula* and relate to modern day?"

Mr. Reinhart expected a couple of hands to be raised, specifically Jaycie Brogdon's. But a hand went up from the back of the room. To Stu's surprise, it belonged to Gabe Coleman. Stu was familiar with Gabe and his little friend group, which included the likes of Tomas Fischer and Hector Stroud. They had a negative reputation among the teachers and faculty. They never participated in class discussion —that is, if they showed up to class in the first place. Worst of all, if the boys were all together in a class, they would feel emboldened to speak out, disrupting the ongoing lesson. However, this period of Gothic Lit saw the Fischer friend group fractured, including only Gabe and Jax. Perhaps with only half the group present, there was a chance of real participation.

Stu pointed at him. "Sure, Gabe, what do you have for me?"

"I heard that the upcoming eclipse is going to be bad because it could bring total darkness to Blair. I even heard some saying it could be dangerous, that hosting Fall Fest in celebration of the eclipse is irresponsible. Is that true?"

"That's an interesting take," Stu said, turning to the board. He used chalk to scribble the words, "vampirism" and "solar eclipse," drawing a line connecting them both. "Perhaps there is a correlation between a vampire's ability and the darkness brought on during an eclipse, right? Very interesting. Now, as far as the safety of Fall Fest, I'm sure everyone involved is taking the proper precautions to make sure everyone in Blair is safe that day."

"That's not what I meant," Gabe said. "Is it true that vampires get stronger during an eclipse? Like, what if Blair is in *total* darkness?"

"Well, I don't think we'll be in *total* darkness." Stu faced the class attentively. "If anything, we'll lose light for a few minutes, but that's all."

"What if we do lose it completely, though?" Gabe persisted. "I heard this eclipse is special. Like, a once-in-a-lifetime kind of thing. I heard that we could be in pitch black for up to two whole days."

Mr. Reinhart chuckled, his face growing warm. "When I said let's relate *Dracula* to modern day, I meant let's stick to *this* reality. We're getting into hypotheticals now, the stuff of legends. Let's try to focus on themes."

"It reminds me of that vampire movie, 30 *Days of Night*. My dad showed me once. It's about this town in Alaska that sits in complete darkness for thirty full days. They were like sitting ducks when the vampires came. What would happen to Blair in that kind of scenario? What if the eclipse leaves us in complete darkness?"

"That's just a movie, Gabe," Stu said.

A sitting duck.

Just like Martin, Stu thought. *That poor kid...*

Dead. Soaked in blood, covered in dirt.

They had been so bad to him.

Sitting ducks...

An entire town left in the dark. Helpless against the potential havoc waiting within the impending eclipse.

Sweat began to accumulate at Stu's temples.

He shook his head. "Alright, um, let's go over some reading milestones. Why don't we aim to finish chapter one by next week? About twenty pages..." He trailed off. He raised a shaking hand to the board to write "chapter one" but couldn't perform the task. He dropped the chalk on the hard, tiled floor, and it snapped in two. The only thing he could think about were the claw marks running up and down Martin's arms. The deep, gashing bites on the boy's neck and shoulders.

If only he could have gotten away from this place.

Stu panicked. A roomful of student faces watched him as he

froze in front of the classroom, sweat now rolling down his back and face. He stammered for a second, unable to think of anything to say. He had to segue back into the lesson, but his mind played over and over the scene near Owl's Head Park. Stunned into silence, Stu darted for the door and retreated into the hall.

Chapter 16
Jaycie

Saturday was such an exceptionally clear day, it was almost cruel. The fall foliage was bright and vibrant, and the temperature hovered at a comfortable seventy degrees. It was like Mother Nature was playing a sick joke on the town of Blair, given the funeral taking place today. The day of mourning being so bright and sunny was like salt in the still-fresh wound that was the death of Martin Welch.

The Brogdon family arrived on time at Blair Cemetery, where Martin Welch was to be buried. The rolling grass looked like an ocean of green, with headstones like cement buoys drifting with the current. Townsfolk filed in through the cemetery gates, dressed in black, floating mournfully to the designated grave site.

The bright sun reflected off the car ahead of them, and Jaycie closed her eyes, lifting a hand to shield herself from the glare.

As they parked, Jaycie had a somber thought: This was the first time they had been out together as a family in a very long time. About two years, if she had to guess. She couldn't remember the last time a Brogdon outing wasn't missing someone. Whether Dad had a work thing, or Jax was off with friends, or Jaycie herself opted to stay home and study. The thought filled her with sadness.

The summer before Jax and Jaycie's freshman year stood out to her. Had it been that long? Her brother was still barely five foot four and would shoot up another half a foot by the end of their sophomore year. They spent a week at their lake house near Lake Placid in the Adirondack Mountains. Then, to conclude their summer in true Blair fashion, their parents brought them to Fred Brown's farm. Apple picking just before the school year started was a Brogdon family tradition. Martin had joined them on this particular outing, making it all the more special.

Jax wasn't even Jax yet. He was still going by Jackson—he would always be Jackson to her. But he wouldn't adopt his abbreviated nickname until their junior year. She remembered him with his pile of textbooks, too, giving it his all. It always took Jax extra effort in studying, though. This made Jaycie sad. She wished she could give some of her innate ability to her brother, so he could have progressed with her and they'd have more of the same classes, anything she could do to slow down the process of them drifting apart. She would do anything to strengthen their family ties, but the current of the ocean that was pulling them apart seemed to be stronger.

She remembered her brother genuinely trying. The history class they had together as freshmen was special because it was one of the few classes the twins actually shared. Jaycie moved on to advanced courses rather quickly, while Jax would continue on at a regular pace. While there wasn't anything inherently wrong with Jax's pace, Jaycie thought they'd share more classes together. She recalled Jax doing well in their history class. They studied together, and they helped each other remember important dates and names. Those times made Jaycie happy.

Then Jax stopped trying. When Tomas Fischer showed up, Jax's efforts went off a cliff. Jaycie grew especially concerned when Jax gave up playing the guitar after a mysterious hand injury. He claimed he'd hurt himself skating, but his story didn't add up. There were no scrapes or cuts on his knees or elbows—this injury was too precise to have come from a fall.

Their trip to Fred Brown's farm was pleasant. It was a day similar to this one, come to think of it. Sun shining hot and bright before the start of autumn. Dad wore his Montauk tank top, while Mom wore sunglasses and a dress. They spent hours picking apples and taking pictures near the bales of hay that surrounded the perimeter of the farm. Jaycie's favorite was feeding the goats—especially the baby, named Pumpkin, who had a distinct brown patch around one eye. When they got home, she'd helped Mom bake pies with the fresh apples.

Jaycie took that trip for granted. She'd figured they would do something like that as a family again. Just the four of them. However, another year passed, and it wasn't so. Then, going into junior year, it was something else. She hadn't thought that the next time they'd all be together as a family would be because Martin died. It made her feel like they didn't even like each other anymore. Like they only just tolerated each other through dinner during the week before going their separate ways. She thought perhaps Martin dying was the final nail in that coffin. Her family would never be able to share in each other's joy again—because, for Jaycie, it felt as if joy were a piece of her heart, gnawed out and never to be shared again.

Dad parked the car, and they all got out. Jaycie looked around and recognized people from BHS. She saw Mabel with her family, and her heart fluttered—she couldn't wait to catch up with her, even though she was feeling extra vulnerable. Rose was here with her family too. Seeing everyone with their families made Jaycie's chest swell with emotion. She wondered if anyone else was feeling the same kind of distancing wedge being forced in between them and their families. But then she saw Mr. Reinhart arriving with a few teachers from BHS instead of their families.

Did every family eventually fall apart?

Finally, Jaycie spotted Mr. and Mrs. Welch sitting near the area where the service would take place. Their grief was inescapable. It was emanating from their bodies, saturating the air over Blair Cemetery like the smell of popcorn at a carnival. With them was Father Benjamin, the priest from Holy Cross Church. The Welches weren't Catholic, but Father Benjamin was okay with doing a funeral for them regardless.

Jaycie spotted the casket and felt sick. Up until now, she'd felt a strange sensation, like the day was moving in slow motion. However, the sight of Martin's casket, positioned above the gaping, ominous hole in the ground, gave Jaycie a sinking feeling. The morbid sight of it caused her to well up.

As they lined up to find their seats behind the Welch family, Jaycie's dad put an arm around her. She could no longer contain her grief. Just as the memorial was about to begin, Jaycie lowered her head and began to cry.

Chapter 17
John Darski

The communities of Blair operated in individual bubbles that often overlapped with one another. The high school faculty often socialized with each other and were friends with many of the other locals, including small business owners and blue-collar workers. This small-town overlap was the reason why news typically spread quickly to the far reaches of the community, and not always in the most accurate way.

John Darski sat on the outside of one of these overlapping circles. He had grown up with Henry Donoghue and graduated from Blair High School with him in 1975. Henry acted as a sort of connective tissue for the town of Blair, his pub being a common ground for different generations to come together.

John knew the memorial service for that boy from BHS was taking place today. However, he was only distantly connected by way of Henry Donoghue and Stuart Reinhart. He was also neighbors with one of the teachers from the high school, Alan Marcus, but they weren't necessarily on friendly terms. While it would have been a nice gesture to show up to the funeral, John ultimately decided against it. He couldn't bear to be around that much grief. It made his skin crawl. He preferred to keep his distance.

Instead, he set up camp along the beach where the Winooski River flowed into Lake Champlain. This time of year was perfect for rainbow trout, which were plentiful in the Winooski. Most weekends in September and October, John would set up camp Friday night and fish on through the weekend.

Hook, Line & Sinker, John's fishing shop, was a staple of northeastern New York. The shop was intertwined with the main artery of Blair's Main Street, but he had customers from all over, including folks from across the lake coming in from Vermont. Fishing enthusiasts, amateur and professional alike, patronized the shop for John's expertise and premier equipment. He always provided the very best service, and every purchase came guaranteed with at least one pro tip from John himself.

The weather going into the weekend had been too perfect to not set up camp that Friday night and try to get in some early fishing on Saturday. John told his friend Henry to send his regards to the mourning family and promised he'd have a beer ready for him when the service concluded on Saturday.

Henry Donoghue and Ray Parilla were the most frequent to join John at his beachside fishing campout. Henry usually stopped by on Friday after the pub closed, capping off the night with a couple of beers.

Ray, affably known as "Blinks," would join them late Saturday morning after completing his delivery route. He wasn't the fishing type, but there was always a chair available for him, plastic legs dug into the sand with a beer in the cup holder. By the time he arrived, the lines had usually already been cast into the river. Ray had a fishing line assigned to him—the word "assigned" used loosely. Ray would peek at it periodically, but he spent most of his time helping himself to the cooler stockpiled with John's beers. He was more interested in chatting it up with the boys, and his favorite subject was town gossip.

John didn't mind sharing his gear or his beer. He enjoyed the company. Besides, Ray would always come ready with this garlic-lemon salt his wife would make, which went perfectly with fresh caught trout—almost always caught by John himself. If the weather was nice enough, they'd grill it up right there on the beach. Not a bad way to spend a Saturday.

On this early autumn Saturday morning, John woke up in his camp without any of his usual guests, as they'd be joining him after the conclusion of the Welch funeral.

He unzipped his tent and stepped out onto the beach, stretching his legs and hearing his joints pop. The sun had barely begun to peek out over the horizon, casting a bright shine along the river's surface. The air was crisp, and he inhaled, appreciating the beautiful morning he'd been given.

John fetched himself a beer from the cooler and dug his bare feet into the cold sand. He'd task Ray with collecting more wood for the fire when he arrived later in the afternoon. Ray could at least do that, make himself useful while he yammered on about what kind of trouble the neighborhood kids were causing this week, or how Blair has changed over the years, or his favorite go-to: the incident at Perkins gas station last year.

The opposite bank of the river was still blanketed in morning darkness, as the rising sun had yet to touch that side of the Winooski. John's vision, blurry from sleep, still picked up on something in the trees on the other side of the river. He squinted, barely making out a human-shaped shadow across the way.

John knew this was an impossibility, because there was nothing on the other side of the Winooski River except the wilderness surrounding Halfmoon Cave. The Winooski acted as a natural border to the south of Blair, keeping all residents and businesses to the north of the woods.

But there was that old legend about the cave on the other side of the river. A town legend that promoted the idea that a witch was living in Halfmoon Cave. Growing up in Blair, John even heard some people add to the legend, saying that every summer, the witch rises from her shadowy grave to eat children. This, John knew, was made up to scare kids, which he thought was in poor taste.

John shook his head and gave the figure a courtesy wave. There was no movement or response, so he rubbed his eyes and squinted harder to get a better look. His vision was rough in the mornings. In recent years, it had only gotten worse. He was certain he needed glasses, but he continued to put that off. Usually by the afternoon John's vision was normal, so he wasn't in a rush to see the optometrist just yet.

As his vision came into focus, John thought he saw a woman on the opposite side of the river, standing on the beach. At least, it was the outline of a woman. He couldn't quite make out a face or any discernable features. His eyes only allowed him to see a dark blur draped over a light blur. His imagination pieced together a pale woman with a tangled mess of black hair covering her face, wearing all white. Was she watching him? Where had she come from, and who was she?

John took a swig of his beer. Was his imagination getting the better of him? He wasn't sure. But he wondered if she had been there the entire night. Was she watching the tent as he slept? If this was a woman wearing all white, he would have seen her at night. The white would have reflected in the moonlight, and there was no way he would have missed her.

Unless it wasn't a woman at all.

Just then, he felt something cold and wet dripping on his right hand. He looked down and saw the beer in his hand overflowing.

"Shit." John placed the bottle in the sand and grabbed a towel to wipe his hands. When he looked back, beer was foaming up the neck of the bottle, spilling down into the sand.

"What the fuck?"

He looked across the river, back to the spot where he'd thought he saw the figure. It was gone, replaced by a deer grazing the grass along the riverbank.

He sighed restlessly and pulled his jacket on. The morning chill had struck his nerves, and he was suddenly very cold. He lit the fire once again and waited for the afternoon to come and his company to arrive. In the meantime, he would distract himself by rigging the fishing lines, because the more he thought about the legend in the cave, the more he suspended his disbelief.

Chapter 18

Stu

Stu left Blair Cemetery in a haze. It felt like he had been going through the motions. Day in and day out, as if he were trudging through mud since he found Martin's body near Owl's Head Park. The trauma was an inescapable cloak of darkness, making it difficult to focus on much else. He had trouble recalling most conversations at school; whether with his colleagues or his students, it was just noise. Unless it had to do with Martin...

And the impending eclipse.

The local forecast spoke about a powerful eclipse expected to occur over Blair next week, but was there really something unique about it? Something to fear?

Once every 230 years...

Was something from Blair's past casting such a long shadow? Or was Stu being paranoid?

He did know he needed to get back and take Paula on a walk. Stu felt like if it wasn't for his dog keeping him on somewhat of a routine, he'd float away into uncontrollable bouts of anxiety, disengaging from others. But he still owed her a proper walk through town, a perfect excuse to force himself to see other people.

When he let himself into the house, Paula jumped on him. He scratched behind her ears, pleased with the warm welcome.

"Ready to visit our friends?" Stu asked. The dog's bushy brown tail waved back and forth in approval.

It was a fifteen-minute walk from Stu's house on Bluebird Drive to the Mitchells' coffee shop on Bean Road. Typically, he and Paula would jog to the shop, feel the brisk autumn air of Upstate New York. Fresh air followed by a caffeine hit used to be the best way to start his weekend. If the weather was nice enough, the pair would often head to Delta Park Beach after their coffee run. Stu would let Paula off the leash, and she would get her zoomies out in the sand. Before, there was never a need to keep Paula so close. She wasn't the type of dog to dart away from her owner, even as a pup. But this afternoon, as they slowly walked Blair's downtown, Stu gripped Paula's leash a little tighter.

As they approached the corner of Bean and Holy Cross Road, Stu couldn't stop his eyes from darting around. He glanced down each street they passed, paying close attention to their surroundings. The routine darkness of a Blair winter seemed to be creeping in prematurely, dusk ostensibly forcing its way into the afternoon sky. It seemed as if it were more than just the death of Martin Welch. Yes, the boy's death had marked a clear shift in the town. It ushered in an invisible gloom, but there was something more. There was a living, breathing darkness residing here now—one which Stu could not figure out until, like a jump scare from a seventies Satanic panic horror movie, it was directly in his line of vision.

Sooner or later, the good times had to end.

It appeared at Stu's feet in the form of a shadow—the outline of a cross in the road like a bad omen. Stu followed the shadow, his eyes slowly looking up above him at the church's spire, where he found the brass cross inverted atop its perch. Hanging there like an angel shot down from grace and hanging on for dear life. The sight of the upside-down cross hanging high above Blair's Main Street made Stu's heart race, but with a tug from Paula, he continued walking toward the coffee shop.

Perhaps the good times were over.

The front door's bell chimed as Stu and Paula entered the shop.

"Hi, Stu," a young woman behind the counter said.

"Hey, Jill," Stu nodded. "Where's Zach today?"

"Oh, he hasn't been feeling well this week, so I went ahead and opened up without him. Well, I *forced* him to stay home today. You know how he is. I told him he should get his rest now, that way he'll be back on his feet sooner."

"Good call," Stu said. "Poor guy. Send him my well wishes, would you?"

"Sure will," she said. "And hello to you, Paula." She stepped out from behind the counter and gave the dog a generous ear scratch. Paula's tail waved in approval, and her back paw scratched involuntarily at an invisible carpet.

Jill stepped back behind the counter, washed her hands, and began to prepare Stu's coffee. She knew his order by heart.

"How are you holding up?" she asked gently. Stu knew she didn't want to pry, but he was sure the answer was written all over his face. Jill, who graduated from BHS a decade ago, had always been one of Stu's most emotionally intelligent students. Stu had always figured she would find the first express ticket out of Blair and start a life somewhere else. Then she met Zach, and they got married and started their coffee shop in town. Now, having their first child on the way had effectively killed any prospect of leaving Blair. But she seemed happy, and that was enough for Stu.

Stu pulled up a counter stool and sat down. Paula followed his lead, lying down near the legs of the chair. Stu shrugged. "I'm holding up about as well as the church cross." He gave a wan smile and sipped his coffee. "Do you know how that happened?"

"I figured it was the storm," Jill said. "They said lightning must have struck the top of the spire, knocking the cross off balance. What are the chances, right?"

Stu contemplated this. He didn't recall a storm...had he slept that deeply?

He's the one who found that boy.

A whisper came from the back of the coffee shop. Stu heard it, and it sent a shiver up his spine. Jill heard it too, and she pursed her lips.

An older man approached the counter. Meanwhile, Jill turned to the espresso machine, replacing the used grounds. Stu turned to give a polite nod to the man, who had a look of deep concern on his face.

"This isn't the first time something like this happened," the man said. "Just the first time it's happened to a *human.*"

"How do you mean?" Stu asked. He wrapped both hands around his coffee, feeling the warmth spread to his palms.

"You know that farm down by the Winooski? About five miles from here?"

"Of course," Stu said. "Fred Brown owns that farm. I know him well."

The man took a deep breath, then continued, "Well, word is he's been having issues with his livestock. On three separate occasions, Fred found one of his goats dead. And I don't just mean dead—I mean mutilated. Completely maimed. Similar to that Welch boy...

"A few months back, Fred got all new wire fencing around the whole property because coyotes kept getting in and killing his chickens. Now, a couple of half-eaten chickens is one thing—something every farmer has to deal with at least once or twice in his life. This was different, though. This was no coyote. Coyotes can't take down a full-grown goat...no, not like that. And coyotes typically consume their prey. Maybe not fully, but they eat. The goat...it looked like it'd been killed for sport. Excuse my French, but it scares the hell out of me."

Paula made a whimpering sound, and Stu grimaced. "I helped Fred set up that new fence. There's no way a coyote could have gotten past it, I promise you that."

"What do you suspect it is?" Jill asked, now fully engaged in the story. "If it's not coyotes, what could it be?"

"Well, I don't know," the man said. "Hard to tell. Whatever it is got in and out without damaging the fencing. I spoke to Fred the other day, and he said whatever it was may as well have just opened the front gate and strolled right in. As crazy as that sounds, it's the only thing that made sense. It couldn't have hopped the fence, it's so tall even a horse would have trouble getting over it. Almost makes me think it was a human that did this. But no human—at least, not one in their right mind—would do such a thing. And Fred said he could clearly see teeth marks around the goat's neck. Teeth. Sharp canines did this, and nothing else."

"It almost sounds like a cryptid," Jill suggested. "If I didn't know any better, I'd say it was a vampire, like from those stories you taught in your literature class, Mr. Reinhart."

"Right...but come on, vampires aren't real," Stu said. But as the words left his mouth, the older man gave him an accusatory glare, as if to say, *That's real fresh coming from the one who teaches* Dracula *in school.* While the idea was easy to dismiss at face value, Stu couldn't help but wonder. He thought about Martin. The manner in which the kid had been found. It was a brutal, gory mess.

Stu hadn't given a lot of thought to *what* could have done that to Martin, only *why*. He instinctively concluded it must have been an animal. But this seemed much more calculated than an animal mauling.

No human—at least, not one in their right mind—would do such a thing.

Stu felt the old man's eyes studying him. "We've got to get going," Stu said, finishing his coffee. He gave Jill an appreciative smile and repeated, "Give Zach my regards."

Paula was up on her feet, taking the cue from Stu. They left the coffee shop and began walking home. A new thought was haunting Stu: *Whoever killed Martin might have been human.*

* * *

The paved road gave way to gravel as Stu drove southeast off the Winooski and toward Fred Brown's farm. He thought he'd go check on his friend after hearing he was having trouble with his goats again.

Fred Brown owned a fifteen-acre property that stretched from the edge of Blair to the Winooski River in the southeast. It also just touched Lake Champlain in the east.

Fred and his wife, Martha, raised a small herd of goats and a few sheep. They also had a chicken coop extending from their house, which they'd built themselves, for eggs. In the autumn, many people from Blair and even Plattsburgh would come in for pumpkins and apples and the variety of pies Martha made. The apple pie was a big draw, especially for Stu, but there was nothing more popular than Martha's maple berry pie. That was something special.

Stu parked in the driveway, gravel crunching underfoot as he stepped out of his car. He could see signage hoisted atop the farm's entrance, declaring the annual Fall Fest was coming. The festival, a Blair staple, was hosted at the Brown farm each year. This year, it was scheduled to coincide with the upcoming eclipse. It was a once-in-a-lifetime celebration, bringing together two unique events.

Once every 230 years.

Stu felt like the cherished Fall Festival would now be tainted by the lingering aftermath of Martin's death.

"How are you, neighbor?" Fred asked, greeting Stu at the car.

"I'm doing alright." They shook hands. Fred had a strong handshake. His hands were calloused but well-manicured for a man who had put in decades of hard, manual labor. "I wanted to come by and check in on you and the wife. I heard you were having some trouble with the goats again."

"I appreciate that," Fred said. He squinted in the bright afternoon sun. "News travels fast in Blair, but that's right. Something must have gotten in again during the night. Whatever it was got to one of the goats. I'll show you where it happened."

Stu followed Fred to the perimeter of the fence. A thought occurred to him. "The goat you found...it's been removed, yeah?" He couldn't bear to witness another gruesome aftermath.

"Oh yeah," Fred confirmed. "Officer Gary White was here after I reported the incident, and he stayed to help me remove it." Fred turned toward Stu and shook his head. "I can't even imagine how you must be feeling. Finding a goat is one thing..."

Stu waved a hand, frowning. He didn't want to talk about it now, but he appreciated Fred's understanding.

They continued to walk, bypassing the fenced-in area behind the house. About eight or nine goats were roaming the pasture, bleating and grazing on grass. However, there was one goat in particular that caught Stu's attention: a large, black goat staring in his direction. The eyes had a deep, thousand-mile stare, and if Stu didn't know any better, he would have assumed the goat was watching him. The goat's eyes had small black pupils surrounded by a yellow halo—like an eclipse. It also had the biggest horns Stu had ever seen on an animal.

"Do goats typically grow horns that big?" Stu asked as they passed by.

"Sure, sure," Fred nodded. "It's rare, but a buck can get scary big sometimes. Matter of fact, this is a new fella. My own goats have never gotten that big, but Midnight here, well, we found him wandering the woods recently and decided to adopt him. Hopefully he'll settle in and act as a deterrent to any future trespasser."

As they continued their walk, Stu couldn't help but look back at the muscular beast. It was far less active than its comrades. Its head tilted in their direction—it was almost certainly watching them.

"So what exactly happened, Fred? How many did they get to?"

"Just the one goat, thankfully." Fred sighed. "Could have been a lot worse, I suppose, but since we only have a dozen, losing one is a sizeable loss."

"Do you know how it got in?" Stu asked.

"Well, no," Fred said. "But I know where." He walked them over to a section of fencing at the far end of the property, close to where the forest met the Winooski River. The grass here was overgrown and darker than the grass near Brown's home.

Stu saw it just as Fred pointed it out. "Over there."

Dark red stained the grass in streaks leading up to the wooden fence. It looked like something had been dragged in or out of the property.

"The fence itself isn't damaged," Fred explained. "But clearly, whatever it had been was tall enough to get over the fence. I don't know what we're going to do about it."

Stu took a sharp breath. He could still feel the goat's yellow eyes watching. All of this preceding Fall Fest...the eclipse. What did it mean? Was it some kind of warning?

"Well, if you need any help, Fred, I'm here."

"Thanks, Stu," Fred nodded. "I just might take you up on that offer. With Fall Fest coming up, we could always use an extra set of hands. The volunteers are great, but you know how it goes. We're also installing some floodlights in case the eclipse makes it hard to see. I want people to get home safely."

"You can count on me," Stu said. "And I'll be the first in line for pie, as always. How is Martha, by the way? She's usually out here with you."

"Martha is hanging in there." Fred put his hands on his hips and sighed. "She woke up with a fever this morning. She was so pale. She's been in bed all morning, resting. That's why we couldn't make it over to pay our respects to Martin Welch.

"She hasn't been sick in ages," Fred continued. "She hasn't caught anything more than a cold since the kids were younger and they'd bring the bug home from school. Poor thing."

Stu shook his head. "Well, listen, if you need, I can run into town and pick up some supplies for you. It's really no inconvenience to me."

"That's very neighborly of you," Fred said. "If Martha isn't out of bed by tomorrow, I'll be sure to give you a holler. Thank you, Stu."

Fred took both of Stu's hands and shook them as if Stu had just offered to re-fence the entire farm himself.

"It's no problem at all," Stu said.

As he left, Stu's mind began to wander. He couldn't help but try to piece together the strange series of events taking place in Blair. The arrival of this strange new goat right before one of the other goats turned up dead. The death of Martin Welch and how Martha had fallen ill. There seemed to be a trend of sickness and misfortune swirling around the town, one which Stu hastily theorized could be a harbinger for this once-in-a-lifetime eclipse.

Chapter 19
Interlude: 1793

It took one month for the story of what Isaac Burton had done to reach the town of Blair. In that time, panic had swept through most of New England, but it was only a prelude for what was going to happen at home.

Burton, a congregational deacon captain from Vermont, had done something unspeakable. Perhaps it was in the name of love, but more than likely, it was in the name of pride. In the name of protecting himself.

He had exhumed the body of his late first wife, Rachel, who had passed away from symptoms similar to those currently plaguing his second wife, Hulda. She had lost a significant amount of weight and had begun to cough up blood.

In the ever-changing landscapes of science and medicine in 1793, Burton's actions were thought of as a means to combat a spreading disease. Much of what we understand today may seem trivial—but in 1793, it was scary. For example, in modern days, one wouldn't think twice about taking an ibuprofen for pain relief. However, the confidence with which early doctors diagnosed ailments they'd never seen before was astounding. Cocaine was commonly used to relieve simple toothaches. Arsenic was used to combat venereal disease. One of the most gruesome methods of fighting disease in the early eighteenth century, however, was the treatment for tuberculosis, or TB.

In 1790, TB was known simply as "consumption." Now, thanks to research, we know TB is a bacterial disease, but in 1790, this was a novel idea. Fear spread through communities, as they couldn't figure out this anomaly of a disease and what was happening to their loved ones. As their families suffered, people went to extremes to try and fight the spread of the disease.

The story of Isaac Burton exhuming the body of his first wife was only the first in a series of events that would later become known as the New England vampire panic. But the panic spread beyond the borders of eighteenth-century New England.

The theory was that if liquid blood was found inside an exhumed body, or if the body seemed fresh, then the dead might not have been dead at all. Instead, they believed the dead person had been *feeding* on the living, and they concluded that the blood found inside these cadavers belonged to patients currently suffering from consumption.

As loved ones continued to suffer and a cure was desperately sought, bodies were exhumed and reexamined. Burton's story was one of the first to reach the isolated town of Blair, but it wouldn't be the last. As the disease swept across northern settlements, horror stories became more frequent, and more disturbing.

Ultimately, Isaac Burton's extreme measures did not prevent the death of his beloved Hulda later that same year.

But life in Blair would continue on. The Fischer family raised their goats and their three children. They palavered with their neighbors. They went about their lives. All while something dark loomed just over the horizon from the east.

* * *

The Fischer boy returned home, leaves crunching underfoot. He could see his breath as he exhaled, visible in the early autumn frost, as was commonplace in the settlement of Blair. His stomach rumbled as he approached the end of his chores for the day. He had just delivered the last of the goats' milk for the month, but his focus was on getting home and removing his walking shoes, having lunch, and reading a story to the goats.

As he followed the path home, he glanced at the neighbor's property, which stood gracefully on the outskirts of town. He always glanced over at that house in hopes of seeing her.

Unbeknownst to the boy, having a neighbor so near his age was a rarity. Settlements like Blair were so sparsely populated, the youth's duties often fell under the same categories as their parents and other adults, which often forced children to grow up quickly as they took on responsibilities for the livelihood of the family and the community as a whole. There was little to no opportunity to interact with children their own age. Even in the town's schoolhouse, students of different ages were often mixed together in the same classroom.

The eldest Fischer boy was no exception. He'd grown up fast after taking on the role and responsibilities of being second-in-command to his father.

However, their neighbors had a daughter his age. He would often see her helping with chores of her own while he went about his deliveries. Her name was Clara, and he thought she was beautiful. In their tiny world, she was, in a way, the boy's shining light. She was the sun, and he was a flower, blooming at the sight of her brightness.

This new feeling intrigued the Fischer boy, and he began to ask his parents questions.

"How did you and mom meet?" the boy inquired.

Nathaniel Fischer smiled, knowing exactly what his son was getting at. "Well, when I was a boy, about your age, I helped my father the way you help me. We had neighbors in town, and they had a daughter who was my age. And, well, it started with me running errands across town and seeing her as I passed by. I knew I would marry her the moment we met. And it was true. When we turned eighteen, we were married."

The boy smiled thoughtfully. "I want to take care of my own goat farm and have my own family one day. Just like you, Dad."

"You will," Nathaniel said. "But you must remember to do your chores. You take care of these goats now, and they'll take care of you later. They'll be yours one day."

The boy nodded.

"Now go check on the goats and make sure they have everything they need. Walk the perimeter of the fence, just like I showed you, and make sure there are no gaps or broken fixtures."

The boy obliged and went outside to the goats.

His mother, Dorothy, entered the kitchen as he left, as if she'd been waiting for the boy's departure. Nathaniel faced the window, his back turned toward his wife as he watched his son approach the goat pen.

Dorothy knew her husband had heard her enter, but she remained quiet. She stepped toward the sink and saw the flower, which was perched inside a clay vase. Sitting there, almost taunting her. She knew the flower had come from that woman. That outsider.

But she didn't want to say it. She was afraid to say it.

Not only because of the consequences, of what would happen to a wife who spoke out against her husband. Who took a stand. Put her foot down. But also because she didn't want to confirm that what she suspected was real.

She knew in her heart it was true, but if she addressed it aloud, it would become something they had to deal with.

Instead, she picked up the flower, wrapping her hand around its delicate stem. She couldn't deny the flower's unique beauty—she hated it even more for that reason. Yet she took the flower and threw it into the trash behind Nathaniel's back.

"I'm determined to protect Blair," Nathaniel said, still facing out the window but finally addressing his wife.

"What do you mean?" she asked.

"I've received word from Vermont. A terrible disease has taken hold," he explained. "It seems to be spreading, and I'm concerned it is only a matter of time before it reaches Blair."

"What kind of disease?"

"It's unlike anything we've seen before. It has been said that people grow weak, as if they're withering away. Their life draining from them. Unbreakable fever, pain, weight loss. And a cough so uncontrollable it produces blood. It becomes increasingly difficult to breathe. The most frightening part—death does not seem to end the suffering. Consumption continues to devastate, even in death. Perhaps death is only the beginning of suffering.

"Knowing this, it is my duty to make sure this ugly disease never reaches our community. It cannot reach Blair, do you understand?" He finally turned around, his eyes burning with a voracious lust for something more dangerous than simple protection. For a moment, Dorothy thought she should run, take the children and leave Blair. Leave her unfaithful husband and start a new life...

Yet she knew that was impossible. She couldn't get away from him. Nathaniel was a man with power and connections. What would become of her, the woman who left the New York member of the House of Representatives?

"However, if consumption *does* reach Blair," Nathaniel continued, "that flower holds the power to quell its terrible symptoms. Maybe even heal those afflicted. So, I am telling you now, do not interfere."

Dorothy looked at her husband, forcing a smile. She felt a crawling disgust inside her stomach at the thought of him sneaking off at night again. But she had to know where he'd learned this information, even if that knowing would make her sick. She didn't want such a terrible fate to claim her family. Her boys, who she loved more than life itself.

"How did you come to know this?" she asked.

"Word from Vermont," Nathaniel Fischer said. "Their congressman, Isaac Burton...he exhumed the body of his late wife and found something horrific. This disease arrived at their town straight from Hell, it seems."

"And this flower," she said. "You know for certain it will protect us? Do others know?"

"Not yet," Nathaniel said. He gently picked the flower out of the trash bin and placed it back into its clay vase. He handled it with greater care than when he'd held his oldest child for the first time. "But I have confidence that this is the only way. This flower is the one thing we have which they do not, and therefore it is the key to our safety."

Chapter 20
Jax

A wise man listens to advice...

Jax walked north on Holy Cross Road, alone, as the sun set behind the church's broken spire. He needed time to himself—he felt as if he hadn't had a chance to process his thoughts about Martin. Foolishly, when his friend had been declared missing, Jax didn't take it seriously.

He thought back to the summer vacation when Martin had joined his family at their cabin in Lake Placid. It was Jax's favorite memory with Martin, one he hoped to hold near and dear for as long as he could. Jax recalled showing Martin a prank he used to play on Jaycie. They shared a room at the cabin, and he would leave a recording playing inside the room, hidden under his pillow, and then hide in their closet and jump out and scare Jaycie while she was looking for Jax under his bed.

This time, with Jax and Martin both in on the prank, a recording of Jax's voice wasn't needed. He had Martin hurry outside to find Jaycie on the porch.

"Quick, Jax was feeding a fox at the bedroom window, and the fox got in! We need help getting it back outside before your parents find out; I don't want us to get in trouble!"

Jaycie rushed back into the bedroom, ready to scold Jax for letting a wild animal into the cabin, but she found nothing but an empty room with an open window...

When Jax jumped out of the closet, Jaycie screamed so loud, a bird cawed in response. All three were laughing so hard, rolling on the floor in an uncontrollable fit.

Even later that night, when they brought it up again, Martin laughed so hard his root beer shot out of his nose.

Those were the times he missed. The times before Tomas Fischer...

Now, with Martin Welch buried in Blair Cemetery behind the church, there was no denying it. With everyone in town either going home or to the bar to mourn the death—or, for his friends, getting ready to attend the party at Tomas Fischer's house—Jax knew this was the only moment he'd get to be truly alone with his thoughts, uncompromised. So, he walked toward the cemetery.

A wise man listens to advice. Jax rolled the quote around in his mind. Strange how, in this moment of solitude, those words were what he thought about. But it made sense. He had heard this quote once, a long time ago, inside this very church. He forgot the context but remembered how his father would repeat it from time to time when trying to instill a life lesson. Jax didn't necessarily hate the message, but he thought it didn't hold much weight due to the fact that it had come from the church. His father couldn't come up with his own way of saying this?

Besides, Jax couldn't remember a single time when taking advice had paid off for him. He especially couldn't think of how listening to advice might have helped Martin Welch.

His old friend Martin. Someone who *did* listen to the advice of those who were supposed to know better. Martin did everything right, and look what happened to him. Look where it had landed him in the end.

Jax wrapped his hands around the cold metal fencing that circled the cemetery behind the church. It was dark, but he could see into the graveyard, the headstones of people who used to take advice, who used to fall in line and do the right thing. No matter what, they ended up here, alongside the others.

"Look at you," he said to himself. "What do you know? You're dead!"

Jax walked around to the side of the church. He plunged his hands into the cold, loose dirt, ran his hands along the siding, and cast the words NO GOD onto the clean side of the building.

He took a step back to look at what he'd done. For a moment, he didn't know what he wanted to do. It was time to go to the Fischer House, but he knew going would push him further into the inevitable. He looked down at his hands, at the scar snaked across his palm. The inevitable, he knew, was drawing closer, and he would soon have to make good on the vow he'd made to Tomas Fischer.

Chapter 21
Stu

Sometimes, the darkness of a place hides in plain sight.

Stu set out to uncover that darkness, and he knew exactly where to go. He had recently read, "When all else fails, give up and go to the library," and that tickled his teacher brain. So, he followed his instinct.

The Blair Public Library had seen better days, but it still held much of its original charm. The exterior looked like an old bank vault, with its arching iron entryway surrounded by dark brick. The lights inside were dim and the furniture outdated, but its collection of literature about local history was unrivaled. Their collection also included books that covered the history of neighboring towns in Upstate New York and New England.

Stu approached the front desk to say hello to Addy Westbrook, the tenured librarian, but he was met with an uncharacteristically suspicious glare.

"Before you head in, I have to ask you to check the bulletin board." Addy pointed. "We have some updates we want to make sure all of our guests are aware of."

"Oh, sure," Stu said. He glanced at the latest printouts pinned to the corkboard. In the center of them all, donning a large red, white, and blue font, was an article from a group called Freedom Readers. It was a list of books being banned from the Blair Public Library. The article concluded with a warning: If anyone were caught pushing any of these books deemed "unacceptable" by Freedom Readers, they would be subject to lawsuits. This included purchase or borrowing for the purpose of sharing these books within schools and other public places.

Stu looked back at Addy apprehensively. *Really?* he thought as he glanced at a couple of the titles. *Looking for Alaska* by John Green, *The Bluest Eye* by Toni Morrison, *And Tango Makes Three*... that innocent little penguin book. Finally, he noticed *Dracula* by Bram Stoker.

"I'm just stopping in to check out some books on Blair's history," Stu explained to Addy. "History books aren't being banned by Freedom Readers too, are they?" He tried to lighten the mood but was met with only a resentful glare.

Addy took a deep breath, her nostrils flaring. "That reminds me, when you have a chance, please send me your updated syllabus for this school year, Mr. Reinhart. E-mail is fine."

"Uh, got it," Stu said, unsure of how to feel. He went ahead and checked out the books he needed and took them to the seating area in the back of the library. The windows extended from the floor to the ceiling, allowing for a nice view of Lake Champlain while providing lots of natural light.

Stu split the books into two stacks in front of him: one stack for the history of Blair, another for New England. Blair's history was rich and complex, and included a lot of crossover with neighboring Vermont. There were also a lot of dark secrets which had been kept hidden for the most part. Secrets people were not proud of, kept suppressed by generations of those living in Blair.

Stu knew a famous story about Bartholomew Riggs, who lived in Blair with his family. He was partly responsible for the very first *Farmers' Almanac*, written in 1792—if only Stu could get his hands on a copy. It was rumored that this inaugural edition had predicted a great eclipse which was said to take place in 1793. With this in mind, Stu hoped he could find connections in the history books.

Stu started with books from the top of each stack: *A Supernatural History of Burlington, Vermont* and *Blair: A Hidden History.*

He began to flip through the pages, bringing each book to the section which mirrored the other, starting with the 1700s. He high-lighted the notable trends for the region, especially in the late eigh-teen century. Consumed by the sweeping vampire and witch panic, entire towns went to disastrous lengths to combat an evil that had been conjured up by their need to place blame for whatever they couldn't explain. Doing things to combat an evil, and becoming evil in the process.

He read how, in 1792, the residents of Burlington gathered together against suspected vampires. It was well-known that innocent people were executed on suspicion of being supernatural creatures. One of the most well-documented cases happened to Bartholomew Riggs. His entire family, accused of being vampires, were hung at the gallows, their necks broken. They were left to hang there and suffo-cate while pearl-clutching onlookers watched them take their final breaths.

Stu imagined it to be horrific, watching four sets of legs dangle in the air, twitching until death took them away. This included innocent children. Stu shuddered at the thought. How barbaric people could become when they had fear in their hearts.

After the suspected were confirmed dead, they were taken down, dissected, and set on fire. People stuck around. They watched. As the flames crackled, a false sense of security blanketed the town. Until the process was repeated a few weeks later. Another sick child. Another farmer finding dead livestock. Another innocent person convicted of being something they weren't. Another mob of angry townsfolk looking for answers.

Demanding justice.

And justice would always come. It was the only way to quell the fear that ran rampant through towns all across the United States. Similar to how the mob came for Frankenstein's monster with flaming pitchforks. People needed a scapegoat.

Stu had read that the panic was a result of tuberculosis. People at the time called it "consumption" and thought that the dead were rising from their graves and feeding on the living. Stu didn't want to jump to conclusions, but a dead child, a mutilated goat at the Brown farm. An impending eclipse anticipated to happen once in a lifetime...

Stu feared history was beginning to repeat itself. It all felt too familiar.

He flipped through the chapter on death and sacrifice. Old photos depicting dead bodies who looked like Martin. In every photo, the victim was facedown, surrounded by dirt, in a grave that seemed to have been dug by hand. Lying in a shallow grave.

It gave Stuart the chills. The more he thought about it, the more he wondered just how close he was to the very thing that had killed Martin. Was it watching him? It couldn't have been far. Perhaps it had just happened when he found Martin that morning. Perhaps it had been scared off by the approaching footsteps and Paula's barking.

Stu slammed the book shut; he was nearly gasping for air. He could almost feel breath on his shoulder.

"Jesus Christ," he muttered. It couldn't be. Nobody would believe him.

Stu had read many books in his life. He had been teaching *Dracula* to his Gothic Literature class for the past six years. Yet he'd never happened upon anything that made him believe any element of the supernatural was real. Until now.

The people of Blair would swear *he* was the crazy one for even suggesting what he was thinking to be true.

Yet there was validity to it...

History, Stu thought, was like looking into a mirror.

Chapter 22
Ray Parilla

Donoghue's Tavern opened in 1996 right off of Blair's Main Street. Henry Donoghue, the newly retired fire marshal, opened the pub, mostly needing something to do with his time post-retirement. The bar promptly became a staple, a gathering place for many of Blair's locals, and it stayed that way ever since.

The bar hadn't been updated since opening its doors. Some of the décor was rather charming, even retro. The dark, hardwood bar and stools were a standard in many establishments, and the exposed brick wall was an aesthetic many modern places strived to achieve. However, the cigarette vending machine—left abandoned and empty since New York State banned cigarettes in bars in 2003—was an eyesore.

A who's who of regulars filed into the tavern on Saturday after Martin Welch's funeral. Mr. and Mrs. Welch had a small post-funeral gathering at their home that included only their closest family and a few friends. Everyone else went on to process their grief in their own ways. However, as sunlight faded, the community needed a place to get together and talk. Henry needed it too, to be around people.

Donoghue's enforced a strict no politics policy, to keep the atmosphere as light and nonconfrontational as possible. "There's enough nagging bullshit outside these walls. I don't want to deal with it in here," Henry would say.

Funnily enough, contentious conversation was never much of an issue, aside from the standard tantrums and bickering that came along with watching sports on the TV behind the bar. Even Ray Parilla, with his reputation of being a gossip, successfully toed the line and touched on iffy subjects without being antagonistic.

Ray earned his nickname "Blinks" because after every sip of his old-fashioned, he would wriggle his mustache and blink twice before swallowing. He didn't mind the name. He just took simple pleasure in having his drink and chatting with his neighbors after his shift delivering the daily paper.

Whatever news he gathered on his route he usually brought back to Donoghue's and repeated verbatim to his fellow bar-goers. Cliff Lassen, another regular, who considered Ray a good friend, found it particularly entertaining. One morning, he shared a story with Ray about his neighbor across the street getting drunk and locking himself out of the house in nothing but his bathrobe. When Ray repeated the story back to Cliff the same night over drinks, it was clear Ray had absorbed Cliff's story, went about his day sharing it with anyone who would listen, and forgot where he had heard it from in the first place. Cliff didn't mind. At least Ray got the story right.

Ray was never as popular as he was the previous summer, however. After news broke of an attempted robbery gone wrong at the Perkins gas station—one of the businesses on his delivery route— he was the one everyone in town approached to get the scoop. He'd never received so many free drinks in his life.

Donoghue's patrons discussed their lives, their wives, and what they thought would happen next in the town of Blair. Inevitably, today the conversation steered toward the funeral, and speculations on the boy's fate were brought up by none other than Ray.

"Devastating shit," he said as he cleared his second drink.

Henry could only shake his head mournfully. He wiped down the bar top with a towel before placing Ray's third old-fashioned in front of him.

"I just keep thinking about Stu," Ray continued. "Finding the kid like that. That's the kind of thing that sticks with you, ya know? I don't know what I'd do if it were me," he said. "I'd probably go crazy."

Cliff answered with a simple "Yep."

"Has anyone figured out what *actually* happened to the kid?" Ray asked. He rotated his glass on its coaster, his brow wrinkled in contemplation.

"At this point, I suppose we may never know. I tell ya, that definitely scares me." Cliff shrugged and finished his pint of beer.

"I just hate it for the Welch folks," Ray said. "Such fine people. Last year they gifted me a bottle of whiskey for Christmas. They didn't have to. I mean, I come here to do all my drinking, and a gift isn't necessary. I'm only doing my job. But it shows the type of people they are. They love this community, and they always do what they can to show appreciation to all of us."

The chatter hushed as the front door opened and Stu made his way into the tavern. The sun was already going down as he approached the bar, giving both Ray and Cliff a pat on the shoulder.

"How is everyone holding up?" Stu asked, trying to break the obvious silence. He motioned toward Ray's half-drunk lowball glass, and Henry began setting Stu up with his own drink.

Stu took a seat at the end of the bar, beside Ray. "You don't have to stop talking on account of me," he said. "I know you're talking about the Welches; it's okay, guys."

"We were just saying how the Welches are such stand-up people. Of all people for this to happen to..." Ray said. "It's a damned shame."

"Ah, I hear that," Stu said, taking a sip of his fresh drink. "But we're all good people in this town. We may not be perfect—I mean, we all have our shit. But we try, don't we? I can confidently speak for everyone when I say our hearts are in the right place. When it comes down to it, we've always been there for each other. I love this town so much." Stu got choked up and had to stop for a moment.

Ray lifted his own glass and filled the silence. "I'll drink to that. I'll drink to this town every day of the week."

"You *do* drink to that every day of the week," Henry said.

"Ah," Ray grinned. "And so I'll *keep* doing it!" He clinked his glass against Stu's, downed half of his old-fashioned, wriggled his mustache, and blinked.

Stu smiled wistfully. "Thanks, guys. It's been eating at me, what I saw. I feel like I've been going crazy trying to piece together what happened, you know? Like, what kind of darkness must have fallen upon this town for something like that to happen to us?"

"Mm," Cliff mumbled, glancing in Stu's direction. "It's making us all wonder..."

"Well, if it's any consolation," Ray said, "we're in this together. Like Stu said, the people of this town have always had each other's backs, and I don't see *that* changing any time soon."

"Right," Henry said, giving the bar one more wipe down. "We'll get through this, just like everything else. And no matter what happens, whatever it is this town is going through, we'll make sure that darkness, that bad undercurrent, will never win. Not in this town."

"Indeed," Ray said, downing the rest of his drink in two gulps. "On that note, I hope you all have a decent evening. I can't be hungover for my route tomorrow." He pulled several bills from his wallet and arranged them on the bar top. Henry nodded in appreciation and took Ray's glass for cleaning.

"Have a good night, Ray," Stu said, slapping his back. He peered at the gap between himself and Cliff and opted to stay where he was.

* * *

Ray walked south on Heidelberg Drive, keeping to the road's shoulder. He had made this half-mile slosh-walk—as he liked to call it

—many times before. He could have navigated his way home with his eyes closed. He lived in the cul-de-sac at the end of Holbrook Court, where the Winooski River bent into a horseshoe shape. Ray's wife was likely in bed, reading a book, waiting for Ray to get home.

At this hour, he only needed to make a quick glance down Porter's Point Road to check for cars as he crossed. Traffic died down significantly after ten p.m., with only the occasional car pulling in or out of the Perkins gas station, which was located at the town's intersecting crossroads.

Well-practiced in his slosh-walk, Ray made good time from Donoghue's as he navigated the shoulder of the road, leaves crunching underfoot.

Houses grew fewer and farther between as he progressed toward Holbrook Court, leaving wide gaps of wooded area that fed into the steep bank of the Winooski. These gaps were filled with darkness, which Ray never really paid much attention to. There was never a need to.

He did wonder about his little slice of the river off Holbrook. It was an interesting anomaly in the Blair landscape. On a map, the bend in the river looked like the state of Michigan. Ray had never been to Michigan, having been born and raised in Blair and never really venturing out. But he felt like he would have blended right in, especially in the late 1960s. The state was home to punk rock legends such as Iggy and the Stooges. Blair wasn't lucky enough to have a true music scene like Detroit. Blair did have its own legends, but not the kind Ray liked to think about.

A little bit farther down, where the Winooski passed in front of Halfmoon Cave, Blair harbored the legend of a witch. Ray didn't necessarily believe in such folklore, yet he did avoid that part of the river. He never forgot the story of a young Blair couple whose daughter drowned there—a true tragedy. While the death was officially ruled an accident, some of his neighbors blamed it on the Halfmoon Cave witch. Sadly, the couple left Blair and moved away to... well, Ray couldn't recall.

Ray made a right turn onto Holbrook Court, the effects of several helpings of whiskey serving as a nice distraction. With his hands shoved into his pockets, he hummed along to one of his favorites, "Search and Destroy": "'And I'm the world's forgotten boy, the one who's searchin', searchin to destroy.'" He kicked pebbles and twigs and other nonsense as he walked. In fact, he was so confident in his drunken ability to walk home, he didn't even lift his head up when a rustling sound came from the trees in the darkness. He was focused on the ground, kicking debris in a childlike manner as he approached his house.

In Ray's defense, the rustling from the trees was disguised by the wind. It came in short, breezy waves, concealed by the howling of the wind. Ray could feel the gusts against his jacket, making his ears cold. However, what Ray could not hear was the scratching coming from behind those trees. Movement, deliberately timed with the sound of rustling leaves, followed Ray home, masked by the natural sounds of the night. As if something lurked in the woods, hungrily anticipating his arrival.

As Ray stepped onto his driveway, he gave a final, hard kick to a can, and it shot off into the woods, landing somewhere along the bank that sloped down into the Winooski. Ray could hear the can land among some shrubbery. And then all was quiet on Holbrook. He reached into his pocket for his keys when he heard a rustling in the brush where the can had landed.

Ray paused and said playfully, "Who's there?"

He reached down and picked up a tree branch. Then he slowly approached the wooded edge of the cul-de-sac, chuckling. "Do I hear a critter? I'm sorry if I disturbed you with my can." He almost couldn't contain his drunken giggle as he stepped over the curb and into the woods. He squinted for a moment, trying to adjust to the darkness of the woods behind his house. His porch light didn't reach this far.

"I had a few drinks tonight," Ray explained to the darkness. "Do you critters like to get drunk too? Hell, I suppose you don't. Or maybe y'all partake in critter weed? I won't tell anyone if you do." He pinched two fingers together, making a toking gesture and laughing at himself. He slowly stepped deeper into the foliage, angling down and following the slope. The rustling sound returned, this time farther down, as if luring him into the water.

Then the sound suddenly appeared behind him, catching Ray off guard. He stumbled on a branch and slid down the riverbank. He tore his jeans on the way down and stopped right at the crest of the water.

"Goddamn!" he exclaimed, sobering up. "I may have had one too many. Say, would any of you critters mind sharing some of your critter weed?" He chuckled again as he pressed his hands into the dirt and pushed himself up. The water reached up to his knees. The cold river water was sobering, but not as sobering as the realization of how far off the road he had gotten.

When he looked up, Ray could see the incline of the riverbank in front of him. It was lined with shrubbery that intertwined with the obscured purple of the Devil's Spiral flower, native only to the section of the Winooski River that abutted Halfmoon Cave. The flower had apparently been introduced to Blair by the Halfmoon Cave witch herself.

Ray squinted, measuring how far he had to climb to pull himself out of the water. His vision was still blurry, but it seemed like someone was standing at the top of the slope. The dark silhouette of a figure hovered over him, watching.

"Hey, who's there?" Ray called out. He got no response. He felt his vision double—perhaps the water hadn't been as sobering as he'd thought. "Do you mind giving me a hand? I slipped, and I'm a little tipsy, ha." He chuckled nervously, but the childish humor had left his voice. He slipped again on the loose mud of the riverbank, and he fell to his knees, the palms of his hands breaking his fall. He wiped his hands on his jeans and felt a stringy residue. When he looked down, strands of ropy black hair clung to his muddy hands.

"Fuck," he grunted. "Disgusting."

He dug his feet into the incline, determined to get out of this clumsy situation, and began to ascend. His breathing was labored; he could feel an acid burn climbing his esophagus.

"Now I need a hot shower. Shit. Got work in the morning," he huffed. "Smell like the goddamned river."

His hazy vision betrayed him as the black mass now appeared directly in front of his face. Ray found himself crippled with fear. The pale visage of a boy cut through the darkness. He opened his mouth, and hot breath discharged into Ray's face. A waft of sour, metallic air stung Ray's nostrils. He felt as if he were going to eject the whiskey from his belly.

It was over quickly. Ray wouldn't make it out of the river. As the darkness wrapped its hungry mouth around his face, Ray saw the pale, dead-eyed stare of something old and hungry.

Chapter 23
Jaycie

J aycie peered out the window of the car's backseat, watching the darkened terrain of Blair roll by like a flip-book. Mabel sat up front, with Rose behind the wheel of her father's SUV. The far end of Overlake Drive was narrow and winding as it led them to the lakefront properties.

The Fischer House was shrouded in mystery. Jaycie knew little of the historic building on the outskirts of Blair, only that it had been around since Blair was merely a settlement, not quite part of New York territory under English rule and geographically cut off from the rest of New England—the town was figuratively an island of its own. However, Jaycie always felt a pang of apprehension around the house, especially since her brother, Jax, started spending more and more of his time there.

Jaycie didn't like Tomas. Her brother had changed a lot since he started hanging out with him, and not for the better. Bullying at BHS skyrocketed after Tomas arrived, and most people either turned a blind eye or were complicit—because supposedly Tomas Fischer's father had money. But there was no proof of that, and it didn't excuse the things he did to others. Jaycie had watched Tomas directly influence Hector and Gabe to do his bidding, to make the lives of the students of BHS worse. She watched them do things like steal backpacks and throw them in the dumpster, pour garbage onto people, and mark lockers with graffiti, including offensive slurs. She knew she would never forgive Hector for the time he stole Martin Welch's saxophone and coated the instrument's wooden reed in rat's blood, causing Martin to have to miss an audition.

All while Jax stood by. The Jax she knew would stand up for people, not simply stand by as if he were on some kind of a leash.

The SUV rolled toward the house, and Jaycie's anxiety grew. Mabel and Rose would be with her, yes, but they didn't see what she saw. They didn't see Jax's behavior drastically shift since he started coming here. But it wasn't only Jax.

Jaycie had always been afraid of this house. Even as a child, she had the better sense to know that the house wasn't haunted, exactly—that was ridiculous. However, the house was like a shell, holding a greater evil inside. How could a house stand abandoned for so long yet still seem maintained? There were no signs of degradation, no overgrowth, no wear and tear, yet the structure remained deserted. The old house was like a filing cabinet, holding dark secrets from Blair's past within its walls. Until a year ago, when Tomas Fischer moved in with his father. But it still felt abandoned, the way Jaycie always remembered it, holding a darkness only eclipsed by the morbid fact that this "party" was taking place so soon after the burial of Martin Welch.

As they turned onto Thayer Beach Road, Jaycie felt certain she was making a mistake by coming, but it was already too late. There was no way Rose was going to turn the car around now. Jaycie was going to this party whether she liked it or not. She felt like her clothes were too tight, as if her jacket was constricting her body like a snakeskin.

Above beautiful Lake Champlain, the sky over Thayer Beach

seemed to be darker. As if the sky above the Fischer House was permanently darker than the rest of the sky—but maybe her mind was playing tricks on her. Of course it was darker out here; they were no longer downtown, and there were fewer lights. But it still felt wrong.

A gothic monolith of a house sat at the end of the too-long driveway. The road turned to gravel, and it felt as if they had made a turn into the eighteenth century. Jaycie looked out the window and was breathless, taken aback by the grandeur of the home. The architecture was too perfect. Three symmetrical gables enclosed windows that glowed a welcoming yellow, shining like a beacon against the façade of the house, which was stark black.

There was an almost regal personality in the house's posture. It seemed to be aware of its greatness, of its historical significance, while it overlooked the sparsely populated Thayer Beach on Lake Champlain.

A figure stood at the end of the driveway, just beyond the front entrance of the house. Jaycie's stomach turned when she recognized it to be Hector Stroud. Of course he was here. She was still mad at him for stealing her sandwich the other day (and smearing that sandwich on Calvin's locker).

Hector had always been a little shit. He was one of the classmates Jaycie and Jax grew up with. Although their junior high school class was small, the twins never really associated with Hector.

He was always kind of a bully, even before Tomas, taking out the anger rooted in his home life on his classmates. Therefore, he never really made friends. Just a messy-haired, pimple-faced kid with anger issues and a mean streak. Which was why Jaycie found it odd when she first saw Jax with Hector last year. It seemed as if Tomas were some sort of nexus with a gravitational pull, luring in the more troubled kids of BHS. It broke her heart to know her brother was tangled in with them.

Jaycie never thought much of her homemade lunch. Then Hector would show up with something he'd picked up from the McDonald's drive-through, and Jaycie would realize how lucky she and Jax were, the care their parents took to make sure they had a decent lunch every single day.

Things didn't change much from junior high to high school, but Hector's sense of style improved...slightly. In junior high, he wore a Nike hoodie (one in desperate need of a wash) even though he didn't play any sports. In gym class he wore highlighter-yellow basketball shorts, which were distractingly bad. In addition, he always wore the same worn-down pair of sneakers with the pump soles, which were marketed to make you believe you could run or jump just like a real athlete. Hector's pair, however, collected dirt and debris, which he tracked everywhere he went.

When they finally got to BHS, he traded in his obnoxiously bright athletic wear for dark, long-sleeved thermals, usually with a dark, puffy vest over top. Now his attire no longer acted as a reflector for headlights at night.

Jaycie always did her best to avoid Hector, but it was difficult sometimes. As time went by, she was amazed at how she grew *more* repulsed by him.

Rose parked the SUV, and Hector approached as they exited the car.

"Welcome, ladies," he greeted them. His voice was much calmer and (dare she say) smoother than Jaycie remembered, even compared to earlier in the week when he'd savagely taken her sandwich. Was this the same person?

In fact, Jaycie couldn't recall seeing Hector at all since the lunch bag incident, the school hallways being drastically less chaotic and stressful in his absence. She'd assumed he'd fallen ill but thought it better not to ask because, well, she didn't want to jinx it.

"Tomas is pleased to be hosting you this evening." He offered Jaycie a hand as she exited the SUV. She politely took it, smiling at the gesture. She looked up and was surprised to see his face completely clear of acne. Not even any visible scarring to indicate he'd ever had so much as a zit. His brown hair was still long and messy, cascading in front of his strikingly dark but surprisingly welcoming eyes. They were warm—unlike the touch of his hand, which was as cold as ice. Jaycie dismissed this detail as she stepped into the cold night air, wondering how long Hector had been standing outside waiting for their arrival. He didn't even have a jacket.

Rose and Mabel also exited the car, and Hector gave each a welcoming smile and polite nod. *Who is this person?* Jaycie wondered.

"You ladies are a little early—I hope you don't mind waiting in the parlor while Tomas finishes getting ready. He is running slightly behind schedule due to a prior engagement. The rest of our guests should be here within the hour."

Prior engagement? Jaycie thought. That sounded convenient and suspicious.

"Sure, sounds good to us," Mabel said, looking at Jaycie. She raised her eyebrows in amusement. So she, too, had noticed Hector's almost comical change. Jaycie relaxed for a moment, knowing that Mabel thought this was as ridiculous as she did.

"Excellent!" Hector exclaimed. "I will escort you to the parlor and then check in with Tomas. I'm sure he appreciates your patience."

The three girls followed Hector through the front door. Jaycie craned her neck, looking up at the estate as they entered. She briefly caught the silhouette of a person in one of the darkened windows on the top floor. It was only visible for a moment, as if the shadows were playing tricks on her. But it reminded her of the silhouette she'd seen in the window at school, when she was talking to Mr. Reinhart. The same feeling of being watched returned, putting her back on edge.

"Is Jax here?" Jaycie asked as Hector led them down a long corridor toward the parlor.

"Jax will be here soon," Hector reassured, his voice deceptively calm and steady, as if to lure the girls into feeling secure.

As they plunged into the depths of the Fischer House, the temperature seemed to drop. The parlor smelled airy, like the freshly distinct smell of the air after it rained. It reminded Jaycie of when her parents would take her and Jax hiking in the Adirondack mountains. The morning after a heavy rain, the smell of the outdoors would drench their cabin on Lake Placid. It was fascinating how this room smelled exactly like that.

Jaycie closed her eyes as they took seats inside the parlor. The sounds of Mabel and Rose chatting with Hector grew distant. All she could feel was the coldness of the room and the sense that something bad happened in here. Had someone died in here?

Yes, there was another scent, just below the airy, rain-soaked surface. It was metallic, like blood.

She wondered if anybody else felt it.

Hector turned toward her. "You okay, Jaycie?"

Jaycie opened her eyes and realized she had broken out in a cold sweat. She glanced around, embarrassed to find that no one else shared her unease. She smiled wanly. "I'm okay, just a little cold."

"Oh, yes, sorry about that," Hector said. "This house has a very old heating system, which doesn't reach into every room. The parlor, being in the back of the house, is just out of range. I can grab a blanket for you if you'd like."

Jaycie nodded. As Hector went to retrieve her a blanket, she took a moment to fully take in her surroundings. The parlor felt very old money. The dramatic, dark-wood-coffered ceiling reminded her of being in a museum. A highly detailed, carved mantelpiece dominated one side of the room, which was very clean except for some residual soot inside the fireplace, which looked to Jaycie like it hadn't been used in some time.

On top of the fireplace was a single flower. Its delicate purple, velvety petals seemed out of place in the otherwise cold and dispassionate room. However, it, too, felt old, like everything else in the room. But the flower was beautiful, unlike anything else inside the overly calculated house. It was beautiful in a timid manner, like someone trying not to overstate their own features, but Jaycie could tell the flower held secrets. Perhaps even dark ones.

Gabe Coleman entered the parlor, holding a cup in his right hand, a glass chalice that matched the rest of the house.

"I'm afraid I've got some bad news, ladies," he said, feigning concern. He took a sip from the chalice as he sat down on the wide, upholstered sofa. "Unfortunately, the other guests we were expecting tonight have canceled." He put on an air of disappointment. "Last minute too. It's really sad, if you ask me. You can't rely on anyone these days."

"I find flakiness to be quite rude," Hector added. "We try to do something good..." He shook his head.

"Wait, *nobody* from school is showing up?" Jaycie asked. "I thought everyone knew about tonight's party."

"No, no," Hector said. "It's not like we invited *everyone* from Blair High School. This was meant to be an exclusive party. A housewarming, if you will. Tomas only invited a handful of people. He was looking forward to mingling and getting to know more people before graduation. But, unfortunately, everyone canceled."

"That sucks," Rose said. She took the chalice from Gabe's hand and took a sip. Jaycie watched her wearily. Her friend was far too upbeat and nonchalant about the fact that it would be just them and the boys. Her infatuation with Tomas was going to get her into trouble.

"Who else was supposed to come?" Jaycie asked, but Hector's attention was turned toward the parlor entrance, where Tomas was now standing with Jax in tow.

"Thank you all for being patient tonight," Tomas said as he walked into the room. His presence was striking. Jaycie had felt him standing in the doorway before she even turned to see him. "It's unfortunate that our other expected guests won't be joining us, but we'll make the most of the evening anyway, right?" He smiled as he approached the three girls on the sofa. Jax took a seat next to Hector, smiling weakly at his sister.

Tomas shook each girl's hand individually, smiling as he did so. He looked different than he did during the day. Tonight, his pale face was mannequin-like—waxy and delicate. Yet he was brimming with confidence, standing tall. Almost arrogant, like he had them right where he wanted them.

When he got to Jaycie, he took her hand, kissed it, and smiled, looking deeply into her eyes. She had never been this close to Tomas before. His hands were cold to the touch, almost freezing. His gaze was even colder, and Jaycie grew uncomfortable. She looked away.

"Since tonight is turning out to be a more intimate event than originally planned," Tomas said, "I want to take the opportunity to speak candidly. As you all know, the tragedy of Martin Welch has been weighing on this town. I'm sure hearing details of the way he was found must have scared you. It scared me." He shook his head. Hector and Gabe nodded in unison. Almost as if it had been rehearsed.

Jaycie watched Tomas intently. It was true. Sadness and fear for Martin Welch pervaded the town of Blair, but she found it odd that Tomas would say this after missing the funeral.

"It almost feels like, after they brought us all together that morning to tell us what happened, the school has done nothing to address anyone's concerns. The whole thing just feels swept under the rug. I don't know about any of you, but it makes me feel like they don't care about our safety."

Jaycie then noticed Tomas looking directly at her again. How long had he been staring, watching her with that cunningly uncomfortable smile stretched across his face?

"I do want to take a moment to express my appreciation to each of you for coming here tonight," Tomas continued. "I know perhaps some of us might not have gotten off to the best start, but tonight is meant to be an olive branch during these difficult times. It's comforting to know that flakiness isn't a widespread problem among neighbors. Especially during times like these, it's good to know who your true friends are." Tomas raised his chalice. "To us."

Everyone followed suit, with Jaycie uncomfortably drinking from her red plastic cup of water. Rose took Tomas's chalice and put it to her own lips...was that the second person she'd shared a glass with?

"I do want to extend an offer," Tomas said. "Sort of the reason for tonight's gathering in the first place. I know a lot of people at school have been on edge this week. A lot of townsfolk in general, actually. There isn't really anybody taking initiative to put us at ease about the situation. I feel like it would be the neighborly thing to do to fill in that gap. So, here is my proposal: We form a sort of coalition, if you will. A neighborhood watch, responsible for identifying suspicious activity and problems before they become more serious. Because, frankly, they gave us no answers regarding Martin's death, and the lack of closure does not sit well with me."

"It's getting late; I think we should go," Jaycie said, turning toward Mabel and Rose. She'd heard enough, and the morgue-like feeling inside the parlor was getting under her skin. The chill felt draped across her flesh, as if she were being caressed by the dead. This was supposed to be a fun, casual party, not some kind of initiation into a so-called neighborhood watch. *Now* Tomas wanted to act like their friend? Plus, the last-minute cancellation of all other guests was a major red flag. It made Jaycie suspect no one else had been invited in the first place.

"It's so early though," Rose groaned. "We can call you an Uber if you don't want to stay. I feel like we just got here."

Jaycie looked down at her phone, a lump in her throat. "I already tried, but there's no service here. None of my apps are working." Her feelings of dread were compounding by the minute.

"It's okay," Jax said. "I'm actually kind of tired myself." He looked over at his sister for the first time, as if he knew what she was thinking. It validated her feeling that something bad was going to happen if they stayed. She wasn't sure if Jax was being protective, or if he knew what that something was. "You can ride with me if you want," he offered, and Jaycie gladly accepted.

Jax lowered his head as he and Jaycie said their goodbyes, as if he didn't want to look at Tomas. Jaycie looked at their host, however, and what she saw was troubling. The look he was giving the twins was one of vitriol. *Uncalled for*, Jaycie thought. *Fuck his party, and fuck him*, she thought as they left.

Chapter 24
Mabel

"Since this party is down to"—Tomas waved his index finger, counting each individual who remained in the parlor—"the five of us, I have a proposition to make.

"There's a place nearby that's supposedly haunted by ghosts of Blair's past. Legend has it there's even a witch who still lives in Halfmoon Cave. I've heard she finds children and eats them. Perhaps this witch is responsible for the death of Martin Welch, hmm? I say we go down there to investigate. What do you say?"

"We're down to explore," Rose laughed. "I don't know what kind of bedtime stories *your* parents told you, but we don't believe there's some witch living in Halfmoon Cave."

Mabel sat listening, bothered that Rose had decided to speak for her. She'd heard the stories of the Halfmoon Cave witch and wasn't entirely sure if she believed in the old legend or not. However, she didn't want to test the theory, especially not now, when Rose seemed a little tipsy from whatever was in Tomas's cup. Her quick resignation to his charm was concerning. Mabel wondered if she should have left with Jaycie and Jax. It would have been better than exploring the woods near Halfmoon Cave.

"I think it's a great idea," Hector agreed.

"So it's settled." Tomas stood, gulping down the last of the liquid in his chalice and setting it on the mantel. "This party is now officially the first meeting of Blair's neighborhood watch. Our first order of business is investigating Halfmoon Cave. Come, follow me."

And so they went, venturing out into the cold night. They walked until the sand of Thayer Beach merged with the rocky path leading up to the cave.

As they came upon the mouth of the cave, Gabe joked, "Do you feel that?"

Rose and Mabel were standing very close to one another. "I don't *think* I feel anything," Rose said, playing along.

Mabel, on the other hand, felt her skin crawling in fear. She *could* feel something. Something deep in the recesses of her mind. It sounded like it was in her head but far away at the same time. She could hear what sounded like a beating heart, throbbing in her ears as they drew closer to the mouth of the cave. The black opening was creepy and uninviting. Although she didn't believe in the supernatural, she still felt a presence from inside the cave. They were not welcome here, and she knew it.

Tomas stopped and turned in front of the cave's entrance. "The safety of Blair is paramount," he began. He was facing the small group and addressing them formally, his tone shifting from casual excursion to all business. The black mouth of the cave surrounded him like a dark halo.

"The incident which preceded Martin's death was a preventable one. There must never be a repeat occurrence of such a tragedy in Blair. I won't allow it. I'm willing to do anything to keep this town safe. My family, the Fischer name, has a long history with Blair, and I am determined to protect it. This town belongs to us. It's time we start taking pride in what's ours."

Mabel tensed, grabbing Rose's hand, who was fully entranced. Mabel wasn't expecting a simple party to turn into discussion about their dead classmate.

"I'm willing to take an oath, right here, right now, to never let anything bad happen in Blair again," Tomas declared. "We must keep the darkness out of our home! What do you say; are you with me?"

Hector and Gabe responded in unison, "We're with you, Tomas!"

"I have an idea." Tomas grinned. He reached down and picked up a stone from the ground. A sharp, arrowhead stone. "A promise... and if any of us break it, our blood will be spilled onto this very dirt." He raised the stone high above his head with two hands. As he did so, the beating heart began to throb louder in Mabel's ears. She could feel panic setting in. She didn't like where this was going, and she didn't want to be a part of it, but she feared what would happen if she turned to run. She feared the consequence of saying no.

At that moment, thunder cracked in the sky, followed by a lightning strike somewhere behind the cave. It was very close to where they stood. The flash of light illuminated the dark sky. Mabel jumped, clinging tighter to Rose's arm.

Tomas brought the stone down and pointed the sharp edge into the palm of his left hand. He paused for a moment, looking up at the four people in front of him. He smiled. "I'm willing to bleed for Blair. Are you?"

Mabel felt a lump in her throat as Rose nodded her head. She was powerless to stop what was unfolding. She was frozen in fear.

Tomas drew the stone's edge across his palm, parting his skin, allowing blood as black as the mouth of the cave itself to trickle down his wrist. Mabel winced at the sight, pulling Rose closer.

No, no, no, no, this can't be happening. I shouldn't be here.

When Tomas was finished, he held the stone out in front of him and approached Hector. "Are you with me, brother? Do you take this oath?" he asked. Hector nodded, and Tomas drew the stone across his upturned palm. The same black blood beaded from the wound, trailing a line down Hector's forearm. A single drop landed in the dirt at their feet. The ground drank thirstily.

Tomas repeated this with Gabe. And then with Rose, who went along, to Mabel's dismay, taking this oath without hesitation. Mabel shivered at the thought of the medley of blood on the stone pushing into her skin until it broke.

Finally, Tomas stepped in front of Mabel. She felt helpless to refuse what was being asked, no, *demanded* of her. But she knew something worse might happen if she didn't go along.

There was never anyone else meant for this party. It was always meant to lead here.

Tomas looked deep into Mabel's eyes until she turned her palm upward, helpless to resist. Tomas took her hand in his. How dreadfully cold his hand felt against hers. He held the stone's sharp edge above her skin. She watched, trembling with fear. The look in Tomas's eyes struck a primal chord in Mabel, a third instinct inside of her fight-or flight-response: the instinct to remain stuck in place, rooted to the ground in hopes that whatever happened next would be over quickly. Tomas's eyes didn't have the far-off look of a psychopath in a horror movie. No, this was different. There was something dormant in Tomas's eyes. It was the aggressive look of an animal after a long hibernation, desperate for its first meal in months.

He drew the stone across her palm, and she could feel her skin separate, warm blood trickling down her wrist. She winced and drew back, but it was already done. A million thoughts raced through her mind. How *dirty* this was. How this went against everything she said she stood for. The disease, the dirt, the unsanitary conditions. She felt nauseous as she continued to hold on tightly to Rose's arm. The throbbing of the heart she could only assume came from inside the cave now sounded like the pounding of a drum.

Tomas stabbed the bloodstained edge of the stone into the dirt. "I say we take a little souvenir from this place. A reminder of our agreement. A promise to anyone who tries to take this town from us, that they will pay with their own blood."

Mabel felt sick. What had she just agreed to?

Tomas gathered five round stones from around the mouth of the cave. He set one in his left palm and passed the rest out to everyone. "Roll it around in your hand," he said. "Cover it."

Mabel watched as Rose unflinchingly followed Tomas's instruction, smearing her blood on the stone's surface. Mabel felt disgusted. She closed her eyes, took her stone, and shoved it into her jacket pocket. This all had to be over soon. She was ready to never speak of it again.

Tomas stood tall, surrounded by the dark, a monstrous grin stretched across his face as droplets of blood fell from his fingertips. "That makes six..." he declared. "And soon, the day the sky turns black, others will join us, and we'll be bound together, forever."

A rumbling came from deep within the cave—almost like a scornful cry. Mabel regretted moving the stones. The way they'd been arranged in front of the cave seemed purposeful. It felt as if they had disturbed something. But it was too late. Her blood was already painted on the stone.

* * *

On the drive home, they rode in silence. Mabel's ears were cold from the outside chill. After wrapping her sliced hand with a bandage, she raised them in front of the heater. She didn't want to put her hand into the same pocket as the stone. In fact, she felt inclined to throw the whole jacket away.

She peered over at Rose, who was focused on the road ahead—she didn't seem bothered at all. *Am I the one being ridiculous?* Mabel thought. They'd been a bit tipsy earlier and not fully making sense. They were just stones, after all. And it was just a cave. Animals lived in caves. The dark woods had given her the creeps, and the alcohol only heightened her anxiety. She'd sensed every little crack of a branch or animal sound as if it were something else. They were fine. They were just kids exploring the woods.

Yet it felt as if they'd stolen from the woods itself.

Rose pulled the car over. Mabel looked up, and they were in front of her house.

Mabel took a breath. "Thanks for driving me home," she said and got out. She felt like something was off. Rose hadn't said a word the entire drive. What if their actions in the woods had deeper consequences? What if they'd disturbed some kind of natural order?

She let herself into her home, and Rose drove off.

They had stolen from the woods. Mabel prayed the woods wouldn't eventually come looking for what they had taken.

Chapter 25
Stu

Stu bolted upright in bed, soaked in a cold sweat. He didn't remember trying to read after he got home from Donoghue's, but he was cradling one of the paperbacks he'd taken home from the library. That, too, was damp with sweat.

He wiped the saliva from his chin and checked the time—1:30 in the morning. He felt groggy, unusual...it seemed like his desire to figure out what was happening in Blair was inching toward obsession.

It's not obsession if there is something to uncover, Stu thought. And there *was* something to uncover, he knew it.

Stu wasn't a big drinker, but given the mood in town after the Welch funeral, he'd needed a little something to numb the pain.

Paula, who was curled up at the foot of the bed, was also awake and alert. Her ears were stiff and pointed toward the window. She was growling lowly.

"Shh, it's okay, girl," Stu said. He placed the book down neatly on the nightstand, grabbed a bottle of ibuprofen, and threw two tablets under his tongue. The bitterness spread in his mouth as he chewed, rubbing blurry sleep from his eyes.

The moon was shining brightly through his window, which bothered him. He always took great care to make sure everything was in order before going to sleep, which meant closing his bedroom curtains and making sure any books he was reading were placed back on the shelf where they belonged. How much had he had to drink? Apparently enough to toss out the habit of neatness he was accustomed to.

Stu got out of bed and drew the curtains, feeling a cold draft coming through the window. He shivered and checked the thermostat. Strange. He'd set the heat to run at a steady seventy-one degrees. He could feel warm air pushing through the vents, yet the temperature at the window was drastically lower than the rest of the room. Colder than any draft coming in through a window should be.

Stu returned to bed, giving Paula a scratch behind her ears for good measure. He threw the covers up to his shoulders and settled in. He was so tired, but his mind refused to be quiet. He knew there was some kind of connection between what happened to Martin and Fred Brown's goat. A gnawing, unrelenting awareness prevented him from falling back to sleep. The likelihood of both Martha Brown and Zach Mitchell falling ill on the same day... It was mounting, like some evil entity was haunting the town and was now hovering directly over his bed, its hot breath blowing directly into his face. He began to sweat again.

There was an undeniable presence in the room with him. He could feel it—breath in his face. A hot, damp whiff coming from just above the bed.

Stu considered his research. The town and its lore. The nature in which he'd found Martin. The nature in which Fred had found one of his goats. It coincided with what he'd read. Blair's history seemed to be repeating itself.

No. That's impossible.

Was it? He rolled the idea around in his mind as he flipped his pillow to the dry side and tried to settle in. Comfort continued to evade him. Instead, fear blanketed him, and his skin broke out in shivers. Somehow, whatever was responsible for the bad things happening in Blair was now visiting him too. Like a game of hot and cold, the clue right in his face. Would he wake up with a fever like Martha Brown had?

Paula began to pant, mouth open and tongue out, as if she, too, couldn't get comfortable. The heightened feeling of a presence inside the room sent Stu into a tug-of-war with logic. On the one hand, he was a reasonable skeptic. Seeing was believing; therefore, he wasn't one to jump to conclusions without evidence. However, the research he'd started at the library, the books he'd brought home with him... perhaps these ideas were getting to him, worming into his brain. Perhaps all the evidence he needed was right under his nose, looming like the anticipation of the coming eclipse.

Once every 230 years...

Vampires in Blair...

As he lay there, forcing himself to only focus on going to sleep, awareness took hold. He heard every sound inside the dark room acutely. Every creak and stirring within the house.

He heard a *skreech skreech skreech* at the window, and his skin broke out in goosebumps. Paula jumped out of bed, barking at the window, her hackles raised.

Stu drew the curtains back again, but there was nothing at the window. Only the night sky and the moonlight. He looked up, down, and side to side out the window. There was nothing in sight that might scratch at the window like that, no nearby tree branch as a possible culprit. And his bedroom was on the second floor, so it couldn't have been an animal...or a person.

"No. No way," he said, almost laughing. "I know how this works. You're not getting in my head." But as he said this aloud, he realized whatever it was had already taken hold. He was responding to sounds outside his window. He was already overthinking the situation. Overthinking a simple scratching sound. A sound he wasn't entirely sure was even real. Coming to this conclusion helped him come to his senses. Logically speaking, he had been through and seen a lot over the last week. It made sense that he'd be on edge. Yet as he returned to bed, lying flat on his back, another thought entered his mind. In the 1790s, the people of Blair genuinely believed there were vampires. They acted on this belief. There were records of exhumed bodies not just in Blair, but in New England, in Europe. Evidence. What would drive so many people to do such a thing without a hint of truth? He could understand how someone could revert to irrational thought...

Stop it.

"Come on, Paula, it's okay," he called. The dog hopped up and circled the foot of the bed, as dogs do, to find a comfortable landing spot. She finally curled up next to Stu, and he buried his hand in her fur and sighed. "It's alright, girl." But it was himself he was trying to convince.

Something bad was happening to the town of Blair. Whether it was vampires or not, whether it was old local legends coming to life, Stu was afraid. He had lived long enough to know when his imagination was running wild and when something was irrevocably wrong.

Stu felt something change inside him. He'd seen things before that he wished he could erase from his memory—people saw things they wished they hadn't all the time. Driving by a car accident and glancing at the wreckage. Those videos on the internet of people falling or getting into various mishaps. Those kinds of videos litter the internet like their own kind of sick virus. Entire websites dedicated to snuff and gore. All it took was looking in the wrong place at the wrong time, and an unwanted image was burned into your memory forever.

Still, no amount of desensitization could have prepared Stu for what he saw that morning at Owl's Head Park. It was like an echo, except it got louder the longer it sat with him. Like a bright yellow spotlight shining down on...

Eyes like an eclipse.

That black goat at Fred Brown's farm...it had watched him, like it knew something. Like it knew Martin Welch was only the beginning. Its dead-eyed stare, like the animal was taking pity on Stu for what was to come. Like it had seen it all unfold before and this was just another rerun.

Like it was hiding some morbid secret.

Stu felt sick. He would check on Fred again in the morning. No matter how much Fred insisted that he and Martha were fine, Stu would show up for them. That's what neighbors did. He'd go get supplies in the morning and go right over. Although he hadn't missed a school day in years, this was important. They would cover his classes. The well-being of his friend and neighbor was more important than his perfect attendance.

He sent a quick e-mail from his phone; Alan Marcus would cover his class for him, he was sure. He put his phone down on the nightstand and then stared out the window all sleepless night. While the scratching sound didn't return, Stu still felt its presence until the morning.

Chapter 26
Jaycie

Jaycie couldn't sleep. She was thinking about Mabel and Rose staying behind at the Fischer House. She felt as if she had abandoned them in that place with those boys. If something bad happened to them in that house, she couldn't help but feel like it would be her fault.

Her room felt so far away from everything. It felt as if her bed were a raft on a dark river. She turned onto her side, closing her eyes. She would surely fall asleep if she just lay there long enough with her eyes closed. It was a trick she knew for a fact would not work. It never worked.

Ever since she was a child, this tactic had only amplified whatever her imagination was projecting. When Jaycie was little, she'd see the shadow of a jacket on the back of a chair as something else—as a monster. She would turn over, pull the blankets up over her head, but the shadow would still be there—the presence. Not being able to see it only made her think of it more. But the more she looked at it, the more it looked like a figure, not a jacket, her imagination morphing the shadows into something ominous. Her innocent, hastily tossed aside jacket. If only she'd hung it up in the closet like Mom had instructed.

Jaycie continued to lay in her bed, thinking of her friends. Unable to focus on simply going to sleep, she became acutely aware of every sound in the dark room with her.

She heard a scratching sound at her window, and her skin broke out in a prickly chill. She peeked out from under the covers, eyeing the window. There was nothing out there but the shining light of the full moon.

Her imagination, however, disagreed. This had always been the case —her mind worked in interesting ways, to say the least. Ways that frustratingly challenged her logic instead of validating it. The curse of having an overactive imagination. It started when she was a little girl, when she first fell in love with books. One book in particular stuck with her. It had since been ruined by the author, yet the story left its mark. In this book, a couple of "imposters" tried to take the place of a little girl's parents—the idea alone scared her enough. But what was really disturbing was that in order to complete the replacement, the girl's eyeballs had to be replaced —with buttons. Jaycie was afraid of someone or something coming into her room, gouging out her eyes, and stitching buttons over the sockets.

While the book itself was not *that* descriptive about the process of the eyeball replacement, Jaycie's mind filled in the blanks. Her twelve-year-old imagination conjured up a specific tool that could scoop out eyeballs in one swift motion. She imagined the connective nerves, in the shape of a tail, pulling out of the socket, dripping blood on their way out. The fear was real, and visceral. In fact, Jaycie could *feel* her eyes get heavy at the thought; she would squint hard to make sure they were in just right. She knew it was silly. But the feeling remained.

However, that rush was part of what she liked about scary stories. It was hard to explain, but she was sure roller coaster enthusiasts could relate to the adrenaline rush. Scary stories never really left her imagination. Especially in the dark. Jaycie thought of the movie

Poltergeist for weeks after the first time she saw it. She would be almost frozen in fear whenever she would check underneath her bed for monsters. Not just clowns, but *anything* could be hiding under there, waiting to attack. Then what? What did monsters do when they caught you? Did they eat you? Did they remove your eyeballs and replace them with buttons?

Did they turn you into one of their own?

That thought sent chills up and down Jaycie's spine. She thought again of her friends, and also her brother.

I don't want him going there anymore, she insisted in her own mind. Thinking it, willing it to be. She didn't know what she would do with herself if something happened to any of the people she cared about. She wouldn't be able to sleep until she knew everyone she loved was safe.

Chapter 27
Interlude: 1793

Thou shalt not commit adultery, the seventh commandment clearly stated.

So, Dorothy Fischer prayed. It was the advice she'd been given as a little girl. Before she had a husband and a family of her own, Dorothy was told to begin and end each day in prayer. Pray during good times and be thankful. Pray during adverse times and ask for strength. So, that's what she did.

She prayed for her husband, Nathaniel. She prayed for her children. And she prayed for the protection of her home and the village of Blair.

Dorothy believed her husband was a good man, despite his infidelity. It broke her heart, but she believed Nathaniel only wanted to protect their family—to protect Blair from that terrible disease known as consumption. She believed it in her heart. He would never deliberately seek out an affair. No, he could *never*...

For the time being, prayer would suffice as remedy. Prayer would fill Nathaniel with remorse and bring him to his knees in forgiveness. And soon, all of this would come to an end.

Dorothy prayed for something else too. A blasphemous incantation. A use of prayer that held contrary to the very concept of the act. She knew this was a sin, but she didn't care. Her desire was stronger than even her own faith.

Dorothy Fischer prayed for the death of that woman. The whore who had taken liberty with her husband. She prayed for this because in her heart, despite what the seventh commandment stated, Dorothy believed her husband had been compelled to his sin by an outside force. The outsider, known only as Grace, needed to be punished. Only then would Nathaniel be unburdened by his unfaithfulness.

* * *

The eldest Fischer boy noticed the goat one day after he felt a particularly negative energy from his parents. He did not see them argue, although he was certain they had. His mother had been praying an awful lot recently, much more than usual. His father was home less frequently, and when he was, there was a tension in the home which seemed to follow him. It hung in the air like dampness. The tension had coincided with the arrival of the new goat. The boy was not sure which had come first, but he was almost grateful to have a new friend to talk to.

This goat was different from the others. It was a large black goat, with menacing eyes and a rough stance. Its shoulders were a hulking, intimidating mass behind the large spirals of its horns. The boy approached it anyway. If he was going to be a man and have his own family one day, complete with his own herd of goats, he mustn't be afraid. Children are afraid. Men are supposed to be brave.

"Hello there," the boy said, introducing himself. "I don't think we've been acquainted yet. What is your name?" The boy reached out to pet the animal's snout. There was something different about this goat. While the other goats bleated with joy at the boy's touch, this goat remained silent, aloof. The boy looked into the goat's eyes, and it was as if a deep, dark abyss was staring back at him. As if the goat was studying the young man.

"You'll have to tell me your name eventually," the boy said. He figured being a welcoming host would be the best way to earn this goat's trust. He'd had to earn the trust of all of the other goats in the family, who he grew to know well.

He spoke to all of them. As a young boy with an active imagination, he thought it would be rude to not address the goats individually as he fed and cared for them. It was a respect he paid the animals, and one they paid him back. Of course, the boy knew the goats would never answer him with words, but the animals recognized his tone of voice and his gentle, kind approach. They responded with bleats and *maaas*. But this new goat...

"Alright then," the boy said. "Maybe some other time." He turned around to pour feed into a bucket for the herd. While the other goats hurried over to eat their fill, the new goat continued to watch, as if it did not need food. As if it were beyond the need for sustenance.

"I hope you don't mind, but I think I'll take the liberty of giving you a nickname—until you tell me your real name, that is. How does Midnight sound? I like it. Midnight." The boy pondered for a moment.

"Okay, Midnight, I'll see you tomorrow!" The boy went about his day, leaving Midnight and the rest of the goats to roam the pasture. He felt lucky to have a new friend.

Chapter 28
Jaycie

For the first time since she was a freshman, Jaycie ate breakfast alone in the school cafeteria. She was worried about Mabel and Rose. It was Monday morning, and she hadn't seen her friends since the party.

She knew they were *alive*, at least. Sunday, she sent a text to their group chat, checking in. The girls both responded with heart emojis, but nothing more. It was not the response she wanted. Yet it was *some* kind of response, and Jaycie supposed she could breathe a little easier knowing nothing horrific had happened to them the other night at the Fischer House. She would have to ask them for details about what happened after she left—her gut still told her it was something, but she had to hear it from them. Breakfast was supposed to be the time for that, but since both girls were late, she would have to wait even longer, until their free period later on.

* * *

Five minutes after the bell, and Mr. Reinhart still had not shown up for third period Gothic Literature. The classroom of sixteen waited patiently, mostly, for their teacher's arrival. It was unlike Stuart Reinhart to be late for class. Yet it seemed like Jaycie was the only one concerned with the fact that everyone seemed to be running late today.

Jaycie occupied the first desk in the row closest to the window. She was looking out over the school's campus, examining the field, her mind filled with speculation. Jax sat directly behind her, impatiently tapping his fingers on the desk.

Mr. Reinhart's Gothic Lit class was the first class the twins had together since they were freshman. It made Jaycie aware of the two years in which they hadn't had a single overlapping class. Unfortunately, they also shared this class with Gabe Coleman. Jaycie gave him a weary glance as he took his seat. She was still in the dark about the events from the other night. How was it that Gabe showed up to school, but the girls hadn't?

"Where do you think he is?" she heard someone ask from the back of the classroom. She could feel their restlessness rising like a smoke signal.

"I heard he went crazy after he found Martin Welch," Gabe said. "I heard they might force him to take a sabbatical because he's so paranoid now."

"That's not true," Jaycie said, keeping her eyes fixed on the door.

"It is true," Gabe sneered. "Everyone knows he freaked out and stormed out of class last week. My mom works for the school, and she knows. Mr. Reinhart is mental."

Jaycie rolled her eyes. "You're unbelievable."

It was only five past the bell, and the general rule was to wait at least fifteen minutes before students could dismiss themselves. Then, they were required to either go to the library or to study hall and sign in. The school needed to know where the students were since the school was responsible for their whereabouts. Going to the cafeteria was not allowed, and leaving the school was strictly prohibited.

"Jax, let's go," Gabe said loudly from the back of the room, with no consideration for any of the other students. "He's not showing up, and this class sucks anyway."

Jaycie finally turned around and gave Gabe a harsh look. Gabe smirked, raising his voice louder. "If you're going to be a pussy and stay here, I'll meet you out back by the bleachers when your balls finally drop." He stood up, swinging his backpack over one shoulder. His desk made an obnoxious screech as he stood, but the sound was not as jarring as his attitude. Gabe brazenly exited the classroom, the door slamming shut behind him.

Jaycie glanced back at Jax, knowing he was debating whether or not to follow Gabe. She wished he wouldn't, but she felt he may have already decided.

A second screech came as Jax stood up from his desk and approached the door. As he reached for the doorknob, the door opened. Jax froze in place, standing in the doorway with his backpack on.

"Mr. Brogdon, if you could have a seat, that would be great," Alan Marcus said as he took his place at the head of the classroom. He motioned a hand toward the vacant desk behind Jaycie, inviting Jax to sit.

Jax's face turned red. For a moment, Jaycie felt her brother was actually considering ignoring Mr. Marcus altogether and following Gabe. To her relief, Jax took his seat once again, begrudgingly, and Mr. Marcus cleared his throat.

"I'll be filling in for Mr. Reinhart today, and possibly for the rest of the week," he explained. "This is a last-minute arrangement, so I'll need someone to fill me in on class assignments and reading." A smug grin appeared on Mr. Marcus's face as an idea entered his mind. "Jackson Brogdon," he said. "Could you summarize what the class has been up to so we can move forward accordingly?"

Jax looked up at the front of the classroom, unable to answer. Sure, he was occasionally absent-minded during class, but Mr. Marcus's audacity to single him out like this blinded Jax with rage. He remained silent.

"Mr. Brogdon," Mr. Marcus said, "I believe it is in your best interest to pay attention in class—especially a creative class like this. That is, if your intentions of joining the art program at Tufts is a serious aspiration. I don't think you're doing yourself any favors by trying to skip out of class early considering the conversation we had last week. Wouldn't you agree?"

Jax remained silent. Jaycie could feel the temperature in the room rising, as if her brother were a space heater occupying the desk behind her.

"Can someone else tell me where Mr. Reinhart left off?"

Another student raised their hand, but Mr. Marcus ignored it. Instead, he turned slowly toward Jaycie. What happened next made her wish she had left the classroom too, or not shown up at all.

"Perhaps the intelligent Brogdon twin has some insight?"

Jaycie's face turned red, and before she even had a chance to think up a response, she heard the screech of Jax's chair again as he stood up and stormed out of the room, slamming the door shut with all his might. The chalkboard rattled against the wall, like an earthquake had just struck the classroom.

The grin on Mr. Marcus's face made Jaycie want to get up and follow her brother in protest, but she stayed, afraid of the potential consequences on her own school record. She slouched in her desk, glaring at Mr. Marcus.

"I believe you had your hand raised." Mr. Marcus pointed to a student in the middle row, but Jaycie couldn't be bothered to look and see who it was. She hung her head in shame, reeling from having to watch her brother storm out of the room in anger.

* * *

When class let out, Jaycie went searching for Jax. To her misfortune, she found he'd already caught up with Tomas, Hector, and Gabe out at the bleachers near the track. She knew they were generally up to no good when they were hanging out by the bleachers, so she decided it was better not to approach.

Instead, she made her way to the school library, hoping to finally find Mabel and Rose. To her delight, her friends were sitting at a small table just past the row of computers. As she approached them, she felt a weird mix of relief and unease. They hadn't spoken in days, not since the party, yet here they were, sitting in the library as if everything was normal.

However, as Jaycie drew closer to her friends, she could see that things were not normal. The girls seemed different, *haunted.*

Mabel had a book open in front of her, but she was looking off into the distance. Her shoulders slouched forward, and she was wearing an oversized hoodie, the ends of the sleeves balled up in her hands as if she were cold. Jaycie only ever saw Mabel in baggy clothes at their movie night sleepovers. Mabel always put effort into how she looked, her outfits trendy and her haircut maintained. The faded hoodie and messy bun made Jaycie worry. What happened for Mabel to suddenly halt her routine?

Rose, on the other hand, sat with a scornful look on her face. It seemed directed at no one in particular, but it was still off-putting, and it made Jaycie hesitate before taking a seat with them. She also noticed Rose's uncharacteristic posture. She sat with her hands underneath the table, out of sight. Both girls seemed like they were hiding something.

"I've been so stressed about you two," Jaycie said. "I was expecting to hear from you after the party, and I've gotten radio silence. What's up?"

"What's up is that you left early the other night," Rose said. "You really should have been there, Jaycie. It wasn't cool of you to leave."

Jaycie was stunned. She didn't think it was a big deal that she'd left. Jax went home early too, and he was hanging out with his friends by the bleachers right now, as if nothing happened. Why was she the one being criticized?

She looked at Mabel, worried that her friend would double down on Rose's sentiment, but she just sat there, downcast. Her eyes were watery, as if she were going to cry at any moment.

"I didn't think leaving would be such a big deal," Jaycie said. "Why won't you tell me what happened? I still want to know how the rest of the party went."

"That's none of your business now," Rose spat. "If you cared so much, you would have been there." She tossed her hair to the side, as if showing she was done and there was no further conversation to be had.

Jaycie looked at Mabel, confused, but she continued to look down blankly. This was so out of the blue, for both of them. It didn't make sense. Unless...

Tomas. Everyone in his orbit somehow changes.

"There is a darkness in Blair," Mabel said flatly. "It has crept in, and now it lives here. A darkness." She sighed deeply.

"She's right," Rose added. "And if you're smart, you'll stay away from it. It's like a rot, and it's eating away at our town."

"And now it lives inside me," Mabel added.

"What are you guys talking about?" Jaycie felt so overwhelmed she thought she might cry. Instead, she balled her hands into fists and squeezed. "I left with Jax. You're not mad at him! Stop talking weird. Is this some kind of joke? What happened to your hands?"

"It's not a joke!" Rose snapped. "You should go. We shouldn't be seen with you."

Jaycie rolled her eyes and stood up forcefully. "Whatever. When you're ready to be serious, you can talk to me. This is stupid and immature." She stormed out of the library and headed for her locker at a brisk pace. She didn't think she had it in her to continue with the rest of her classes for the day. At the very least, she needed some fresh air.

She ran into Calvin on her way out. He waved.

"Hey, lab partner," he called out.

She paused and considered whether she should just keep walking. She didn't feel like talking to anybody. But then she looked down the hall and saw Calvin's locker. She thought about last week, when she helped him clean the tuna off his locker. Talking to Calvin couldn't be any worse than the exchange she'd just had with her friends.

"Hey," she managed to get out without breaking down.

"You okay?" Calvin asked. "You sound exasperated."

Jaycie put on a smile and said, "I'm fine. It's just girl drama. It'll be alright. What's up?"

"I saw flyers around for this Fall Fest happening next weekend," Calvin said. "Do you know about it? Is it cool?"

"It's...fine, I guess," Jaycie said. "No, yeah, it's very cool actually. We go every year. This year they're supposed to do something special since it's the same weekend as the eclipse. You should go. Definitely."

"Do you want to go with me?" Calvin asked. "I don't really have anyone to go with, and I'd rather not go alone."

"What do you mean, like a date?" Jaycie asked. "Because..."

"Oh, yeah, I know," Calvin chuckled. "Definitely not a date. Just wouldn't do myself any favors if I showed up alone, ya know? I've already been labeled as the weird new kid."

Jaycie laughed out loud.

"Besides, I know you like Mabel," Calvin said. "It's kind of obvious. Not to sound clingy or anything just because you helped me clean my locker last week, but you're kind of my best friend here in Blair."

"That's very clingy," Jaycie said. "Reel it in, new kid."

Now Calvin laughed out loud. "Alright, here; take down my number and text me where to meet. I think it starts on Saturday."

"Sounds good, lab partner," Jaycie said. She put her number into Calvin's phone and texted herself. "See ya then." At least there was one person in her orbit who was still acting normal.

Chapter 29
Jax

The top row of the bleachers at the far end of the school's football field was the perfect spot for sneaking the occasional cigarette during school. This vantage point allowed whoever sat there to see who was approaching from all directions. Straight ahead, there was a full view of the field, most of the campus, and the high school building itself. Behind the bleachers was the faculty parking lot.

"It's about time," Gabe said as Jax caught up with them. "I thought you were going to stay behind and wait for someone to show up to that class." He was already taking a drag on a cigarette and passing the pack back to Hector.

"Someone did show up," Jax said. "Mr. Marcus. I was on my way out when he stopped me, otherwise I would have been here sooner."

"Oh, your favorite try-hard egomaniac," Tomas smirked, ashing his cigarette. He had his hood pulled up, covering half his face, the way he always did while they were at school.

"Fuck that guy," Jax said, his hand shaking as he reached for his own cigarette. He wanted to know exactly what happened at the Fischer House the other night after he left. While he had an idea, he tried to suppress the thought. Worse, he didn't want to be punished for questioning it. He felt Tomas glaring at him, as if he knew what Jax was thinking.

Hector reached into his backpack; cigarette perched in his mouth. "Hey, check this out," he said, and he held his bag open for Jax and Gabe to peer in. Inside was a bottle of Fireball whiskey. Hector had been able to conceal the bottle all day.

"I think the coast is clear," Gabe said. There was no one in sight except for a single student making laps around the track. His name was Ralph, and he was dressed in gray sweats with the school's logo on the front. He didn't give a shit and wouldn't be an issue.

The sun was out, but there was a considerable chill in the air. Jax stuck his hands into the pockets of his sweatshirt and pulled his hood over his head.

"Don't worry," Hector said. "This stuff will warm you up." He glanced around, took a swig from the bottle, and passed it to Jax.

"Hold on," Jax said, lowing the bottle. In the distance, Alan Marcus was walking down the access road from the school into the faculty parking lot.

"Speak of the devil. I fucking hate that guy," Hector said, ashing his cigarette. "He is such a prick for no reason."

"Right? I told him I wanted to apply to Tufts, and he basically told me to fuck off," Jax said. "He could have at least helped me apply. Why does it matter to him whether I'm accepted or not? Just do your job; you don't have to be a dick about it."

"Ha, you want to go to Tufts?" Gabe laughed. "What's wrong with staying in Blair?"

Jax shrugged and took a sip of Fireball. Hector was right—it did warm him up. He felt the burn the moment it touched his lips. He kind of hated it, but he swallowed it down. He guessed they called it Fireball because it felt like actual lighter fluid moving down his esophagus.

As the burning sensation dissipated, Jax looked up to see Tomas glaring at him. It wasn't like Jax had forgotten the promise he made...

the oath he took. He carried it with him every day. However, he still felt that pull in his heart, the desire to one day leave this town and see the world.

"Nothing's wrong with staying in Blair," Jax explained. "I just thought it would be cool to travel a little bit."

Tomas just listened, unimpressed. A single eyebrow cocked, a cynical reminder that Jax should know his place.

"Hey, look," Gabe pointed toward the track. "The new kid again."

"I *really* hate that kid," Hector said as he yanked the bottle from Jax's hand and took a gulp. "Doesn't belong here." He shook his head, staring at Calvin Roberts as he walked by unknowing. Hector blew smoke out of his mouth and nose, contemplating as he watched the new kid.

Tomas was watching too. Stone-faced and emotionless, as if he were looking at a piece of debris being carried by the breeze. His eyes glinted with demonic loathing.

"He's not *that* bad," Jax said, his attention turned toward Mr. Marcus. "He doesn't do much to bother anyone." Yet Jax knew he couldn't convince Tomas otherwise. The contempt he showed for Calvin was no different than the contempt he showed for everyone else who lived in Blair.

"What's with you, Jax?" Hector turned toward him slowly. "First you want to leave Blair and go to Tufts. Now you're defending the Black kid. I said he doesn't belong here. What part of that don't you understand?"

"Chill the fuck out," Jax said. "Mr. Marcus is an asshole, and the hate he gets is warranted. The Roberts kid doesn't bother anybody."

"Well, he bothers me," Hector said, flicking his cigarette into the grass behind the bleachers. "If you hadn't left early the other night, maybe you'd have a better understanding of the situation this town is in."

"Are we going to do the thing?" Gabe asked.

"No time like the present, right?" Tomas said smoothly. He

motioned toward Hector's bag—he had been hiding something more than just Fireball all day. On cue, Hector brought out the chloroform they had stolen from the science department supply closet.

"And Jax, to prove his loyalty, is going to lead the way," Tomas declared, as if punishing him for his desire to leave Blair.

Chapter 30
Calvin

Calvin held his backpack close and walked briskly across the football field. It was about a twenty-minute walk from school to home (cut down to ten minutes on his skateboard), and the fresh air helped cool him down after drum practice.

From the corner of his eye, he spotted the small gathering huddled atop the bleachers—the same jackasses responsible for hitting him with spitballs and leaving the mess on his locker. He continued to look straight ahead, trying not to make eye contact or even gesture in that direction. He wanted nothing to do with that group. *People like that are only strong when you're afraid*, he thought, and Calvin refused to show any bully that he was afraid.

He knew they were watching him, so he put his chest out and his head up. He wouldn't be intimidated. Besides, he felt good, endorphins flowing post-practice. He felt confident, ready for jazz band tryouts at the end of the week.

He continued on, walking over the well-maintained field. However, when he subtly glanced over, his concern was validated. The group of boys were now standing, looking in his direction. Calvin took in a steady breath through his nose.

Just keep going, ignore them. They're just trying to scare you. Keep walking like nothing is happening.

Calvin continued toward the opening in the field gate. He lost sight of the bullies but refused to turn and look in their direction. He refused to give them any sort of satisfaction, but he was concerned. Of course he was concerned. There was something not right about those boys. He had dealt with bullying back home, but this was different. In the city, he'd experienced name-calling and hazing, the type of bullying everyone experiences to one degree or another. He had even been in a fight or two, which didn't bother him *that* much if it meant standing up for himself. Sure, he would have preferred to not partake in physical altercations, but that came with growing up, he supposed. In the city, he'd dealt with boys' ego trips and insults in a brief exchange of hands in a one-on-one situation. At least the assholes who had the nerve to start a fight knew that if you started something, it was your responsibility to finish it. You reap what you sow.

But in Blair...it seemed personal, the way Calvin was targeted. He could feel it. From the onset, there was something different about it. The way they had stalked him in the music hall. There was a meanness, a line they didn't worry about crossing—a look in their eyes that Calvin hadn't experienced before, even with the most lowbrow bigots.

If it were up to Calvin, he would put these assholes in their place. It would give him so much satisfaction to take one good swing at them. Especially the big one, Hector. He'd like to wipe that smug, entitled grin off his face. Ugly, pasty fuck.

But Calvin didn't come here to fight. He only wanted to go to class, do his best, and save up enough money to buy his own drum kit. He didn't want to partake in small-town drama.

Yet small-town drama was heading his way, closing in from behind. He could hear the squelch of sneakers on damp grass, the breathing and shushing among them as they sped up to close the gap before Calvin could get to the fence. He didn't dare turn around, but he felt them approaching.

Then he felt hands on him, grabbing the collar of his shirt. Calvin instinctively twisted around and pulled with all his weight, causing his aggressor to trip. However, the numbers game was quickly a factor. Gabe came in fast, grabbing Calvin's other arm, allowing Hector to get back on his feet quickly. He took a swing and connected with Calvin's stomach, forcing the air out of him.

A third boy came up from behind—was that Jaycie's brother? There was something in his hand that looked like a white, rolled-up T-shirt. Jax stopped in his tracks, in a moment of self-awareness, it seemed.

"What are you doing?" Hector turned back to Jax, screaming in his face. He ripped the T-shirt from Jax's hand and stepped behind Calvin, reaching a hand around his face.

Calvin instinctively held his breath as the hand covered his nose and mouth with the T-shirt. The cloth had a subtle scent of sweet citrus, barely noticeable; however, his lips burned upon contact.

What the fuck? Was this chloroform?

Calvin tried to force himself out of Gabe's grip as Hector held the T-shirt over his face. He could feel both boys trying to push him down, get him onto the ground.

Calvin managed to break Gabe's grip, delivering a shoulder block to the boy. The momentary freedom gave Calvin the chance to wrench Hector's arm, freeing him of the chemical-doused T-shirt. Calvin spat and wiped his mouth with the back of his hand. His instinct was to run, but then he saw Tomas Fischer watching everything unfold from the safety of the bleachers. From this distance, he could see Tomas's mouth pulled down in a scowl while the top of his face was cloaked in the shadow of his hood. Calvin raised a middle finger at the orchestrator of this attack.

When Calvin turned to run, he was stopped by the symphony of shouting that had descended upon the field. The whole confrontation had lasted maybe thirty seconds, but people had noticed.

"Everyone stop!" a teacher shouted. It was Mr. Alberts, the music director, and for a moment Calvin felt relief that someone was finally on his side. But his heart sank when Mr. Alberts glared in his direction. He came running toward the fight, followed by Mr. Quinn, the physical education teacher. Mr. Quinn grabbed hold of both Hector and Gabe, then turned toward Jax and said, "Don't move."

Calvin stood motionless, his head down. Mr. Alberts grabbed his arm preemptively. "What the hell is this all about?" he asked. The disappointment in his voice seared like a knife.

"These idiots tried to chloroform me with a T-shirt," Calvin said. "Don't you realize that's not how chloroform works?"

"Quiet," Mr. Alberts said, tugging Calvin's arm. "That's enough."

"If you idiots paid attention in class, you'd know that," Calvin continued. "But you're too stupid to know this isn't like the movies." Calvin recalled hearing how chloroform can evaporate when it comes into contact with the air, losing most of its effectiveness. While he did feel light-headed, he wasn't even close to fainting.

"I said that's enough!" Mr. Alberts shouted. "Everyone get back inside right now. You're all in big trouble."

* * *

This is it, Calvin thought. *I'm done.*

The four boys were escorted back into the school, through the empty hallways. He could see Mr. Quinn leading Hector, Jax, and Gabe ahead, keeping them away from him. They made a turn down a corridor of offices beyond the teacher's lounge, where students never go. Then Calvin realized—Tomas was not among them. The one who'd likely orchestrated the whole thing got to watch from a distance and then abandon ship while everyone else took the fall.

Calvin could see Jaycie's brother, his shoulders slumped in regret. He couldn't bother to care, though. *Fuck around and find out*, he thought. *That's what you get for associating with scum.*

When they reached the end of the hall, they separated the boys into different rooms. It was probably for the best, but Calvin still had a bad feeling. The music teacher, who Calvin looked up to, wore a face of great disappointment. It hurt, but Calvin didn't understand. He hadn't done anything wrong.

"We're going to have to call your parents to explain what took place here," Mr. Alberts explained. "They'll come pick you up, but first we need to create an incident report."

"No," Calvin said. "Please, don't call my mom."

Mr. Alberts shook his head. "We have to. It's school policy to notify parents or guardians of such incidents."

Calvin's leg jittered in his seat as he tried to hold back tears. It was then he noticed he was inadvertently holding his side. Pain throbbed in his ribs, where Hector had jabbed him.

As Mr. Alberts situated the paperwork, Calvin heard shouting from another room. He couldn't be sure which of the boys it was, but it sounded like an objection to something harsh. He wondered what was being said.

"Calvin," Mr. Alberts said, "you are suspended for a week. For no reason are you to attend anything on school property, or any events associated with the school, for the duration of your five-day suspension."

"*Suspended?*" Calvin stood up, and the throbbing pain in his side sharpened. "I was defending myself! They literally jumped me—they tried to knock me out with chloroform! Why am I getting suspended?"

"Watch your tone, Mr. Roberts," Mr. Alberts said. "You're getting off easy. If you want the same treatment as the other boys, you can consider yourself expelled indefinitely. Fighting is strictly prohibited. Had you run or refrained from fighting back, we would have given you the benefit of the doubt. But we saw you throwing punches too, and there's nothing we can do for you in that case."

"It was three-on-one," Calvin argued. "How was I supposed to run away from that? This isn't fair. You're telling me I should have just let them beat my ass?"

"Watch the language," Mr. Alberts said.

Calvin sat back down and buried his face in his hands. "Now

what? My grades are going to suffer because of this?" He was fighting back tears now. "I have a project with a lab partner. I have band tryouts."

"I'm sorry, Mr. Roberts," Mr. Alberts said. "I don't know what to say."

Chapter 31
Jaycie

The Brogdon household was uncharacteristically quiet during dinner. Jaycie ate what she could before quietly excusing herself. It was awkward, and it felt strange having dinner without Jax. But dinner was always at six p.m. sharp. Jaycie and Jax both knew, if they weren't present, the family would eat without them.

Jaycie made her way upstairs to her room while Dad cleared the table and Mom wrapped up the leftovers—a full plate untouched, which belonged to Jax. Jaycie had just sat down to study when she heard a crash come from the kitchen. She stood up carefully and slowly opened her door.

She could hear her mom sigh forcefully while her dad said, "I'll clean it up."

"Thank you," Mom said. "I love those plates. I lost a handle on them. It's just, my mind is elsewhere."

"Mine too," Dad said.

At that moment, Jaycie could hear the front door open and close, followed by Dad asking, "Where have you been?"

"Just wandering aimlessly, I guess," Jax said "That's all I've got now anyway."

Jaycie recoiled against her door—she knew an explosion was imminent. Her parents' tempers had seethed like ticking time bombs during dinner.

"You have no one to blame but yourself, Jackson!" Dad shouted. "You've been told multiple times to not put yourself in situations you shouldn't be in. We've told you to be mindful of the company you keep. Yet you continue to make bad decisions.. On top of that, you go and start a fight? What were you thinking?"

"Seth, please," Jaycie heard her mom say.

"No, I'm going to tell him," Dad continued. "On top of that, you were drinking on school premises. It's like you're seeking out trouble. Are you out of your mind?"

Jaycie inched out of her door, peering over the banister. She could see into the kitchen. Her heart broke as her family continued to fight.

"That's not fair," Jax said, his head down.

"Fair? I'll tell you what's not fair," her father continued. "It's not fair that we have to sit here and watch you throw your life away. For what? What has gotten into you, Jackson?" At this point, Jaycie could hear Mom break down in tears.

"I thought you were better than this," Dad said. "I guess I was wrong."

"What?" Jax said, hurt.

"I said," Dad said again, raising his voice. Jaycie could see both his hands grasp Jax's shirt and yank him forward, like hockey players do before a fight. Her heart sank. Was her father about to punch Jax? "I guess I was wrong about you."

He let go of Jax's shirt, pushing him away in disgust.

Jax staggered before regaining his balance. Jaycie could then hear footsteps coming up the stairs. Her face turned red as she backed away from the banister. Jax stormed past her room; then his bedroom door slammed shut.

Jaycie quietly looked out over the banister again. Her parents had gone back into the kitchen, their anger and disappointment overflowing into the house.

A few moments later, the door to Jax's room opened, and he came out with a backpack stuffed to the brim. He stopped in front of Jaycie and just looked at her, his face red with harrowing pain.

"Where are you going?" Jaycie asked quietly.

Jax stood there in the hall for a moment, looking at his sister, his face full of regret. "Away, I guess." He shrugged.

"You don't have to do this," Jaycie said. "So you made a mistake—it isn't the end of the world. Mom and Dad will get over it. We're all here for you. It doesn't have to be this way."

Jax clenched his jaw and stared at the floor, as if he were contemplating. But Jaycie knew he'd already made up his mind.

"Where will you go?" she asked, but she already knew the answer to that too. She could see it. She could also see that Jax knew she could see it too. He lied anyway.

"I don't know, I'll figure it out."

"Jax, please, just stay," she pleaded. She felt like a younger sister talking to an older brother instead of her twin who was born seven minutes after her. "Talk to *me*. You can always talk to me, Jax. You don't have to do anything drastic. Please." She could feel her eyes well up with tears.

Jax shook his head and clutched his backpack closer. "I'm sorry," he said. Then he turned and started down the stairs. Jaycie heard the front door slam as Jax left into the night, not even saying goodbye to Mom and Dad. She feared it may be the last time she saw her brother alive.

Chapter 32
Stu

Stu arrived at the Brown farm first thing in the morning. The sun was bright. A paper bag full of groceries occupied the passenger's seat next to him, containing all the ingredients necessary for chicken soup. Fred had said he'd call if he and Martha needed anything, but showing up was the neighborly thing to do. Hopefully, his e-mail to Mr. Marcus from the night before would suffice, and his classes would be covered.

Stu pulled into the gravel driveway and got out of his car. He scooped up the bag of groceries and turned toward the house.

A string of lights had been added around the Fall Fest banner over the driveway. Several canvas booths had been erected as well. Stu could also see the poles around the property for the floodlights Fred had mentioned. This made him think about the impending eclipse. Was the town of Blair approaching disaster, like a car veering into the opposite lane, one you never see coming? Was the eclipse bringing with it a hornet's nest of horrors he once only knew to exist in fiction?

The farm was eerily quiet, but the wind chime hanging on the front porch made a sound even though Stu couldn't feel a breeze. It was unlike Fred to be indoors. Stu couldn't recall a time he ever drove up to the farm without seeing Fred outside, working on something, or at the very least greeting visitors.

Instead, Stu was greeted by a stale, stagnant air and the muted bleating of several goats inside their pens. They had yet to be let out into the open pasture—this was a detail that raised alarm. Fred never forgot to let the goats out first thing in the morning.

As Stu approached the front porch steps, he caught a glimpse of a single goat roaming in the pasture behind the house. It was the large, black goat from the other day. The one with the eclipse in its eyes. Yes, it was watching Stu again, as if it were trying to tell him something. It seemed to say: *I have never been confined to a pen like the others. I transcend captivity. I transcend Blair. And I know something you don't.*

I have a secret. Do you want to know what it is?

Stu took a deep breath and ignored the web his imagination was spinning. The wind chime continued its gentle knell as Stu climbed the porch steps. He knocked on the screen door. It rattled in its frame, and Stu peered inside.

"Hello? Fred? Stu here!" he called out. There was no answer.

Stu let himself in. The air smelled damp. A coppery odor lingered, putting Stu on edge.

"Fred?" he called out again, placing the bag of groceries on the coffee table in the living room. He slowly advanced inside the house and toward the kitchen, where he found Fred with his head down on the kitchen table.

Stu rushed over. "Fred, what's wrong? Are you okay?"

Fred weakly lifted his head to look up at Stu. His face was ghastly, as pale as the moon. Dark circles surrounded his eyes, as if he hadn't slept in days. He was visibly confused and lethargic.

"It's Martha," Fred said slowly, matter-of-factly. "She's getting worse, Stu." His hands trembled, and he reached for Stu. "She's getting worse. I don't know if she's going to make it."

"Then we need to call an ambulance," Stu said as he took Fred's hands. They seemed so small in his own. Weak. Not the hands of the hardworking man he knew. For the first time since Stu had known him, Fred Brown looked truly old. Not just old, but frail. So fragile that he might shatter if he moved the wrong way.

"We should call for help," Stu insisted. He stepped over to the sink to get Fred a glass of water. "What was the last thing she said to you? Have you tried giving her anything? What's wrong exactly? Fever?"

Fred stared off to the side like he hadn't even heard Stu. It was as if he'd woken up, found Martha's worsened condition, and retreated downstairs to the kitchen to rest his head and ponder the situation. As if he were incapable of processing the possibility that Martha might pass away, as if his brain had detached itself from the rest of his body, shutting down to prevent feeling the pain of potentially losing his wife.

Stu slipped into the next room, leaving Fred in the kitchen. He made his way upstairs and toward the primary bedroom, where he confirmed his suspicions about Martha. She needed an ambulance.

It looked as if she'd already been done up by an embalmer—she looked more like a likeness of Martha Brown than Martha Brown herself. A person without a soul. Pale and stiff. Stu could see her chest rising and falling weakly beneath the quilt. Particles of dust danced in the beams of sunlight that leaked into the room from the open window. The dust danced around her body as if she were a sacrifice.

Stu quickly called an ambulance from his cell phone before going back downstairs to keep Fred company while they waited.

* * *

In the short time it took the ambulance to arrive, Stu couldn't keep his mind from wandering. Flashes of the other morning, when he'd discovered Martin Welch, plagued his mind. Something about finding Martha tucked away in bed like that was almost more disturbing than the gory, bloody mess that had been Martin.

When a pair of paramedics arrived, they wasted no time and made their way upstairs to tend to Martha. Two police officers arrived as well. It was standard protocol, to gauge the situation. Fred remained lost in his own way, his interactions limited to slight nods.

"What brought you here this morning?" the older of the two officers asked Stu. His name was Gary White, and Stu knew him from Donoghue's. He would frequent the bar once a week and was typically standoffish unless you were part of his fantasy football league. This put Stu in an odd place, because he had participated once, years ago, before deciding it wasn't for him. It was clear his relationship with Officer Gary had since soured. The younger officer, Stu did not recognize.

"I was here the other day, actually," Stu said. "Fred mentioned Martha had fallen ill. I decided to be a good neighbor and bring them some supplies from town this morning, which is when I found them like this."

"So nothing seemed out of the ordinary during that first visit?" Gary asked.

"Not really. Like I said, Fred only mentioned Martha wasn't feeling well," Stu explained. "One of his goats had been killed, so he took me around the property to show me where something had gotten in. I came by this morning to see if there was anything I could do to help."

"Well, I think you've done enough to help, Mr. Reinhart," Gary said.

"What is that supposed to mean?" Stu was confused by the sly comment.

In that moment, one of the paramedics made her way down the stairs and looked gravely at the gathering in Fred Brown's kitchen. "I'm afraid Martha is dead."

The room spun as Stu processed the paramedic's words. "She's dead? No. She's sick; I just saw her. She just needs fluids. She has the flu or something. She can't be dead."

"I'm sorry," the paramedic said. "It was too late. Had she made it to a hospital yesterday, she might have made it."

Two funerals in a week.

This town can't handle much more of this...

Fred Brown stood and took the paramedic's hands. He was shaking, his mouth agape in a moaning sob. "My Martha? What happened to my Martha?"

"I'm sorry, Mr. Brown. If you would come with us to the hospital, we'd like to check you out too."

Fred left with the paramedics and headed toward the ambulance.

Gary turned back to Stu. "Like I said, I think you've done enough, Mr. Reinhart. What's done is done. Don't go poking around, and mind your business."

"I take offense to what you're saying right now, Gary," Stu said. "It's never been an issue for anybody to stop by here. The Browns are wonderful people, and you know that."

"You know that goat you mentioned," Gary said, "the one that was killed? You're an educated man, Stu. You know that wasn't a coyote that did that, right?"

"I know."

"We investigated that too, after we heard the news. Do you know what we found when we examined that goat? Bite marks all over its body. Marks exactly like the ones found on Martin Welch. And do you know *what* those marks belonged to?"

"No," Stu said.

"Human." Gary leaned in, looking at Stu gravely. "The bite marks were left by human teeth. Whatever—no, *whoever* killed that goat, it was human. One of us. Could have been anyone in this town. It could have been you."

"I don't like what you're alluding to here, Gary."

* * *

Stu left Fred Brown's farm in a haze. He got into his car and began to drive, ignorant to a destination. He needed answers.

Human teeth.

Could someone be so deranged? So sick as to trespass onto someone else's property and sink their teeth into an animal?

Bite marks left by human teeth.

Who could have done such a thing? One of his neighbors? One of his colleagues? An outsider? Stu could feel his stomach twist as he drove north, away from the farm. Could it have been the same person who brutally murdered Martin Welch?

As he drove past the church on the corner of Holy Cross Road, he noticed the brass cross was still hanging upside down atop the spire. It dangled from the top of the steeple like a climber who'd lost their footing on a cliff's edge.

The sight stirred up the dread already rising within Stu. Given recent events, he felt like the upside-down cross hanging high above the town was a warning. A sign of things to come. The church's spire was something the people of Blair saw every day; there was no avoiding it. Yet it had been hanging upside down in plain sight for close to a week now. Had anyone noticed it but him? Was the rest of Blair so preoccupied that they'd overlook this menacing sight?

Sooner or later, the good times had to end...

Stu made a turn and pulled into the library's parking lot. If this town was indeed cursed, the upside-down cross made perfect sense. Martin Welch, the goats, Martha suddenly falling ill. He feared things might get worse before they got better. He needed to figure out the root of this evil before the entire town succumbed to it.

No human—at least, not one in their right mind—would do such a thing.

* * *

Stu took a seat inside the library and gathered up a few books. Something had sparked a memory, and it took him to Blair's history section, where he took out a few books on farmers and the history of agriculture in the small town. These books dated back to the late 1700s and included a history of the *Old Farmers' Almanac*.

First, he pulled up a directory of some of the earliest families in the area, their occupations, lineage, and causes of death. Nothing would be as accurate as the census. He found names and causes of death there and matched them with names he found in the almanacs and history books, all marking the complex and buried history of Blair.

Two interesting causes of death occurred within days of each other, in 1793. The first was a young boy whose name belonged to the Fischer genealogy, a name that had been ingrained in Blair for centuries. According to the census, the cause of death was tuberculosis. However, Stu referenced back to another mention of the Fischer family in one of the history books. It mentioned the death of a boy, his name redacted, who was the son of a goat farmer named Nathaniel. It said that this boy was murdered—not only murdered, but the victim of a witch's black magic. It had to be the same boy.

The second death listed under the directory for that day in 1793 was that of a woman, Grace [Last Name Redacted]. Her cause of death was a single, cold word: execution.

Stu flipped back through another section in the hidden history of Blair book, where he had seen another reference to her. As he thumbed through the pages, he suddenly stopped, reflexively pushing the book away. Folded neatly in between the pages of the book was a tuft of long black hair. It looked like it had been pulled right out of someone's scalp. Stu took a closer look—the hair was singed at the edges. As if it belonged to a burn victim.

Stu felt he may vomit.

He discreetly tore out the back page of another book and used it to remove the hair from the book he was trying to read. He then wiped his hands on his pants and continued his research.

According to documentation, the townsfolk of Blair believed a witch was living among them in 1793. There was no mention of a name, only the fact that she was an outsider, mostly reclusive, keeping to herself. She never married or had children, which in that time commonly drew suspicion to a woman.

It was also said that this woman was an expert in natural medicine. Most of her interactions with others came in times of need. *Typical*, Stu thought, people only looking to others when they needed something, when they were sick or had a toothache and needed a remedy. They needed her when they needed her, but they wouldn't dare get close enough to give her the respect of allowing her into their community. Not an outsider.

The book retold the events: A young boy became sick with TB, and this outsider was tasked with finding a cure. When it didn't work, the boy's father killed himself.

This act was considered a condemnation on the entire town, leaving a bad omen over Blair ever since. *It was the boy's father who let the evil in*, Stu thought, *not the woman.*

During that time, women accused of witchcraft were often burned at the stake. However, this case proved to be extraordinarily gruesome. The book said that her heart was cut out and stored inside a box, buried deep inside an unmarked location in Blair, separate from her body—a detail that turned Stu's stomach worse than the burnt hair. It was extra crude and barbaric, he thought. People who were distressed and felt threatened often went to extreme measures to punish those they felt had wronged them. They acted in horrific ways as a means of their own protection. Stu wasn't surprised by that. People still resorted to barbaric punishments to this day. Human nature hadn't changed much.

A light flickered briefly overhead, bringing Stu back into the present. He was getting lost in the story, falling right back into 1793. He took a breath, closed the book, and stared at it for a moment, reflecting on its time-worn cover. Like a three-hundred-year-old game of telephone.

But how did all of this correlate to what was happening in Blair today? Could there actually be a dead woman's heart buried somewhere in Blair? Or was that part of the story embellished? Whether or not it was true, Stu could feel the presence of this dark secret looming in the distance, waiting to be unearthed.

Chapter 33
Interlude:1793

When the eldest Fischer boy fell ill, no one in the town of Blair could have predicted what would come next. The devastation. His deterioration was swift and unrelenting.

At first, they found it difficult to diagnose the boy. His early symptoms ranged from fatigue to mild fever. Eventually, he developed a cough, one which proved to be increasingly persistent the longer it endured.

Finally, the town's doctor concluded everyone's worst fears—consumption had finally made it to Blair. There was panic among the town. It was no secret, the horror that took place in New England.

"What are we supposed to do now?" one woman shrieked. "I heard they had to burn the organs to prevent the disease from spreading!"

Another resident stated, "No, but the diseased gland *will* have to be extracted from the boy. Remove the part that houses the disease, and all shall be well."

"Everyone, please," the town doctor said. "We will not need to be so drastic. Goat's milk and brandy will flush out the toxins, and the boy will be healthy."

Despite the confidence of Blair's doctor, there was also anger within the town. Blame needed a home. But Nathaniel Fischer was desperate to save his boy.

When the goat's milk and brandy didn't work, they sought other remedies. None were successful. By the fourth day, the boy's cough had evolved into a rasping, hacking whooping.

It was painful, like rocks in his chest. He cried. His family cried. And it was clear they were running out of options. Nothing was working. Nathaniel Fischer could no longer bear to watch his son writhe in pain, losing the ability to breathe in the process.

So, he visited her. Grace [Last Name Redacted]. He knew the visit would upset his wife, but there was no other option. He did not want his boy to suffer any longer.

At first, Grace hesitated. She reiterated that she did not know what side effects the flower might have on a person. But it was either try or watch the boy die a slow, painful death.

So, she mashed the flower into a black paste with a mortar and pestle. "Give him this and have him stay in bed for an entire day," she instructed. "I will come to your home tomorrow. Until then, limit contact with him as much as possible."

"Then what?"

"Then the procedure will rid him of the disease," Grace said. "However, I must warn you: It is not pleasant. Bloodletting is a painful process. But it will purge the body of impurities. Your boy will need time to recover, but afterward he will be strong."

Nathaniel believed her. There were no other options; this one had to work. His boy had to be healthy for the upcoming fall harvest. He just couldn't fathom partaking in the annual celebration without his son.

He looked to the sky as the sun began to set and thought of something he'd read in a paper printed late last year called a farmers' almanac. In it, a man named Bartholomew Riggs had predicted that a great eclipse would coincide with the 1793 fall harvest. Nathaniel prayed that the man was nothing more than a loon, that this prediction would not come true. But only time would tell.

Nathaniel followed Grace's instructions and gave the flower paste to the boy. Then he waited.

The following day, at sunset, Grace visited the Fischer House.

There were stares as she entered the town. They knew who she was. No one's face held more scorn than Dorothy Fischer, who watched as this known whore entered her home. Yet, it was clear a job needed to be done. A last resort. All focus, all energy needed to be directed toward saving the young boy's life.

Grace lit candles around the parlor, and a warm yellow glow filled the void left by the absence of daylight. She then tied the boy down to his bed, which had been pulled into the middle of the room. The poor boy was drenched in sweat, barely able to open his eyes. He was rendered helpless, his arms pulled tightly up above his head. However, the numbing effects of the flower made him feel groggy.

Next, she placed stones around the boy. Two on either side of his head, one under each armpit, one between his legs, and two on top of the mantel.

"The stones," Grace explained. "They hold magical healing properties. They will help draw the sickness out of the boy's body during the bloodletting process."

Dorothy cleared her throat. "Is this safe? I think perhaps we should find another way." She sized up the stranger, giving her an untrusting glance. As much as she loathed this other woman, Dorothy couldn't ignore the fact that she'd seen her hands shaking as she prepared the ritual. She was clearly scared. Did this woman want to do this? Was she being forced? Dorothy almost felt sorry for her. But it was too late to ask questions, to get her side of the story. Her son needed a cure.

"No," Nathaniel said. "We are out of options. This will work." He turned to Grace. "Do it."

Grace did as she was told. First, she placed two silver bowls underneath the boy's elevated arms.

"Bleeding bowls," she said shakily. "To capture the sick blood for disposal." She then set wound dressing and a vial of antiseptic on the table beside the boy's bed. "After the procedure is finished, it is important to sterilize the wound. We don't want to cause an infection, which would make recovery more difficult." The candlelight danced on her cheeks as she spoke.

Finally, she produced what looked like a small metal box. Dorothy tensed and asked, "What is that?"

"This is the scarificator," the woman explained. "It is a more humane, and far less painful, method of drawing out bad blood." Without any further explanation, Grace proceeded. She engaged the spring-loaded lever, releasing blades from the ten slits at the bottom of the device. The blades punctured the boy's skin, and thin streams of blood flowed down his arms and dripped into the bowls.

The boy groaned. Although he hadn't felt the sharp pain of the blades, he could feel the backward flow of his blood and the pressure of the device. He writhed in his bed as much as the bindings around his ankles and wrists would allow. Sweat poured off of him as the blood began to flow.

When the procedure was finished, Dorothy wiped the boy down and helped apply the wound dressing. Then she tucked him in, and he promptly fell asleep.

"Thank you for allowing me into your home," Grace said. "You did the right thing, and your boy will be himself by the morning. He will be healthy and vibrant after a night's rest."

Dorothy nodded solemnly, silently. It was more than Grace expected to receive from her. She stopped on her way out, looked at Nathaniel, and then lowered her head and left.

The Fischer family blew out the candles, letting their home go dark. They trusted they'd made the right decision. That Nathaniel had led them righteously, and that their boy would be well in the morning. They slept.

* * *

In the morning, there was screaming.

Such an abrupt shift away from the silence of night—it was as if the chaos of the screaming had been brewing in the darkness. The calm of the night was only an illusion. Instead, death had come.

When Dorothy discovered her deceased son, a great, wailing cry of grief sounded from her like a tidal wave. It signaled to all of Blair, before even the rooster's crow, that death had arrived.

His skin was as pale as goat's milk. He was cold and unresponsive. Yet his eyes remained open. His dead eyes staring at the parlor ceiling. He did not die peacefully. Fear was burned into in his vision, an imprint in time. A reminder that the Fischer boy died a horrible, painful death.

Dorothy let out long, heaving cries as she mourned her son.

When Nathaniel came to her side, she grew angry. "You let this evil in! You let a witch perform an unholy ritual on our boy. You killed our son! You let her kill our boy!" she cried.

"N-no," Nathaniel stammered. "It wasn't supposed to be like this…"

He stood and left the room. The morning sky was dark, pregnant with the impending storm. "She should have never been allowed in…" he rationalized with himself.

I was tricked…

Under her spell.

She must be punished.

* * *

A knock at the front door startled Grace. She opened it, and Nathaniel stepped in. He took off his hat and was silent at first. Then he took a seat at the small table.

He was nearly crumpling his hat in his hands, his face distraught.

"What is it?" Grace asked.

"My son is dead," Nathaniel said. "He didn't survive the procedure."

Grace covered her mouth in shock. Her heart sank. She knew what this meant for her. This thing she'd wanted nothing to do with had gone wrong. She remained silent, as she knew the consequence that would soon befall her.

"He is to be buried tomorrow," Nathaniel explained. "Underneath a tree in our yard. He was so young...

"I only wanted to protect him. To protect Blair. But an evil has made its way here, and it seems there was nothing I could do to prevent it.

"I must know..." He trailed off. "Are you, indeed, a witch?"

"If you must ask such a question, why did you come to me at all?" Grace asked.

"I was out of options," Nathaniel said. "I would have done anything to save my boy. You know that. Even if it meant endangering my community. Without my boy, I have nothing."

They sat in silence as a ray of morning sunlight crept in through the window. Nathaniel feared it may be the last time he would ever see the sun rise. It would certainly be Grace's.

"So, are you a witch, or are you not?"

"I am no such thing," Grace said. "I am a woman. I study plants and medicine. I am a loner. That is all I ever was, and all I ever will be. If that answer does not suit you, I apologize."

"Was the flower not meant to protect? You said it had healing properties, did you not? Did you not tell me it was so delicate and rare that I must not touch it, as doing so would risk its integrity?"

"I did tell you of its delicate nature, yes," Grace said. "But you didn't listen to me, Mr. Fischer. I specifically told you the Devil's Spiral had healing properties for *some* ailments. It is not my fault you assumed this meant it could save your boy from consumption."

Nathaniel turned to her in a burning rage. "I recall saying I would have you burned like the witch you are if you spoke back to me."

Grace recoiled.

"You are to stay away until we bury my boy," Nathaniel said. "Then we will determine what is to be done with you."

165

Chapter 34
Jaycie

Jaycie anxiously waited for Mrs. Coleman to arrive at the science lab. She needed to talk to her about the dissection assignment. Calvin's suspension couldn't have come at a worse time. They had planned to take on this project as a pair. Now, Jaycie found herself partnerless.

She thought she should be more upset at the number of people going in and out of her life at any moment. At least Calvin's hadn't skipped out on her purposefully. And Jax...

Jax was dealing with his own demons. It broke her heart, but she remained hopeful he would return home.

Jaycie sat awkwardly on the stool, leaning over the workspace with her arms folded. She didn't even bother to remove her backpack. She could hear the murmurs of the other pairs, discussing their projects among themselves while she sat alone. She felt like she was on display being the only student without a partner.

The clock struck ten o'clock, and the door opened. Mrs. Coleman entered, and Jaycie promptly got up from her station, the metal stool scratching against the floor—now she really felt as if a spotlight had been pointed her way.

She quickly approached her teacher. "Hi, Mrs. Coleman? Can I talk to you?"

The teacher nodded. She seemed to be hiding a pain of her own behind her smile. They moved off to the side of the room near the eye wash and safety station.

"I know we're supposed to do our dissection project today, but is it too late to opt out? My lab partner is suspended, and I don't feel comfortable doing it on my own."

Mrs. Coleman closed her eyes and pinched the bridge of her nose with two fingers. "Oh, Jaycie," the teacher sighed.

"I know I'd be required to submit a paper," Jaycie said. "I'm sorry it's last minute. I just don't know what else to do. I wasn't expecting to have to do this alone."

Mrs. Coleman pursed her lips and looked at Jaycie woefully. "You've never been late with an assignment before. I'll accept a paper from you if you can submit a working outline by the end of the week."

"Thank you, Mrs. Coleman."

The teacher nodded. "However, since the rest of the class will be working on their dissections today, I do have to dismiss you. It wouldn't be fair for you to view their work and then write a paper on it. The research is still your responsibility."

"Understood. I can go to study hall," Jaycie said. As she turned to leave, Mrs. Coleman stopped her. "Ms. Brogdon, are you okay?"

"Yeah, I'm fine. Why?"

"With everything that's going on, if you need someone to talk to, you can talk to me. Or any of the teachers here, for that matter. We know everyone is under a lot of stress. It's good to talk about it. Bad things happen, and it's okay to not be okay. Even teachers deal with it; we're still human, after all."

"Thanks, Mrs. Coleman." Jaycie forced a smile. She'd thought she was doing a better job of hiding her pain. But Mrs. Coleman was dealing with turmoil herself. Jaycie imagined how difficult it must be for a teacher to have a son involved in what happened with Calvin.

Mrs. Coleman was known to hold her students to a high standard, but Gabe fell far short of those.

Jaycie lowered her head and left the lab. She checked into study hall, where she was required to be since she was not in a classroom. She thought she could get a head start on her outline there, but first she took a lap around the desks and computers in search of her friends.

She missed Mabel and Rose. She was worried about them. And she still felt this strange, unresolved energy with them.

If she'd done something to upset them, to make them angry with her, she wanted to fix it. She began to feel guilty for not reaching out more, but she didn't want to be annoying and text constantly either. She felt self-conscious sending one of those, "Hey, long time no talk, stranger," kind of texts.

To her dismay, neither of the girls were there. Jaycie sighed and found a seat at a vacant computer. She might as well start outlining her research. However, her mind was everywhere except on the task at hand. The girls had to be avoiding her. It was especially out of character for any of them to skip the cafeteria before homeroom each morning.

Jaycie couldn't concentrate on a paper, so she picked up her phone and opened the messaging app.

Hey, you okay? she texted Calvin. She put her phone back down and then watched as three dots appeared and then disappeared.

Nobody wanted to talk to her.

But then a response came through.

Calvin: Been better. Sorry I couldn't be there for D-Day.

Jaycie smiled. D-Day, known as Dissection Day.

Jaycie: It's okay. Coleman says we can hand in a paper instead.

Calvin: Cool.

Those three dots appeared and disappeared again.

Calvin: We still good for FF this weekend?

Jaycie: Is it still on? Heard about Martha Brown...

Calvin: Think it is.

Jaycie: How?

Calvin: Volunteers, I guess? I don't know, you're the local

Jaycie: Touché

Calvin: So? Yes?

Jaycie: See you then

A thumbs-up reaction appeared over her text bubble. She put her phone away and smiled. Fortunately, she still had someone she could talk to.

Chapter 35
Stu

The Blair High School teacher's lounge was quiet enough that Stu could get some reading done before his next class.

The ethereal fog trailing him since the death of Martin Welch had thickened.

Now two bodies.

Stu had found two residents of his community dead, and anxiety was sinking its hooks even deeper into him. Then there was the gnawing truth that Ray Parilla was also missing, yet to be found. Would Stu be the one to find *him* too?

He couldn't take much more of this. He could feel his sanity cracking under the weight. His beard was growing in thick, as he'd abandoned shaving since accidentally cutting himself a week ago. How things had seemed to only get worse since.

He took a seat at the end of a long table with a book he had borrowed from the library,

Tuberculosis & Witchcraft: How an Unknown Illness Triggered a Second Salem Witch Trials. The hard look Addy Westbrook, the librarian, had given him as he requested this specific book made him feel self-conscious. But this book wasn't necessarily problematic; it was his right to learn.

For the most part, his friends and neighbors had been kind. They understood he was going through a hard time after seeing the things he saw. Everyone in Blair was distressed in their own way. Addy was probably sensitive to such books since hearing of Martin's death. Everyone reacted to tragedy differently. Stu wanted to educate himself, while others might prefer to distance themselves from the horrors. Both were valid reactions.

The way Officer Gary had looked at him the day Martha died, however... The line of questioning made Stu feel like he was in the line of fire. Made him feel like he was guilty of something.

Stu was aware that some people were looking at him differently since Martin Welch's death. Discovering the body of a young man had put him under a microscope.

But he had to figure out what was going on in Blair. He couldn't accept that bad things just happen. There had to be a pattern. In fact, aside from Officer Gary's comments, there had been no mention of what exactly happened to Martin. No official cause of death. Sure, Stu had seen the body himself, but...

Human teeth... Whoever killed that goat...

Was it even necessary to know what happened to Martin that day? An autopsy report? The kid had been savagely mauled by something. But the town never did make an announcement, did they? Did they know?

It was human... Could have been anyone in this town.

Stu opened the book and returned to the particularly grim section of events that took place in Blair in 1793. The overlap of events made his mind coil and wind in different directions. Why had no one ever talked about a major eclipse happening in the sky over Blair before? The same year the first *Old Farmers' Almanac* was published, according to the history books, was the same year of...

It could have been you...

Morning, Stu.

Stu learned that tuberculosis was known as "consumption" until the nineteenth century. When the residents of Blair could not determine a cause or a cure for the disease, they blamed it on a suspected witch. It was a scandal that coincided with the great eclipse predicted by that first almanac, an event said to bring more than just darkness to the town.

The sound of liquid being poured resonated somewhere in the background of Stu's thoughts as he read.

Her name was Grace.

He read about her. Cause of death: execution. Buried away from the sun.

To break her hold, she must be set free. To break her hold, she must see the sun.

"Stu?"

Stu recoiled at the sound of Principal Holden's voice. He looked up, closing the book. She stood in front of him, coffee mug in hand. Her eyes were wide, and she looked genuinely scared. Had he been reading aloud?

"Are you okay, Stu?"

"I, uh, yes—I'm fine," Stu said, rubbing his eyes.

Principal Holden pursed her lips and took a seat at the table opposite Stu. She looked at him with concern. But Stu resented it. He felt her judgment on him.

"Stu," she began. She glanced down at the book's cover, her body stiffening, "I'm a little concerned for you. We're flexible about you taking the time you need to sort things out, but this...*obsession* now, with the town's history. It's a lot. I'm concerned you're going down a path of conspiracy."

"I assure you, I'm fine," Stu said.

"I don't doubt that," Principal Holden said. "I just think that maybe you should take some extra time for yourself. Certain pressures can get to a person. It happens to all of us. We all need a break. Think about it."

"I don't need time off," Stu said. "Aren't you curious about the string of people missing? Murdered?" He lowered his voice.

"Stu, we've worked together for a long time," Principal Holden said. "You're one of the smartest people I know. But you stormed out of a classroom. You missed several days of school without telling anyone. You—"

"I sent an e-mail to Alan," Stu said, confused. "I asked him to cover."

Principal Holden shook her head. "I wasn't notified. And on top of this, your behavior has become erratic—you brought up conspiracy talking points in front of the students. The Blair police have done a fine job keeping us safe, and I'm confident they'll continue to do so. Let them do their jobs, and we'll do ours, yeah?"

"I just—"

"Stu, take the week," she said. "Given the current political climate, and with Freedom Readers in town, making sure we don't bring dangerous reading materials into our school"—she pointed at Stu's book—"I think it's best for you to decompress and forget about this whole Martin Welch thing. It'll be good for you. Please, don't make me put you on mandatory leave."

Stu nodded somberly. "I just care about this town, you know? That's all this is. I'm scared."

"I know," Principal Holden said. "We all care about this town. We're all going through this together. And I think the best way to show you care about Blair is to take some time off. We don't want this garnering national attention. Please, take care of your mental health, Stu. That's the best way to look out for our community."

Chapter 36
Tomas

"Expelled..." Tomas let the word roll off of his tongue. He sat in the parlor of his house, sprawled across a throne-like chair, one elbow resting upon the armrest. He wore a veneer of arrogance as he studied the faces in front of him, swirling one finger around the lip of a chalice perched on the armrest.

Hector and Gabe stood before him, flushed with shame. They were accompanied by Rose, who sat on the opposite end of the parlor, disconnected from their interaction.

"In a way," Tomas continued, "this was my fault. I was too eager to flex, I suppose. Too eager to take what is rightfully ours. I should have waited for the darkness."

There was silence inside the parlor as the night grew dark. The air was cold and stale, as if this were a waiting room. A purgatory with sinister intentions.

"And what about you?" Tomas said, lifting his gaze toward Rose. "Were you expelled today too?"

"No," she said coldly. "I went home early today, with a sick note, so I wasn't there to witness you boys fumble."

"Fine," Tomas sighed. "It's going to be fine, and I do apologize for my carelessness. This is on me. When I said we were to rid Blair of impure waste, I meant it. Jumping into this on school property, before the eclipse...it was a misstep. I took for granted that there are some people in this town who still don't understand the pureness of our intentions. Speaking of intention, where is Jax?"

"He's home, I guess," Hector said. "He said he'd catch up later."

Tomas scoffed. "Catch up later... I expect better from him, from all of you. You have to grow up one day. You can't leech off of me forever, but I will teach you to be self-sufficient. The time is now. You must all learn how to survive. Having four mouths to feed is—"

"Three," Rose interrupted in a disinterested tone.

"Excuse me?" asked Tomas.

"Three," she repeated. "I'm not doing whatever *that* is." She sighed. "I'm not playing revenge with you boys. I've decided I don't care about whatever disgusting undead games you want to play. It's all bullshit anyway."

"Are you saying you're backing out of our oath?" Tomas asked.

"That's exactly what I'm saying."

Tomas grinned, amused. "Three mouths, then. I stand corrected. Still, it's more responsibility than I should be taking on. I am not your keeper. You can't understand the insatiable hunger I feel on a constant basis. Yet this really is the only way. To survive. To thrive. To take Blair and make it ours. Take it from those who don't deserve her. Those who take her for granted. I will show you how. Come with me."

"I'll stay here," Rose said. "You boys have fun doing whatever it is you do."

"Very well," Tomas said. "Tomorrow, when the eclipse cloaks Blair in darkness, we do this." He turned toward Hector and Gabe. "Yes?"

The boys nodded in unison.

"Good," Tomas said. "Then we proceed, whether Jax is with us or not."

Chapter 37
Jaycie and Calvin

The sky was beginning to darken, and the floodlights were finally turned on for the first night of Fall Fest. A pair of spotlights were pointed toward the clouds as well, illuminating them so they looked like giant mounds of cotton candy floating above the earth.

Jaycie waved at Calvin as she walked up the path to Fred Brown's farm. "Hey, lab partner." She smiled as she approached. "Hope you weren't waiting long."

"No, not long," Calvin said. "I got here a couple of minutes ago." He was standing near the entrance of the festival, which also served as Fred Brown's driveway, but all cars had been directed to the main road to make room for foot traffic. Calvin's skateboard was tucked under one arm, and he was wearing a gray long-sleeved Henley.

The smell of popcorn and fried sweets filled the air, and Calvin had practiced masterful restraint while waiting outside. He could have gone in and snuck something from one of the many vendors who sold treats from booths and tents, but he preferred to wait for his friend.

"Ready to experience the best part of Blair in October?" Jaycie asked. Calvin obliged.

As they got their tickets, they heard a calliope in the distance. The instrument was a nostalgic touch that Fred Brown included every year. He didn't actually own a calliope, but he liked to play carnival music to set the atmosphere. He always made do with what he had.

As they began to walk around, Jaycie watched Cal take in his surroundings. As far as festivals go, Jaycie knew this one was on the smaller side. Fred Brown owned a large plot of land by Blair standards, but it was still a modest little farm. His home.

Space was finite, but the volunteers, vendors, and everyone involved always did a great job. Fall Fest attracted vendors from Plattsburg and even Vermont, who sold various treats, candles, artwork, and other trinkets. This year, there was a stand at the entrance with someone handing out special glasses for the eclipse.

"Get your protective eyewear!" he shouted like a 1950s carnival barker. "Stay behind tonight and experience a once-in-a-lifetime event on the beach!"

The air was alive with a lightheartedness that belied the reality that someone had recently died in the Brown home. Jaycie tried not to think about it.

The field, which began at the driveway and wrapped around the side of the property, was the path everyone used to get into the heart of the festival. It dipped into the grassy pastures that were home to Fred's goats. There was a small tent where kids could grab a free handful of pellets to feed them. The path was lined with booths covered by red and white striped canopies. Each booth either had games or was selling some kind of carnival treat. Jaycie's favorite was the guessing booth. It was probably the least active of all the games, but if you guessed correctly, you could win an outstanding prize.

She pointed at it and motioned Calvin along. "We have to stop here first," she said. "Jax and I used to do this all the time. One year, right before high school, we actually guessed the closest without going over and won the entire jar of candy. It lasted us until Christmas."

"So, you just guess?" Calvin eyed the booth. A girl from school—he thought her name was Ashley—was watching over the booth and documenting everyone's guesses. There was a large glass jar filled with candy. That was it. It was a little underwhelming, especially compared to the other games, like the ball toss or high-striker, where you could win actual prizes. He saw they were giving out gift cards to the music store at the tent with balloon darts, and he thought that would be perfect. It would get him closer to his drum set.

"Exactly!" Jaycie said. "It's fun, and I'm really good at it."

They each placed their guesses and continued to walk. After trying their luck at the other games, they turned into the next row, where they found a palm reader.

"This looks fun," Jaycie said. "Do you want to try it?"

"Sure," Calvin shrugged.

They sat down at the two stools in front of the booth and were greeted by a stoic woman who Jaycie did not recognize. The sign on the table read ten dollars for a palm reading. Calvin sighed and glanced at Jaycie. He thought ten dollars was a steep price to have someone make up stories, but Jaycie was already reaching into her pocket for some cash. She placed a twenty down on the table and said, "For both of us, please."

Calvin hesitated but eventually obliged and gave up his hand. The palm reader took it and began running her index finger around the crevices of his palm.

"You're feeling a bit like you don't belong," she began, and Calvin raised an eyebrow. "People tell you that you can't or shouldn't be doing something—but you need to follow your heart. You're in the exact place you're meant to be."

Jaycie looked over at him and mouthed the words, *I told you.* Although Calvin wouldn't admit it, he was slightly impressed. He had been expecting something a little more generic from the palm reader, but she'd hit the nail on the head.

"Also, you're going to go through something difficult very soon." Her eyebrows furrowed. "An attack, in a way. You're going to be challenged like you've never been challenged before, but you must never give in. You must fight back."

"Okay," Calvin said. *That was weird*, he thought as he took his hand back. Either the palm reader was a few days late, since he had already been jumped and fought back the best he could, or something bigger was coming.

Now it was Jaycie's turn.

"Oh, honey, you are a unique one, aren't you?" The woman smiled. "I love your energy. Never compromise who you are, for anyone. Your confidence will take you far."

This time, it was Calvin who smiled. He wasn't sure why or how, but this statement confirmed that Jaycie was genuinely being his friend. At first, he'd thought she was only being nice to him because he was the new kid. But it was true; she had his back, and she meant everything she said to him.

"However." The palm reader paused. "I see challenges in your future." She took a deep, shuddering breath. "Heartbreak. Oh, honey." She released Jaycie's hand and covered her mouth. Her eyes fixed on Jaycie's, filled with sadness.

After a moment, she took Jaycie's hand again and continued. "I sense tragedy in your future. You must be strong for your family. No —you must be strong for your community. People will need you."

This time, it was Jaycie who took back her own hand.

"Thank you," she said quietly, and she and Calvin moved on to the next booths.

"You okay?" Calvin asked.

"Yeah," Jaycie said. "I'm just worried about Jax, that's all..." She trailed off, tucking a strand of hair behind her ear. "Hey, we should get maple berry pie from the backyard. It's a Blair staple. There's nothing like it anywhere else in the world."

They got their pie and took it to a seating area that overlooked the goat pasture. They could hear lively clucking sounds coming from the chicken coop. By now, Jaycie was looking around quite a bit, and she was less chatty.

"Are you sure you're okay?" Calvin asked. "It seems like you're looking for someone."

"Actually, I am," Jaycie said. "Mr. Reinhart. He missed Gothic Lit twice this week. It's unlike him, and I'm beginning to worry. I'm sure he'll be here, though. He never misses Fall Fest, and I need to talk to him."

Calvin nodded, taking a sip of hot apple cider. He began looking around the crowd too, hoping to be helpful in Jaycie's search for their teacher.

Calvin didn't mind Mr. Reinhart. He didn't know him too well, but of all the teachers he'd met at BHS, Stu was one of the few who went out of his way to ask Calvin how he was doing.

He looked around and saw people having fun, laughing, spending time with their families. He began to feel a little homesick. It was strange to be surrounded by such warmth while not being embraced by it. It made him appreciate Jaycie even more.

"Is that Fred Brown?" Calvin asked, motioning to a man sitting in a chair on the back porch of the house.

Jaycie turned to look. "That's him," she said. "I don't know how he's doing this. Martha was his world. I know this is what she would have wanted, to keep the festival going, but it just seems impossible. Easier said than done. I can't imagine how he feels right now."

"Oh, hey, I think I see Mr. Reinhart." Calvin pointed off in the distance toward a man standing alone, observing the festivities from afar.

Jaycie stood up and called out, "Mr. Reinhart!"

Their English teacher turned and looked in their direction. When he saw them, he recoiled for a moment, as if to hide, but when he saw that no one else was looking his way, he relaxed. He gave a sheepish wave, eyes darting back and forth as he began to approach.

"Hey, guys. Good to see you both," Stu said innocuously. He

pointed at Calvin's cup. "Hey, you're turning into a local already! Best apple cider around." He sat down next to them.

"Mr. Reinhart," Jaycie said, "is there really something bad happening? I've been hearing rumors."

Stu took a deep breath and looked around. "You've probably heard people jumping to conclusions, trying to connect the recent string of deaths to a single cause—a sort of 'darkness,' right?"

Jaycie nodded.

"Well, that's how it begins," Stu continued. "We start pointing fingers, looking for someone to blame. A scapegoat. That's how neighbor turns on neighbor. Anxiety turns into fear. Fear turns into panic, which eventually devolves into people falling back on their darkest impulses."

"What do you mean?" Jaycie asked. She could see that Mr. Reinhart was shaking, that he needed to get something off of his chest.

"I got into the weeds a bit at the library," Stu said. "I'm still not sure myself what I'm getting at, but I found some information that frightened me. Blair has a problem. Traces of an unresolved atrocity seem to linger in the bones of this town, and we're feeling its effects still today."

"I'm so glad I moved here," Calvin said sarcastically.

"It'll be okay," Stu said. "At least, I think it will. I want you both to know, we'll figure this thing out. Remember, sound minds always prevail."

"I heard a rumor at school that you're going to be away for a while," Jaycie said. "Is that true?"

Stu nodded. "Only for a week. Listen, I don't want to sugarcoat it —you deserve better than that. But, as you know by now, I'm the one who found Martin Welch's body near Owl's Head Park." He lowered his voice. "I was there when Martha Brown passed away in her sleep. You might hear more rumors from people, people who claim they are desperate to find a reason for the bad things happening in Blair. But, as I've taught you in class, you should trust your gut. Occam's razor: The simplest explanation is usually the correct one."

Jaycie nodded again, although she wasn't sure she fully understood. This was something Mr. Reinhart had brought up in class before. Then she remembered *Dracula*...

"Mr. Reinhart, why do they want to ban *Dracula* from our class?" Jaycie asked. When she saw the shade of fear in her teacher's eyes, she knew she was on the right track.

"I don't know if I have a good answer for that," Stu said. "But it seems like some people in Blair have their mind made up about what's causing all the quote, unquote 'bad things' happening here."

* * *

The gloom of nightfall fell quickly over Fall Fest. The floodlights kicked on, shining artificial light over Fred Brown's farm. Everyone looked to the sky, waiting for any sign of the eclipse. But, to their disappointment, there was none.

"Attention friends and families," a volunteer announced. Jaycie recognized her as Jill Mitchell, owner of the coffee shop. "Thank you for coming to the first night of Fall Fest. While the eclipse is expected any time now, we might not see any activity tonight. This part of the festival is closing until morning, but if anyone would like to stay around for eclipse watch, there are areas set up on the beach."

Calvin turned toward Jaycie. "Do you feel like hanging out and watching the eclipse?"

"I think I'm going to go," Jaycie said. "I should probably have dinner with my parents. We're hoping Jax comes home."

Calvin nodded.

Mr. Reinhart stood up. "I'm going to get home too. This whole eclipse makes me apprehensive. Be careful."

Chapter 38
Jaycie

The silence at the dinner table was palpable as Jaycie, Mom, and Dad finished their meal. It had been an awkward night. It felt as if they hadn't had a proper conversation since the night Jax left. Only tension and resentment remained in his absence.

Jaycie was mostly quiet as Mom and Dad tried to make small talk —a sad attempt at behaving like a family. Jaycie fussed with her food, using her fork to push it around the plate. Eventually she gave up on pretending to eat and asked to be excused. Mom nodded, and Jaycie got up and brought her plate to the sink. As she cleaned it, she noticed something on the refrigerator she hadn't seen before. A prayer card from Martin Welch's funeral.

She remembered seeing a stack of them at the service itself, but she hadn't wanted to get any closer to the body, so she avoided that table. She didn't realize her parents had brought one home. She thought it was a little morbid.

She took the laminated card from the fridge and turned it over in her hand, examining it. The picture of Martin was unsettling. He looked alive in the photo, his hair done neatly, combed to one side. He sat with good posture, wearing an innocent smile. But Jaycie saw through this snapshot in time. Martin was dead, and nothing was bringing him back.

The most offensive element was the prayer printed on the back. It was titled, "Safely Home," and it began, "I am home in heaven, dear ones; oh, so happy and so bright! There is a perfect joy and beauty in the everlasting light. All the pain and grief is over, every restless—"

Jaycie couldn't continue. She began to feel angry. The choice of prayer was bullshit, and kind of in poor taste, in her opinion. What joy was there in Martin's fate? None, Jaycie thought. Joy would have been Martin going to the college of his choice. Joy would have been him learning and exploring the things that made him happy. Living a full life. Leaving Blair and meeting someone to grow old with. That would have been beautiful.

Not being found facedown in the dirt.

Jaycie hastily returned the prayer card to its place on the fridge, despite her urge to throw it in the trash. When she felt a hand on her shoulder, she turned around, startled.

"Mrs. Welch was handing them out at the end of the service," Mom said. "I know it meant a lot to her that we were there for Martin."

"Do you think there's something wrong in Blair?" Jaycie asked. "That there's a reason for the things that have happened?"

"No, honey," Mom said. "There's nothing wrong with Blair. The people of this town are strong; they have faith. It's all just part of God's plan."

"You don't ever think that God's plan is kind of shit?" Jaycie said, exasperated. She felt her mother recoil a little bit, but she wasn't sorry. It was true. If there was a god, he wouldn't have let Martin die like that. And if there was a god, he'd bring Jax back home.

As Mom opened her mouth to answer, their attention was caught by the lights. The lights in the kitchen flickered briefly, the way they would during a heavy thunderstorm. It only lasted about ten or twelve seconds, but when the lights returned to their normal brightness, the darkness outside was palpable. Out the window, they could see only black, as if the moon and stars had all ceased to exist.

"I'm sorry," Jaycie said. "I—I'm going to go to bed now."

Chapter 39
Jax

I just wanted to let you know I miss you, Jax thought as he sat in the dirt next to Martin's grave. The cold soil in between his fingers was the only feeling he could summon, as if the last vestige of his friend's presence.

"I didn't mean to be so harsh the last time I was here," Jax said out loud. He glanced at the faded NO GOD still smudged on the church's exterior. "I just... I guess I'm still working through things. I miss the old days, you know?" he said, as if Martin's headstone would answer him.

Jax looked up at the sky. The sun had almost fully set. Still no sign of an eclipse. He wondered, *How can an eclipse happen at night?* He supposed he would have to see it to understand.

"Fall Fest started tonight," he said. "I know you used to like that. They're probably closing up by now. I don't think I can go knowing you won't be there.

"I just feel like I can't find the joy in anything anymore. You knew that, I guess. That's why we stopped talking, because the only thing I've been good at lately is ruining anything good in my life. I'm sorry..."

The sky quickly grew dark as the sun fully set. Shadows moved over the grave markers, spilling darkness into the cemetery.

"The last time I was actually happy, I think, was that summer before freshman year, when you came to our cabin up in Lake Placid. It was the last time things felt...normal? Like, TV-sitcom normal. Whatever the fuck normal is supposed to be. I guess I felt optimistic back then. It was before I knew what it was like to let people down. To let myself down."

Jax got quiet. He knew he was rambling, unloading his thoughts. Then he felt the air around him shift. As if back for an encore, the sun seemed to materialize from within the darkness of the night sky. It crept up behind the unsuspecting moon. Two orbs, high and pronounced, reminded Jax of the original *Star Wars* movie, moon and sun both glowing in the sky like twin leviathans. It was unlike anything he had ever seen in real life.

As the two orbs converged, there was a vibrant burst of light. Jax squinted, shielding his eyes from the overwhelming brightness. The sun shined powerfully behind the moon, casting the night sky in a faux-daytime hue.

The brilliance of the phenomenon lasted only a moment before the sky over Blair returned to pitch darkness. The twin orbs in the sky were now indistinguishable from one another, a single black globe stalking the earth from space. Its reflection cast a gray illumination, giving the illusion of a world in grayscale, a black-and-white TV show. It felt like the eclipse had transported Jax from an ordinary place, a place he was familiar with behind the church, right into a horror movie.

With the shift in perspective, there seemed to be a new presence in the cemetery with Jax. Surrounded by tombstones, markers of Blair's residents past, Jax no longer felt alone—and he shivered. He heard a creaking sound from behind Martin's headstone, like a heavy door opening very slowly.

"Martin?"

Chapter 40
Calvin

alvin walked along the Noblewood Park trailhead, which led from Fred Brown's farm down to the beach. Several Fall Fest attendees did the same, bringing along their prizes from games played and won, paper bags filled with fried dough covered in sugar, and their special protective eyewear.

The beach was situated south of Blair proper and just east of Fred Brown's farm. It was split into two sections by the Winooski River, which ran through its middle as it emptied into Lake Champlain.

Calvin looked around and thought the beach was, in fact, the perfect spot to view the once-in-a-lifetime cosmic event. The vast night sky expanded overhead, and while the moon wasn't visible behind the heavy cloud cover, when the eclipse started, whoever was on the beach would surely have a front-row seat. There was a group of people who had clearly set up on the beach prior to leaving Fall Fest for the night.

He found a spot where the sand met the water, a quieter spot away from the larger crowd, as he just wanted to drop in and see what all the chatter was about. He wasn't feeling much like socializing without Jaycie, but he was curious.

He sat down on his skateboard, letting his sneakers dig into the sand. He dropped his drumsticks on the ground next to him and relaxed.

Calvin looked out toward the water. Lake Champlain certainly was beautiful. The way the waves gently rolled up to the sand was quite calming. Under the night sky, the water looked as clean and smooth as dark silk.

He looked around, taking mental note of those in attendance. He recognized a few people—there was the girl who worked at the coffee shop and her mom, who worked at the grocery store. She always rang Calvin up when he would stop in for groceries. He liked the girl just fine, but her mom gave him bad vibes, perhaps because she always gave him a strange look when bagging his groceries.

There were other familiar faces, such as the parents of Martin Welch. While the mood on the beach was mostly upbeat, the Welches looked like they were only there because they had to be.

There were also some unfamiliar faces. A group of guys Calvin did not recognize hanging out at the far end of the beach. They shared beers, laughing loudly as they drank. A couple of them tossed around a Frisbee; others kicked back as if they were attending some kind of tailgate party. Someone was even playing music from their car: "It's The End of the World As We Know It." *And I feel fine,* people sang gleefully. A little tongue-in-cheek humor to set the mood for this novel event.

Stupid, Calvin thought. He suddenly felt apprehension toward this post-festival gathering on the beach. He didn't know why, but it felt wrong. He felt foolish, but he wondered how an eclipse could even take place at night. It was like everyone was gathered to bear witness to the implausible. And the implausible began to feel dangerous.

In a moment of self-awareness, Calvin thought maybe he didn't want to be here anymore. It felt foolish to mess with the unknown, especially with little more than generic protective eyewear.

Despite this, the watch party continued, and the music blared on.

Perhaps this truly was the end of the world, and everyone was singing along to their demise. He looked around and saw more people congregating on the beach, waiting for an event whose potential nobody understood. What if it was going to be dangerous?

Calvin took a breath and shook his head. Maybe he didn't need to see for himself. He decided he no longer wanted to be here and would make his departure before the sky—

Chapter 41
Tomas

Hector and Gabe crossed into the darkness with Tomas. They walked through the wooded area behind the Fischer House, following Tomas toward Lake Champlain. The overgrown path had thick tree cover, but they could still see that the sky above was suddenly darker than they had ever seen it before.

It has begun.

A feeling of unease cast over the boys as they followed. As they walked through the clearing where land met the waters of Lake Champlain, their shadows disappeared. Then a strange anomaly happened in the sky—day and night seemed to converge. It was suddenly both simultaneously. A murky gray veil covered everything around them, casting them in a heavy curtain of darkness.

You boys trust me, right?

Tomas's voice sounded in the gloom of the eclipse although they did not see his mouth move. There was a disembodied effect to his voice, as if the question had come from inside their minds and not from the mouth of their friend. As if Tomas had planted the question in their minds through the air while the clouds behaved in absurd ways, mimicking a colorless kaleidoscope, casting strange shapes in the sky.

"We trust you," they answered together as they approached the leaf-strewn beachfront.

This section of the beach, much farther north than the more populated center of Blair, north of the Brown farm and Fall Fest, was isolated and barren. The path from the Fischer House led to a tree, the patch of dirt beneath it open and ready like a cavernous maw. Hungry and violent.

Good. Tomas turned around. His pupils dilated to a frightening size, making his eyes look almost entirely black. His lean frame looked like it was being swallowed up by the giant darkness of Lake Champlain behind him, like a black halo. Without the reflection of the moon on the water's surface, it looked like an endless void of darkness.

He spoke, but his lips did not move. *Now that the day is here, we move forward and fulfill your oaths. You will join me, surrendering your souls to me. Do you understand?*

Hector and Gabe nodded in silence.

Good. Then follow me.

Different shades of gray pulsed and swirled in the sky above, like a gothic rendition of *Starry Night.* The moon became visible again, a black orb filtering out all sunlight and casting a harsh burst of silvery, oppressive gloom.

The boys watched, unsure if what they were seeing was real or an effect of the anomalous event in the sky. Then their friend's figure changed before their eyes. As if he were growing taller before them. His fingers elongated into snakelike hooks. Tomas wasn't thriving inside the darkness. He *was* the darkness. The ancient fear passed down by generations of Blair's lineage manifesting in the flesh.

Despite not casting a shadow, Tomas obscured the boys from the glowing gloom in the sky as he approached them underneath the tree.

* * *

Rose sat by herself in the empty parlor as the boys left to do whatever it was they meant to do in order to satisfy their oath. She was getting bored inside the house by herself, bored of this oath game they were playing.

She was growing to resent Tomas for making her care about this stupid shit in the first place. She figured most of this was a lie. For what, she didn't know. But where was Tomas Fischer's supposedly rich father? She was beginning to suspect there was nothing remarkable about the Fischer House after all. It was old, yes, but the more she looked around, the more it became clear that there was no wealth. Money would typically bring with it some level of care inside the house.

Instead, there were cracks and water stains running across the parlor ceiling. There was a persistent chill throughout the entire house and ice-cold water from the faucets. If there was wealth, shouldn't there be a basic level of comfort as well? How could Tomas Fischer live like this?

She should have been spending her senior year of high school having fun. Instead, she was spending it here, ostensibly *not* having fun.

Restless, she stood and went to the kitchen for a bottle of water. The wooden floors creaked as she moved between rooms. The lights in the kitchen didn't work, but she could navigate the vast stretch of room by the dim glow of gray twilight that spilled in from outside. When she opened the refrigerator, she discovered it didn't work either. The unlit fridge was empty inside, its walls stained with mold.

She rolled her eyes and slammed the door shut. How could she ever fall for such idiocy? Yet that night, outside the cave...Tomas had been so convincing. In his presence, the truth had seemed obscured. Now that Rose was alone, it became clear—this was all a lie. Tomas was living in squalor. He was an imposter with pathetic ambitions, nothing more. A loser who wanted to rule over this shitty little town, a town that barely mattered when compared to the rest of New York...a worthless town full of worthless people, herself included.

Rose wandered outside, done with the sad state of things inside the house. The darkness of night embraced her like a blanket. She kicked pebbles as she walked, rustling up dirt and leaves. She bent down and picked up a tree branch, poked plants with it and used it as a walking stick against the rolling terrain.

The cool, damp October air was brisk against her face. However, she didn't feel the same chill she'd felt in previous years. The breeze flowed through her knee-length cardigan. She let it dangle open, allowing the cold air to caress her skin. Goosebumps broke out over her skin, especially on her bare legs. A waft of something charred crossed her nostrils and made her wonder what was out here in the woods along the edge of Lake Champlain.

She was getting closer, once again, to Halfmoon Cave. Ever since the night of Tomas's party, she hadn't been able to stop thinking about the cave, and the stone. The blood-drenched stone she'd painted with the promise of her loyalty to whatever stupid cause Tomas had in mind. She felt as if something had been disrupted, not only within the woods, but within herself. She felt like a piece of her insides had been taken away. Literally carved out with a knife. The void pulsed inside her, like whatever contained her ability to feel joy or happiness had been gnawed out.

She sighed heavily, as even the gentle caress of the cool breeze failed to elicit any sort of reaction from her. She had to know why.

Returning to the place where it began, Rose could feel a presence. Perhaps the legends were true, those stories of a witch she and many others who grew up in Blair had been told. She could feel centuries of myths inside the cave, myths that were not meant to be uncovered.

Rose found the mouth of the cave. There were imprints in the dirt where the stones had been removed. The stamp of something that was never meant to be disturbed. She knelt down and produced the stone Tomas had given her from her pocket. It was coated in a dry, dull veil of her blood. Evidence of the oath she had stupidly taken that night flashed in the reflection of the white moon.

She took the stone and placed it back where it belonged in front of the cave. Then realization swept over her as she laid eyes upon the broken stone formation. It occurred to her the possibility of what they had unsettled. They had broken a seal. The stones were meant to serve as a threshold, to keep evil inside the darkness of Halfmoon Cave, just like the stories said. The burial of one of Blair's darkest and oldest secrets, caged away and never meant to be let out.

No. I don't want to be a part of this game anymore.

The calm of the night sky above shifted into something both vivid and obscure. It happened so suddenly, it startled Rose.

The day the sky turns black, others will join us.

It was happening. The eclipse.

Rose felt a sudden panic flutter up inside her stomach. She had to move quickly. She didn't know why, but she felt a sudden, desperate urgency to undo what she had done. To back out of this agreement, this oath.

She quickly grabbed the remaining stones from the ground, as many as she could hold in her arms, and rushed over to the lake. She stumbled into the water until she was knee-deep. The calm current of water was ice-cold against her skin, but Rose didn't flinch. She dropped all of the stones but her own into the water, watching them sink into the gloom. Her breath grew erratic as she fought off the icy cold. She then took her own crimson-coated stone and dunked it into the water. She tried scrubbing away the blood with her fingertips. The red streaks faded from the hard surface. It was working. She would wash away the evidence of what she'd agreed to that night; then she would toss the stone deep into the depths of the lake. Then she would run away. Find somewhere else and never think about it again. Maybe cross the lake into Vermont. Or perhaps go north into Canada. Anything to rid herself of the sinking feeling of despair that weighed her down like an anchor.

Rose lifted her stone into the moonlight, into the terrible, swirling nightmare of sky above. She blinked hard, checking the stone's surface for remnants of dried blood—then she felt it. A presence behind her in the obscure gray darkness. The presence from inside the cave. No, not from the cave— She was confused. She could smell charred flesh, but also something very old. It was watching. Yes, from inside the cave. But that...that was not the presence she felt. This was someone else. Close to her.

Rose's breathing slowed. She felt frozen in place, as if a net had been cast over her head, weighing her down. She was stuck, like an animal caught in a trap. She began to shake.

A figure loomed over her, and she felt utterly helpless.

Then, movement. From behind her. It sounded as if an old door was being forced open, creaking out in the woods. The sound landed in her ears, and she felt the cold touch of something on her shoulder.

Stop.

She dropped her stone into the water and felt her heart sink with it. It was over. She had done the unthinkable. And she was going to pay.

Dearest Rose...

She knew that voice.

You've broken the oath...

From the corner of her eye, she saw a hand stretch out beside her. It was the hand of Tomas Fischer, not hidden by magic or illusion, but the hand of his true form. It was horrifically disfigured, burnt. The crooked fingers dangled off the knuckles, as if they had been yanked from their sockets, yet the index finger contained enough tendons to hold it intact and erect. To point her in the direction of Lake Champlain. Instructing her to go deeper into the water.

Those fingers, smeared in blood and dirt. As they had been earlier today. As they had always been.

Rose stood frozen. She felt insignificant in the looming presence of the figure towering over her. The presence was more than just a lone apparition. It felt like many apparitions at once. Large, looming, and evil.

"I...I'm sorry..." She trembled. "Please. I don't want to."

I needed to trust you...

If you couldn't come with me forever...

You must walk alone tonight...

Rose took a step forward, the riverbed pressing down beneath her feet. She walked slowly into the cold lake, the chill creeping up her thighs and soaking her cardigan. The wet sweater clung to her body. She took a breath as she walked deeper. Then, suddenly, a force pulled her under.

She struggled, thrashing her arms, trying to keep her head above the surface. She opened her eyes but could only see blackness. She was failing. She had lost her equilibrium. She didn't know which way was up, which way was the shore.

She rolled in the water, and for a moment she could see both moon and sun. They were like giant black-and-white marbles in the sky over Lake Champlain, like an ominous beacon. The gray and black sky swirled around the anomaly.

Then something hard nudged her in the stomach. In her confusion, she couldn't tell what it was. It came down again and again, breaking through the surface of the water and assaulting her body. It struck her in the shoulder, knocking her underwater, and she was disoriented once again. Panic washed over her, colder than the icy lake water. Rose struggled to find the surface; she needed to escape, but there was something just above the surface that wouldn't allow her to.

It came crashing down again, hitting her in the chest and causing her mouth to open. A gulp of cold lake water rushed in. She forced herself to the surface, poking her head out so she could take a breath. She was struck again, this time in the head. Her world spun upside down, and all she saw was the blackness of the lake bottom. Her lungs starved for air. A burning sensation filled her chest, and she failed to keep the lake water out of her mouth. She was drowning, she knew it, and she tried to tell herself to remain calm. *At least it will be over soon.* She tried to tell herself that in a few short moments, she wouldn't feel anything anymore. But the pain—the unbearable, burning pain. It was the most horrific thing she could have imagined.

But in a few short moments, she wouldn't have to worry about any oaths, or sicknesses, or Blair itself. Before she closed her eyes, the last thing she saw was the dark moon pulsing in the night sky. She saw double—two moons now. Turning from white. To yellow. To black. Two black eyes watching as she succumbed to the cold water of the lake.

* * *

When Hector and Gabe returned to the Fischer House, Tomas had already made his return. His looming silhouette cast a darkness inside the parlor. The pair entered through the doorway, covered in the dirt and blood-smeared aftermath of their transformation. They saw a shift inside the parlor itself. The darkness cast by Tomas seemed to recede as they entered.

Things had changed.

First, the hunger was already setting in. Though it was more than just hunger—it was a rampant, roiling stomach pain, as if their insides were squirming and convulsing, searching for sustenance.

Tomas looked them over. "I told you. Insatiable hunger."

"We have to go—can we please go eat now?" Hector begged.

"It hurts," Gabe said. He seemed on the verge of tears.

The boys stood in the doorway, clutching their stomachs, trembling as if they had each taken a fist to the midsection.

"It will be fine," Tomas assured them as he stood up, putting a hand on each of their shoulders. "Come with me."

"Where...where is Rose?" Hector asked.

Tomas pursed his lips. "I told you—you choose to follow me, or you choose death. Time is finite, and it must not be wasted on hesitancy...

"Speaking of which, we cannot wait for Jax any longer. When he returns, he'll have his own decision to make. Until then, the time is now. We must eat."

"What do we eat?" Gabe asked.

"We take what is available to us," Tomas said. "What is abundant. This town...I want it. I deserve it. We will strip it to the bone. Peel back the skin and eat from it. I will show you."

Chapter 42
Interlude:1793

Grace wandered the unwelcoming Blair countryside. The pale shawl draped over her head and shoulders covered part of her face—she did not want to be seen. She knew there were eyes on her now. Interrogating, judgmental eyes. They watched her every move.

She pulled the shawl closer to the edges of her face as the breeze rolling in from Lake Champlain grazed her skin. The terrain was gray. Not a glimmer of sunlight, no color cast onto Blair. She feared it was her fault. Her fault for agreeing to open up such darkness.

Fear consumed her, and she thought it best to run. Blair was not the place for her. This place would not become her home. She would gather her belongings and run.

As she walked back to her small cottage on the outskirts of town, she stopped. She noticed a goat standing tall among its herd. While the rest of the goats grazed on grass outside the farm, there was something different about this particular goat. An anthropomorphic quality which no other animal possessed. It was odd, but she almost had the sense she knew this goat. Perhaps they had been acquainted in this life or a past one.

She approached, reached a trembling hand out, and gently caressed the goat's brow. She closed her eyes; she felt as if the goat were waiting for her to speak. To confide in it. To spill her soul. And so, spill her soul she did.

"I did not ask for this." Grace's voice trembled. "I wanted nothing to do with that boy and his family. I wanted nothing to do with that man. But I was afraid. Afraid to say no. I know he is going to hurt me. Exile me from this place."

The goat listened.

Grace recoiled, pulling her hand back. Yes, the goat listened, but there was something more. The beast that stood before her took in the words she spoke to him. His yellow eyes filled with knowledge—wisdom.

"Oh, dark master." Her voice shook. She gently placed her palm on the crest of the animal's forehead. His black fur was as soft as silk. "If you are listening, if you *can* listen, I need you. Please, give me the power to liberate myself from this place. I did not mean to hurt that boy. I was given no choice. I was threatened. I saw no other option but to listen to that man, Nathaniel Fischer. Now his son is dead, and I am to be punished. Please, dark lord, grant me the power to direct revenge upon those who blame me for that which I did not endorse in the first place."

A breeze swept between Grace and the great beast. It smelled heavy, like sulfur, and it carried with it a silent answer, acknowledging Grace's prayer in the affirmative.

"I know they will come for me," Grace said. "They demand justice. But where is *my* justice. Who has *my* back? A strong man he claims to be, yet he is so weak that he cannot protect his own family... please, master, let your power consume me and make me strong enough to endure. Give me the strength to impose revenge before they enact their plan."

The goat blinked.

Grace backed away. She turned and retreated to her cottage. Her temporary home, until death took her. Before standing by and waiting for the inevitable, she had one final task.

* * *

As Blair slept, Grace worked. One final purpose she must fulfill before the end.

She spun dead twine into a sort of wheel shape, a circle containing a six-petaled flower. A daisy wheel, as it was known. She tightened the twine, twisting into the shape the mashed-up residue from the Devil's Spiral flower. The one that had drawn Nathaniel to her in the first place. A curse entwined within the hand-spun wheel. She blessed it. Kissed it. Held it close.

When Grace emerged from her cottage, it was still fully dark. The sun was creeping up behind the moon, an ominous display in the sky casting a gray hue over the landscape.

Punishment was on her mind. For what had been done to her, the pain and fear cast upon her. She'd captured all of that pain and wound it into the daisy wheel. The village of Blair would be forever cursed for the misery they'd directed at her.

Grace carried with her the daisy wheel, this hex. Weaved with intention. Twine and fabric drafted together to contain newfound, potent restitution. In addition, a strand of the boy's hair. Blood from her hands washed into the basin and soaked into the fabric. As far as she was concerned, it was the blood of the innocent. The boy's blood had been spilled in vain. She, too, was innocent. Carrying with her a blessing from the dark goat, Grace constructed this hex.

She found the grave of Tomas Fischer, the plot of dirt underneath the Fischer family tree. Grace nailed the daisy wheel onto the tree trunk, piercing the bark of the tree and the flesh of the community as she did so.

Chapter 43
Fred Brown

Fred Brown awoke from a deep sleep to the shrieking sounds of the animals. He hastily got out of bed and found his robe and slippers in the pale-gray haze of his bedroom. He presumed the peculiar gray coming from outside was a result of the eclipse so many had talked about, but this was unlike anything he had ever seen. It reminded him of watching television as a boy, when pictures were colorless.

He grabbed his shotgun from the closet and made his way downstairs in a hurry.

Fred's sleeping pattern was in disarray after Martha's passing. He had not been himself for days, and there were many sleepless nights. Insomnia had crept in and made itself at home in his late wife's vacant side of the bed. For several nights now, he had been acutely aware of every sound coming from outside, but none matched the horrific shrieking sounds that woke him up tonight. Woke him from the first decent sleep he'd had since Martha died.

The first night of Fall Fest had been a success. Although hosting the event was not the same without Martha, it did bring back a small sense of normalcy. Seeing the strong turnout made Fred happy. The outpouring of support was comforting. The number of people who came to enjoy the Blair tradition, along with the volunteers who made it all possible, allowed Fred to finally get some much-needed rest.

Yet something about the passing of his wife was still gnawing at him. She hadn't just gotten sick. No. Something...*someone* had slithered their way onto his property and hurt her. The same way it snuck in to kill his goats...it also killed his Martha.

Fred grabbed his shotgun, which he kept loaded and propped inside his closet for easy access. When the evil that had killed his goats and his Martha inevitably came back, he would be ready.

Over the years, things would sneak onto Fred's farm and wreak havoc. Usually coyotes. However, he would always make his discovery the morning after. He was usually a heavy sleeper and never heard disaster occurring in the moment. However, the terrible cry he heard tonight gave him chills. His skin broke out in goosebumps as the shriek echoed in the twilight.

When he stepped outside, the pale darkness was like a shroud over his property. He slowly crept along the side of the house until he could reach the switch for the floodlights. When he flipped the switch, a harsh white light doused the farm. What Fred saw when the light spilled onto the goat enclosure made his blood run cold.

Three of his goats had been rounded up and dragged into the center of the pasture. Among them were what looked like three humanoid intruders. Fred had heard of folklore, different cryptids like skinwalkers or Chupacabra who fed on livestock. But this was different. The figures looming over his animals were distinctly human.

"Hey!" Fred shouted. "What are you doing?"

All three figures turned toward him with breakneck speed, their pale faces reflecting the brightness from the floodlight above. Fred squinted. He recognized these faces. They were boys from Blair High School. Boys who had been to his farm before. But now, fresh blood coated their chins, rolling down their necks as if they were feral animals. Their hungry, blackened eyes squinting against the harsh light.

The one in the middle stood, mouth open, jaw unhinged like a snake. It hissed at Fred in disgust. Its eyes bulged from its sockets in anger, so black it was as if the eyes themselves were engorged with blood—likely true, considering the grotesque feast they had made of the goats.

Fred fired a warning shot into the air as he stepped off his back porch and into the goat pen. He could hear the remaining goats inside their pen, crying in terror.

As he approached the scene, he realized who the boys were. Two of their youthful, inexperienced faces flinched in the light—Hector Stroud and Gabe Coleman. Their families lived in town. And the third boy was Tomas Fischer, who lived in the historic Fischer House. A house steeped in mystery and darkness—an old relic from Blair's inception, where legend had it a tragic bloodletting took place centuries ago. An attempted tuberculosis cure gone wrong.

The three boys stood in the middle of Fred's field, bathed in the obscure gray luster. These were *not* the boys he knew. They hissed at him again, like bestial shells of their former selves.

Fred felt as if he were in some kind of fever dream. As if his mind had snapped after the death of his beloved Martha. But what he was seeing was, in fact, real. And it didn't matter if he knew the boys or not—he was going to defend his land.

Tomas threw his hands up, shielding his eyes. He jumped backward in an unnatural movement, levitated in the air, and gingerly settled in place on top of the fence. The boy's bare feet hooked around the top of the fence like talons. Fred didn't ponder the abnormal movement too long. Instead, his main concern was getting these boys off his property and away from his goats. If he were crazy, he would have considered, for a moment longer, the possibility— these creatures were vampires.

But Fred didn't stop to think. His only concern was protecting himself and his property. It didn't matter who or what these boys were. Whether they were boys causing trouble, coyotes, vampires, or whatever the fuck else came from the woods, they were on his property and making a feast of his goats. They were responsible for the death of his wife, and they were each going to take a bullet for that.

Hector did not retreat. Instead, he lunged forward, eyes hungry and frenzied. His blood-drenched teeth bared like those of an animal defending its kill in the wild.

Fred reacted by pulling the trigger of his shotgun.

The boy's middle exploded, spraying the grass crimson. The inhuman scream that followed sent chills down Fred's spine. Fred aimed again, this time at the boy who had retreated toward the wooden fence. Shotgun shells sprayed through the air, blasting the boy and causing him to fall from his perch.

Humpty Dumpty had a great fall. Fred grinned. He stepped away from the porch and moved deeper into the goats' pen. His hands were shaking violently as he broke the gun open and reloaded it with two additional shells. His eyes darted around frantically, making sure he had tabs on all three of his intruders.

Incredibly, Fred felt no true fear. He felt concern for losing more of his goats—he worried that *they* felt pain. Maybe he worried about feeling pain himself, if he should be overtaken, but even then he knew that pain would be temporary. No pain would ever compare to the pain of losing Martha. Nothing else mattered, in a sense. Physical pain would die with him. The pain he felt over Martha would follow him into the afterlife.

Fred snapped his gun closed right as Gabe descended on him, leaping down from a tree branch as if skating on the air. The thing's arms splayed out like wings. Its mouth craned open in a sadistic grin, displaying its teeth. Its protruding canines were much more exaggerated than any teeth a human might possess. The thing landed on Fred's shoulders and latched onto his neck.

For being the size of a high school boy, the thing was extraordinarily light. Fred imagined being landed on by a human of that size would buckle him at the knees, yet he remained upright. However, the thing's weight was the least of his concerns. Fred felt a burning sensation as teeth sank into his neck. Fred could feel the blood being sucked out of his body and into the mouth of the creature. He let out an agonizing cry. He was being fed on like an animal, enduring the pain his goats must have gone through.

Fred jerked the gun backward and smashed the butt into the boy's face. He felt a crushing—he had most certainly done damage. The boy detached from Fred and landed on the ground, twitching like a bug after being hit with a newspaper.

Fred looked down at Gabe's broken face; his forehead was caved in where the butt of the gun had made contact. His face was so pale. Sickly, disgusting, like a cadaver on ice. But the thing blinked, flashing its black eyes and looking directly at Fred.

Fred raised his gun and aimed it at the creature. "Get off my property, and stay away from my goats," he slurred. The words felt soft as they left his mouth. Something was wrong. He was injured, that much was obvious. He could feel blood flowing out of his neck and soaking his robe. He looked down to see it dripping down his chest and arms, spreading out like the branches of a tree. He began to feel dizzy, disassociated from his body.

He could hear a moaning cry near the floodlight, where he'd shot the one boy in the stomach. However, there was silence over by the fence, and he aimed and shot at the boy who was perched on the fence like a vulture. From this distance, Fred wasn't completely sure he had made contact. But soon he knew—he'd missed.

Tomas was on him, drinking from his neck, spilling blood down his robe. Fred couldn't turn his head to look. Something was wrong. The boy on the ground. His eyes locked onto his. He was playing some sort of sadistic game, and Fred was sure he was being held in place by some supernatural power he couldn't fathom.

He weakly lifted his arm and aimed again, the boy already in his sights. If Fred was going out, he was taking his attackers with him.

He pulled the trigger, and the top portion of the Gabe's head was gone. All that remained was the sadistic, blood-soaked grin. His teeth bared, showing the evidence of the feast he'd made of the goats just a moment earlier.

"Oh," Fred said as he felt weakness overtake him. He dropped to his knees, feeling sick.

Fred was punished for what he did. For fighting back. This excursion was for sustenance only. A training exercise. Fred Brown was not supposed to be involved. But he had to step in. He couldn't let his goats be picked off like that. This thing—this vampire—wrapped its hands around Fred's head and bore down, and with one quick motion it snapped his neck. Fred's lifeless body went limp and tumbled to the ground.

The night air would have been completely silent if not for the incessant wailing of the boy who had been shot in the stomach. The wind chime could be heard from the front porch as a slight breeze moved through the farm, carrying with it the scent of death.

Chapter 44
Jaycie

Jaycie's phone began to ring amid her scattered Googling, which was keeping her awake in her bed.

It was Mabel.

She'd hoped it would be Jax, but her heart still leapt at the sight of her friend's name.

She answered the call, preserving the tab she'd been using to research a bit of Blair's history.

"Jaycie..." Mabel's voice came through shakily.

"Mabel, what is it?"

Mabel didn't sound like herself. She sounded afraid, almost desperate. "I—I need you here—I'm scared..."

"I'll be right over, hang tight," Jaycie said.

* * *

Jaycie rode with her dad to Mabel's house. She packed an overnight bag and brought her schoolbooks as well—she didn't want to fall behind on studying because of a last-minute sleepover. But there had been something in Mabel's voice on the phone...a desperate tinge of despair which frightened Jaycie into going to check on her friend.

Jaycie was nervous. Their friendship seemed like such a question mark lately. She didn't realize how much time had actually passed since their last interaction (and how much had taken place since). After that first weekend of limited contact, after she had left the party early, Jaycie felt weird not talking to her friends. But after a while, it seemed to become her new normal.

The last time she'd seen Mabel, she was not herself. Jaycie vividly remembered her baggy sweatshirt, the sleeves balled up in her fists. She was slouched forward, looking troubled. And Rose was outright aggressive. The abrupt shift made Jaycie reconsider her friendships. Made her reconsider her attraction to Mabel. Perhaps this was why the distance between them began to feel more normal as it wore on.

She still cared deeply for both girls. She still loved them; that would never change despite their growing apart. People always grew apart. Jaycie knew this was a normal part of life. She wasn't naïve to the fact that as people got older, they tended to drift apart. As they started families, got jobs, and relocated. She just never imagined her friendships with Mabel and Rose would be floating on opposite currents. She hadn't thought there'd be distance between them this soon.

When she got to Mabel's, Jaycie waved at her dad, and he drove off once she was inside. Jaycie looked around Mabel's house, a place that was almost as familiar as her own home. It looked different. She was experiencing a kind of *jamais vu*, feeling confused, unfamiliar with a place she, in fact, knew quite well.

Mabel's parents were not home, and all of the downstairs lights were off.

"Mabel?" Jaycie called out. "I'm here. Are you upstairs?"

Jaycie made her way up the stairs and pushed open the door to Mabel's bedroom. When she saw Mabel sitting upright on the edge of her bed, Jaycie's heart dropped. Her friend was ghostly pale, as if she'd aged ten years since she last saw her a week ago. Her eyes swam in darkened circles. She looked like she was being swallowed by her gray Plattsburg sweatshirt.

Jaycie dropped her bag on the floor and approached her friend. "Oh, Mabel," she said. She threw her arms around her friend. Seeing her friend like this made Jaycie's eyes well up with tears. It was breaking her heart. And it scared her. It scared her a week ago to see Mabel in a hoodie, clutching her sleeves in her fists as if she were freezing. Now it looked like she was rushing down an avenue of misery.

"What happened to you?" Jaycie asked, taking care not to hug her friend too tightly, as she felt delicate to the touch. She could feel Mabel's breath rattle in her chest as she inhaled.

"The night of the party, after you and Jax left," Mabel explained, "we stayed behind, just shooting the shit with Tomas and the boys. It was harmless at first. You know, we were drinking. Not a lot, but enough that I felt nice.

"It was getting late when Tomas suggested we explore the woods. But then he started talking about the town, and this darkness, and it was just weird. I was apprehensive at first because it was late, and considering the Martin Welch thing, I didn't want to go into the woods. But Rose was there, and so were the boys, so I figured we would be safe. But we went into the woods, and it was awful.

"Tomas started talking crazy, and everyone seemed so adamant about it—everyone was on board. I don't know what I was more scared of: what we heard and saw in the dark woods, or what Tomas was saying about Blair. I think we did something bad that night, Jaycie. I should have gone home with you. I'm sorry. I'm sorry I was cold toward you."

Jaycie held Mabel's sweatshirt-wrapped hands in hers. She wanted to kiss her. Tell her everything she was feeling. "What did you see in the woods?" she asked instead. She could feel Mabel's hands shake. And maybe she was shaking too.

Mabel pulled her hands back and took a deep breath. She pulled up her sleeves, revealing her hands. Jaycie gasped when she saw it, the scabbed-over line that traced the inside of Mabel's palm. The ugly, dark brown line was at least two inches long, worming its way across her palm like a fissure.

"How did this happen, Mabel?" Jaycie asked, dreading the answer. But she needed to know.

"When we got to the cave," Mabel said, "Tomas made us take an oath. I wanted to say no, I really did. But I was more afraid of saying no than I was of joining everyone else. Rose didn't seem fazed at all, so I felt stupid for even questioning it. I didn't want to be the only one out there to say no. It was just us, in the woods alone. I was scared, Jaycie."

"What was this oath?" Jaycie felt a lump in her throat as dread turned to realization. The marking on her friend's palm resembled the one Jax had. The one from the "injury" he'd kept hidden for the past year.

Mabel shook her head. "I didn't want to do it. He said something about keeping darkness out of Blair. It didn't make any sense, I swear. He said he was willing to bleed for Blair. I felt so dirty. I hate it so much. I wish I could take it back."

Mabel leaned into Jaycie, burying her face into her shoulder.

Jaycie ran her hand through Mabel's hair, and that's when she noticed the smell. Mabel's hair smelled damp, like the lake. Like she'd been in the lake. No, it was more than just Mabel's hair. The entire room smelled like Lake Champlain. It smelled unclean. Like death.

"He was here," Mabel whispered.

Jaycie froze. She pulled away from Mabel, looking her in the face. "Who was here?" She felt a chill run through her body. Who could have been here? Who could have brought that smell?

"T-Tomas," Mabel said shakily. "He was here tonight..."

"What did he do to you?" Jaycie said, feeling heat rise into her face. If he hurt her friend...

Mabel slowly glanced at the closet door. Jaycie followed her gaze to discover that the closet door was slightly ajar. She felt her breath catch in her throat.

"Is he still here?" she whispered.

Mabel frowned. Somehow, it was worse than a verbal response.

Warily, Jaycie got up and approached the closet door, bracing herself for an attack. If Tomas was here waiting for her, she wouldn't go down without a fight. She drew closer, her heart pounding in her chest as she tried to steady her breath. She wrapped a hand around the door handle and, like ripping off a Band-Aid, swiftly pulled the door open.

Jaycie let out a scream when she saw Rose's body slouched up against the closet wall. Her dear friend's face was petrified, eyes water-logged and gray. Her arms fell unevenly at her sides, as if broken in several places, and her head lolled on her neck, hanging sideways. Swollen punctures ran up and down her broken arms, blood smeared on her pale skin.

Jaycie backed away from the closet, feeling a pit inside her stomach. Was her last interaction with Rose really that day in study hall? They'd exchanged harsh words, and Jaycie stormed off. How could that be the last time they spoke? How could they never have a chance to smooth things over?

Jaycie looked up in horror. Inside the closet, clothes were pushed to the side, exposing the wall. There, written in Rose's blood, were the words, "You're next."

"Mabel, what the fuck happened?"

"Tomas," she said. "He was here. He killed her. He said she broke the oath. The stupid fucking oath he made us take at the party."

"You have to tell me what this oath is," Jaycie said. "I don't understand."

"Tomas isn't who he says he is," Mabel said. "This legend about Blair...he's actually a part of it. I couldn't believe it at first. I didn't want to believe that such a thing could be real. But he's the result of something heinous that took place a long time ago. He was a child when he died, but he was never truly able to rest because of the nature of his death. He has a vendetta against the entire town of

Blair, and he wants people to suffer the way he was made to suffer all those years ago."

"We can't stay here," Jaycie said, shaking. "Come home with me. We'll stick together and figure this out somehow. It will be okay, I promise."

"Don't promise," Mabel said. "I've been having thoughts, Jaycie. Really bad thoughts. And I've never felt this way before. I want to die so badly. I just want it to end—oh my God, do I want it to end. You promise me, no matter what happens, you'll bring her peace."

"Bring who peace?" Jaycie asked. "Rose?"

"Grace," Mabel said. "From the cave."

Chapter 45
Jax

Jax heard howls of agony coming from the parlor as he entered the Fischer House. He dropped his bag in the front foyer and followed the sound. He stopped underneath the archway leading into the parlor when he saw Tomas sitting quietly. Across from him, writhing beneath a blood-soaked sheet, was Hector, shrieking in pain.

"Holy shit," Jax asked breathlessly. "What happened?"

Tomas continued to watch Hector. "Things don't happen at your convenience, Jax. We weren't going to wait for your arrival. You knew this..."

"Is— Is he going to be okay?" Jax asked, shaking.

"Oh, of course," Tomas said calmly, finally turning to look at Jax. "He'll survive. He's going to be in a lot of pain...but he'll sleep. And he'll heal. And when he wakes, he's going to be hungry. Despite him not having a stomach at the moment...he'll be just fine. In fact, he's going to be very hungry."

"How?" Jax looked at Tomas gravely.

Tomas was on his feet and standing toe-to-toe with Jax in an instant. It struck Jax in this moment just how utterly imposing Tomas

Fischer was. His control over his pure, animalistic aggression was frightening. Within him was the potential to unleash his will on whoever he perceived as a threat (or as prey), and all with an eerie calmness.

"How what?" Tomas asked. "How did this happen? How will he survive? What?"

Jax could only stammer.

"They tried to rid me of sickness as a boy," Tomas explained, turning his back to Jax. "See, my father, he thought he knew best. He thought he knew what was wrong with me. And he thought his mistress held the answer. The cure. So, what did they do? They bled me out. Then they buried me in the ground. Right back there." He pointed out the window into the woods behind the Fischer House. Then he grinned. "They left me for dead...well, I *was* dead, I suppose. But this..." Tomas grazed a flower on the mantel with the back of his hand. "This same flower, which is keeping Hector alive right now, somehow..."

Tomas turned back to Jax once again. "The question is, are you going to honor the oath you took or not? Can I trust you the way I can trust Hector?"

"Yes," Jax said. "I'm with you. I was just scared. I'm sorry. I went home to my family after school because I thought—"

"It doesn't matter." Tomas raised his hand. "You're here now, yes? And you're committed?"

Jax took a deep breath and nodded. "I am."

"Good," Tomas said. He walked over to Hector, put his hand on his forehead, and pursed his lips. Hector stirred, drowsily.

"Please," he begged. "I need more."

"You'll have more," Tomas promised.

"Did it hurt?" Jax asked. "When you turned."

Hector winced. "A little, I suppose."

"How bad?"

"I couldn't tell you about pain in this moment, for obvious reasons," Hector said, lifting the blood-soaked sheet and exposing the gaping gunshot wound in his stomach. "But as far as *that*, no worse than a root canal, I suppose."

Jax looked back at Tomas and inhaled through his nostrils. He nodded. Tomas grinned.

"Drink this," Tomas said, lifting a chalice to Jax.

"What is it?"

"It's a tincture made from the Devil's Spiral. It will keep you alive long enough for...well, you'll see."

Jax let out a sharp breath, said, "Here goes nothing," and downed the mixture. The sharp bitterness stung his throat as it went down. He winced. A fiery heat rose from his stomach as the liquid settled there. When he exhaled, he could feel the chemical breath coating the inside of his mouth. It felt like if someone held a match in front of him, it would certainly ignite.

He was so focused on this new sensation that he almost didn't notice Tomas standing over him. When his cold hand rested on his shoulder, Jax looked up and saw something strange in his friend's eyes. It was like he owned him now.

"Good," Tomas said, smiling.

Jax relaxed. It wasn't as bad as he had anticipated. The burning in his stomach was already subsiding. He felt calm. A sense of peace washed over his face, cooling his senses like the cold touch of Tomas's hand on his shoulder. It was the most peace he'd felt since before the whole chloroform ordeal. Since before Martin Welch's death. The anxiety of the last four years, of feeling like a failure, just seemed to melt away.

Tomas's grin didn't falter as he drove a knife in between Jax's ribs. With one hand still on Jax's shoulder, he pushed the blade deeper into Jax's stomach. Jax felt a burning sensation as the liquid he'd downed a moment ago settled into his stomach. The hot blood flowing from his wound had to have been burning the cold flesh of Tomas's ever-advancing hand.

Jax gasped for air but could pull none into his lungs. His hungry, dying lungs. His vision blurred as his eyes welled with tears. His mouth moved, but only a meek whimper came out.

He thought of Hector. *Considering that he currently doesn't have a stomach, he'll be just fine.* But Jax didn't think this could be fine. Is this what Tomas meant?

This is the oath you took, Jackson Brogdon.

You now belong to me.

Finally, Tomas pulled the blade out. Blood was pouring from the wound. It flowed like the Winooski River during high tide, darkening Jax's shirt and the front of his jeans. He reached his hands toward the wound and felt around the area, and it burned. Everything burned.

Tomas seized Jax from below the armpits and began to drag him. Jax quickly found that his legs no longer worked. They no longer supported his weight, and if it wasn't for Tomas, he would have certainly fallen face first onto the floor. But Tomas held him up. Broke his fall as he dragged him from the parlor and outside.

Jax felt the cool night air caress his face. The cold sweat was now uncontrollable on his skin, and a thought occurred to him: This was a mistake. This wasn't what he wanted. He didn't want to die. He wanted to go home. Despite being the fuckup that he was. Despite having thrown his life away, he wanted to go home. He wanted his parents and his sister. He wanted another chance to fix his relationship with them. He wanted to try again with school. Work hard and ignore the bullies who made him afraid to go to class as a freshman. He wanted to tell Alan Marcus he would try again. He would put his mind to his studies and get better grades. He would earn his place in that Tufts program; he would prove he was good enough. It was where his heart told him he belonged.

But it was too late. His heart was growing weaker. The wound in his side pulsed as his blood continued to soak his shirt. His sneakers made grooves in the sandy dirt as Tomas pulled him away from the house and toward...toward what? Where was he bringing him?

Jax had an idea of what came next. He'd heard accounts of near-death experiences. Out-of-body experiences. Where they could "see the light," where they traveled at unknown speeds through a tunnel and toward what they could only describe as "the light." But everyone knew what that light meant. It meant the end of the journey. It meant death.

All of those stories were lies. There was no light where Jax was going. He could feel himself fading as he was dragged away from the Fischer House and into the woods under the bleak, pulsing sky of the Blair eclipse. The lights of the house grew smaller as his limp body was pulled toward the woods. He could feel his life slowly slipping from his body as the burning sensation turned cold. Tomas's touch grew more distant, even while his grip tightened as he continued to pull. Jax was aware of it all, but there was no light to be seen.

That's when he saw it—a patch of dirt in between the trees. A patch of dirt protected for centuries. Once the grave of Tomas Fischer. Tonight, that grave would be shared with Jax.

There was only darkness, wrapping around him like a swaddle, until eventually his vision went completely dark. There was nothing left to see. He could only feel the cold. Even Tomas's touch disappeared.

Everything felt cold and black as he was pulled down into a patch of dead earth.

Too little, too late.

Chapter 46
Seth and Liz Brogdon

The lights had long been turned off at the Brogdon house. Stillness had settled in among the darkness. Silence.

A peaceful silence, except for the anxiety looming within. The unease of a family divided manifested as energy.

The tension in the Brogdon house bloomed in the still darkness like a flower. Bouncing between members of the family unit. Slithering its way in like an untraceable sickness. Yet the symptoms were there. Jax storming out of the house. Jaycie questioning faith. Seth and Liz were doing their best, but despite their efforts, their family was coming apart at the seams.

The door would always be open for Jax. Their son. Seth Brogdon kept his cell phone by his side at all times, waiting for a call that never came.

The automatic light of the front porch glinted on, as if it were waking itself up. As if on cue. Sort of how a person's bladder will wake them up in the middle of the night to go to the bathroom. The light, in its own slumber, was waiting for something. As if it felt the Brogdons' waiting. Feeding off of the family's anxiety.

Seth's cell phone lit up on the nightstand, vibrating with a notification. He stirred but didn't wake. Then the phone screen's light faded, and the room was dark again.

Silence.

Darkness.

Ding.

Another notification. Another *ding* in the night, attempting to alert the Brogdon family of a visitor at the front door.

This time, Liz stirred awake, turning over. She could see the dim light of Seth's phone on the nightstand. It cast a weak glow in their bedroom.

Ding Ding Ding Ding Ding Ding Ding. The phone exploded in a synchronous wave of notifications as the high-pitched *dings* chimed in the room.

"Babe, babe, your phone," she said, nudging Seth awake.

He grunted, turning over to check his notifications. "It's the Ring camera," he said groggily. He opened the app to find, in horror, someone looking back at him.

A man's face, distorted and cast in gray, eyeing Seth down through the camera lens. His pale skin illuminated in the night's glow. He looked furious, jaw clenched tight, eyes narrowed.

Seth recoiled, shocked by the face staring back at him through his phone. This drew Liz's attention, and she leaned in to see what Seth was looking at. She shuddered at the face crowding their front-door camera. At first glance, he looked like he could have been high school age, but the depth inside his eyes and the lines on his forehead suggested otherwise.

He turned on the audio and heard the man knocking on the front door. Pounding strikes rattled the camera. The sound came through harshly distorted. In between hits, they could hear the man.

"Let me in! I need to speak to her!" he demanded.

"Speak to who? Whoever you're looking for doesn't live here," Seth said through his phone.

The man grumbled something inaudibly and then said louder, "I'm looking for GRACE! She did something bad. She brought darkness to Blair!" The banging on the front door got louder as the man became more insistent. His eyes looked like colorless, lifeless orbs in the night vision of the camera. "I just need to speak with her. I need to understand why she did what she did to my boy."

"You need to leave, or we're going to call the cops," Seth threatened.

"LET ME IN!" The man continued slamming on the door. "Call the damned sheriff! I need to speak with Grace! She killed my boy! She is not welcome in Blair!"

Liz dialed 911 as Seth got out of bed and headed for the stairs.

"Seth, what are you doing?" Liz called out. "Don't go out there," she pleaded, but he was already heading down the stairs, armed with a baseball bat, leaving his phone behind. She glanced at it and saw that the man had become silent. It only lasted a moment, but she was certain that his blank, soulless expression would remain with her for life. His eyes blinked asynchronously before a grin stretched across his face. Then he started laughing and uttered a maniacal, hysterical declaration that Liz did not understand.

"Daddy let her in...

"Daddy fucked the whore and then let her kill me!

"Daddy let her in...

"Daddy fucked the whore and then let her kill me!"

The man suddenly stopped, distracted by something out of view. Then, headlights appeared in the street behind him as a car approached. The last thing Liz saw before the screen went dark was a disturbing grin, and then he turned away. The feed cut off, and the bedroom filled with silence.

When Seth got to the front door, he looked out to find the front porch empty. He raised the bat, unlocked the door, and opened it cautiously. But there was nobody there. Only silence.

The automatic light went on, triggered by Seth's movement. He let out a sigh.

Then, as if he were dreaming, he saw Jaycie getting out of a cab at the curb, followed by her friend from school.

"You girls alright?" Seth asked.

Jaycie led Mabel to the house, not making eye contact with her father. "Yep, all good, Dad." She couldn't tell him what had actually happened. Her parents wouldn't understand. How, exactly, would *this* fit into God's plan? It was a conversation Jaycie thought best to avoid.

The girls made their way up to Jaycie's bedroom. Jaycie pulled an extra pillow and blanket from the closet, but Mabel took a seat on the floor, legs crossed.

Jaycie froze, feeling the terror in Mabel's eyes. Her own hands were still shaking from what she'd seen in that closet. She dropped the pillow and blanket and joined Mabel on the floor. There was a reflection in the window, a split second of someone's face before it dissolved into the night.

"Tomas," Mabel started.

"I know," Jaycie said. She put her arms around her friend, who was still shaking.

"He's using her," Mabel said. "Grace...we woke her up from the cave that night. Now he's using her to turn everyone in Blair against each other."

Jaycie felt cold. "We have to tell Mr. Reinhart. He'll know what to do."

"No," Mabel said. "We can't. Tomas already came after Rose. He'll come after me next. I...I shouldn't be here. I'm putting you in danger now. I should go."

"Stop it," Jaycie said. "You're staying here, and we're going to figure this out together. Mr. Reinhart knows something. I trust him."

"You shouldn't," Mabel said. "The more people you trust, the more you'll be let down."

Chapter 47
Jax

In the moments before he finally woke up again, Jax felt like he was outside of his body. He could see the spot underneath the tree where loose soil covered his body. He could see a strange symbol nailed to the trunk: a circle of twine with six petal-like shapes within. He could feel what was contained within the symbol—the ancient hex—transferring to his body, surging into the remnants of his mortal coil like an electrical current.

This was the oath he had taken. To share this grave, which had once belonged to Tomas Fischer. Jax lay on his back, feeling centuries-old spite bring his body back to life.

Jax sat up. His fingers closed around clumps of loose dirt, the same dirt shared between Hector and Gabe earlier in the night. The sky was a spiraling panoramic nightmare of black and gray, each shade darker than the last. His body was surrounded by the colorless veil cast by the eclipse. He wasn't sure if the dizzy sensation he felt was a result of the eclipse or what just happened to him.

This is death. You have died, Jax.

Jax stood, taking a trembling step back toward the Fischer House.

It was a strange sensation, like sea legs. He looked down at his hands. The scar that marked his compliance with Tomas's oath was gone. His palm was no longer marked for death. His mouth was horribly dry. It felt even worse than the time he caught a bad flu and was so dehydrated his tongue swelled up.

Tomas was waiting for him back in the parlor. He grinned as Jax entered.

Jax knew exactly what Tomas was going to say. It was about the hunger. The voracious desire bubbling inside his stomach. He saw it in Tomas's eyes—he understood the *need*. The uncontrollable appetite surging through Jax's body. The thirst for retaliation.

Tomas and Jax went together out into the night. They stopped in a quiet neighborhood lined with modest homes on either side of the street. The windows of all the houses were completely dark. Except for one.

Jax knew what this was, and he was ready. He was afraid, yes. The journey the boys had taken earlier in the night, the one Gabe did not come back from, the one in which Hector was gravely injured—it scared Jax. But he was more afraid of what would happen if he didn't do this. If he let this new hunger take over. It felt as if his stomach were being ripped from his body. He would give anything for it to end.

Tomas waited in the shadows as Jax proceeded, stalking the house the way an animal hunts its prey.

* * *

The stairs creaked under Alan Marcus's bare feet as he slowly made his way downstairs. This had been his ritual every Friday night for the past eight years or so—his body's internal clock would wake him once his wife fell asleep beside him. He would then sneak out of bed and down to the kitchen.

Realistically, Mrs. Marcus wouldn't have cared if Alan didn't wait until she was asleep to make his way downstairs. The less time they spent in bed together, the better.

Alan, in his navy-blue flannel pajamas, would sneak into the kitchen of their modest, three-bedroom home. He would find his seat at the kitchen island and make himself a midnight snack.

His choice of midnight snack had barely changed over the years. There were slight variations, but the foundation was always a peanut butter and jelly sandwich on a brioche roll. Alan would take a roll and scoop on two heaps of peanut butter and a dollop of jelly, followed by a few slices of Smithfield's precooked bacon. He ate his sandwich cold because he didn't want to wake his wife by activating the microwave or stove. Most of all, he didn't want to rub in the embarrassment that her glutton of a husband was downstairs stuffing bacon into his peanut butter and jelly sandwich.

Alan sat there, hunched over a beer and his PB&J, breathing deeply through his nose as he devoured his snack. He would stare out the kitchen window into the darkness of the backyard. He never looked at anything in particular, as it was always too dark to see anything. This ritual was a meditative trance Alan would fall into as he ate his midnight snack.

Tonight, the darkness felt blacker than it ever had before. But this detail meant nothing to the focused Alan Marcus. His eyes felt heavy. He continued to make love to his sandwich, staring blankly into a dark void. He took a swig from his beer can, and then something caught his attention outside, in the black night.

Alan didn't move. He sat there, staring out the window from the kitchen island. He could feel movement out there. He was confused by the fact that, while there was activity in the backyard, the automatic security light did not activate. Maybe he was seeing things? His tired eyes playing tricks on him, perhaps? Or maybe something *was* out there. Watching him in his moment of vulnerability. His special moment. The one he looked forward to all week, every week. This only private space he had for himself, now invaded by an unwanted guest.

It was quiet. The only sound Alan could hear was his own breathing, air pushing out of his nose as his heart, already thumping from the satisfaction of the salty, sweet concoction going down, gave pause to the sense of being watched. He put down his sandwich and wiped his hands.

There was somebody out there. He was sure of it. Alan slowly, quietly, pushed the stool out and stood up from the island. He approached the sliding glass door that led out into the backyard from the kitchen. He slid the door open and peeked his head out into the cold.

He peered around but saw nothing. Still, he could hear rustling movement nearby.

The automatic security light finally flickered on as he stepped out into his backyard. It revealed the rolling grass of his yard, flowing gently downhill and converging seamlessly into his neighbor's yard. He could see down the terrain to the row of shrubbery that marked the end of his property and the start of his neighbor's. Everything became completely still as the rustling sounds stopped. His breath and his heartbeat were the only indicators of life out in the darkness.

The soft, glowing light went out. The timer was set to auto-dim after a minute of no movement. Alan stood, looking out into the darkness, simply watching. Curiosity taking over. The only light now came from inside the kitchen, silhouetting his large frame.

The security light came on again though Alan had barely moved an inch—as if something had stealthily gone by.

Still, there was nothing out there but darkness. At least, nothing that he could see. But there had to be *something* setting the light off.

"Probably an animal," Alan muttered under his breath. He put his hands on his hips, feeling a chill as the cold grass caressed his bare feet. The night air hit his chest, and he pulled his navy-blue shirt closed. He stepped out, deeper into the backyard, scanning the rolling grass under the yellow light. He stood as still as possible, observing.

The light dimmed, casting him in darkness again. He waved his hand in an attempt to activate the light once more, but it did not turn on.

"Goddammit," he said, squinting into the darkness like a fool. The presence was back. Two, in fact. If he didn't know any better, he'd have said he could hear them whispering. As if one was giving the other instructions.

Upon hearing this, he finally felt afraid. He felt as if he were being stalked. No, worse than that. Hunted.

Alan backed up slowly, retreating to the sliding glass door. However, he turned around to find the door closed and the lights inside his house turned off. It was so dark inside his kitchen, it seemed as if he were peering into Halfmoon Cave. In fact, there seemed to be more light from the ongoing eclipse, with its colorless glow. His breathing grew heavy as he reached to pull the door open, but, to his horror, it was locked.

Panic began to set in as he struggled with the door, pulling with all his might. But it would not budge.

"Jenny?" he called out to his wife, but there was only silence.

He brought his face close to the glass door, cupping his hands around his eyes in an attempt to see inside. Suddenly, the lights in the kitchen came back on, and Alan let out a blood-curdling scream.

Inside his home stood one of his students—Tomas Fischer. The boy was covered in blood, wearing a demonic grin. In his hand, he held up the decapitated head of Alan's wife like a trophy. Her eyes open limply, her tongue lolling out of her mouth, blood dripping onto the tile floor.

Alan's shock was so great he didn't realize there was a second presence behind him. It had arrived so quickly; it didn't register until a pair of hands were wrapped around his neck.

He reached up. Whoever these hands belonged to was extremely strong. He struggled to breathe as the hands tightened around his neck, then his vision went black.

The grip loosened, just enough for Alan's vision to come back.

He turned and caught a face in the darkness. It was another face he knew well. Jackson Brogdon.

Alan was shoved violently to the ground. He looked up to get a better look at Jax, who was now standing over him. While it was, in essence, Jackson Brogdon, he was extraordinarily pale. The boy's shocking blonde hair was uncharacteristically dirty as it fell into his face. Something about his facial structure also seemed different. It was certainly Jax, but *sharper*? If that was even possible. It was as if someone had been given a portrait of Jax and told to carve his face out of stone. His sharp, defined features made him look enduringly angry. Vengeful. And in this moment, in this realization, Alan feared Jax. He felt the sinister intention of his late-night visit.

"Please, Jackson, no," Alan said.

Suddenly, Alan was up on his feet again, being thrown around like a rag doll. Jackson's hands, much stronger than they looked, gripped Alan by his pajama top, nearly tearing the fabric off the man's body. He pulled the teacher up close to his face, and Alan could smell Jackson's breath, cold and damp, like the night air itself. Reeking of death.

The scent made Alan dry heave. "No," he moaned, trying to push the boy away. But he was easily overpowered. Alan felt as if he were in some sort of dream, and he lacked the waking ability to get away from the monster.

Jax threw Alan's helpless body across the yard, shoving him through the sliding glass door and back into the kitchen. The glass door exploded on impact, sending a scattering of broken glass into the house. It littered the bloodstained tile floor of the kitchen.

Alan's lacerated body lay in a heap among the shards. He writhed in pain, chunks of broken glass penetrating the palms of his hands and splitting his shins open. As he tried to crawl away, flecks of blood bloomed from his wounds.

Jax followed Alan inside, walking slowly, confidently, stalking his prey. Shards of glass crunched under his feet. Soon, his belly would be full, his hunger would be satiated. But he wanted to enjoy this moment. Enjoy having this power over this man who had done nothing but hold him back. He wanted to savor his first meal.

"Eat," Tomas commanded.

Perhaps Jax would have made it quick, but Alan had purposefully made sure to not help Jax out. Therefore, Jax would purposefully draw this out as long as possible.

Chapter 48
Stu

Stu knew sleep would be a formidable task tonight. He had foolishly thought going to the first night of Fall Fest would restore some sense of normalcy, but he was mistaken. Instead, he left with nothing but a hollow ache. The fleeting joy he'd once felt for his favorite Blair tradition had gone. Things truly had changed.

Sleep continued to evade him, so he opted for the one place he could go where his grief wouldn't be judged.

Just one drink to cap off the night...

Anything to make him forget, even for a second, that he was living in the strangest time. But he couldn't fool himself, even as he approached Donoghue's Tavern. The obscurity painted in the sky, caused by the ongoing eclipse, was a stark reminder.

Stu was haunted by the truths he'd uncovered in recent weeks. Surely, every town had secrets. Every place had people who actively kept the darkest ones buried. Perhaps he never should have gone down this rabbit hole. He felt like he was watching history repeat itself, and there was nothing he could do to stop it. It felt as if he were the only one aware of the pattern. For that reason, he needed this drink.

When he arrived at Donoghue's, he noticed immediately that something was wrong. The most obvious clue was Ray Parilla's absence—a stark reminder that things were fucked. However, there was something more. The pub's atmosphere felt off, spoiled.

There was an unease inside the bar. Stu felt eyes on him. Not the routine looks folks would give whenever someone came through the door. This time, people seemed to *glare* at Stu as he found his seat. There was an audible throat-clearing as all conversations died when he walked in the door. He almost didn't feel welcome.

Stu was acutely aware of the barstool scraping against the floor as he pulled it out to take his seat. Still, like clockwork, Henry set Stu up with a glass and a generous pour.

"Evening, Henry." Stu nodded cordially.

Henry responded with a curt *mhm* and threw his towel over his shoulder. The bar chatter returned to a modest level, and Stu settled in with his drink. He couldn't make out the conversations, but he heard whispers scattered in among the normal banter. By the tone of it, they were whispers of judgment.

It was uncharacteristic of the crowd at Donoghue's to keep their voices down. Despite a few regulars being out at the beach near Fred Brown's farm to watch the eclipse, there were still enough people in here to make some kind of reasonable small talk.

Stu turned to his left and raised his glass toward Cliff. "Evening," he said, testing the waters.

Cliff sucked his teeth and took a swig of his drink.

"Everything alright?" Stu asked. Cliff had been so blatantly passive aggressive that Stu needed to say something.

Ted promptly came over and took the empty stool between Stu and Cliff. "Stu, we're surprised you would even show your face around here," he said. He then downed the last of his beer and motioned to Henry for a new one.

"What does that mean?" Stu looked at Ted, his frustration growing.

"I mean, aren't you embarrassed?" Ted said. "You were the last person to see Martha Brown alive. The whole town knows you were poking around there in the days leading up to her death."

"Are you accusing me?" Stu said. "I was the one who called the paramedics. I tried to save Martha. How can you say such a thing? You have no idea what it's like to find someone like that."

Ted cocked his head. "You're getting to know that feeling well, it seems."

"Don't you dare." Stu glared back at Ted, pointing a finger at him. "If you're referring to Martin, don't you fucking dare. What happened to that boy has been haunting me for weeks. It makes me sick."

"Alright, everyone relax," Henry said. "No fighting in the bar."

"I'm sorry, Stu," Ted said. "It's just, you know, we're all dealing with a lot. I know you didn't have anything to do with anyone's death. I'm just mad."

"It's fine," Stu said. An awkward silence filled the air as everyone focused on the TV behind the bar. The game on the screen was a replay, but they needed something to draw focus away from the tension.

Ted broke the silence. "Say, didn't that Freedom Readers group put your *Dracula* book on their list? Does make me wonder. You're so obsessed with those horror books, always reading about death and evil...maybe that's the reason it always seems to be you who's caught up in such things in real life."

"I resent that," Stu said. His gaze remained fixed on the TV as he tried not to lose his cool. Ted was just trying to get a rise out of him.

"I don't know," Ted prodded. "A personal kink is one thing, you know? Whatever, to each his own. But you bring that filth into the classroom. You expose Blair's children to evil. It follows you around, Stu. It's concerning."

"I don't need to listen to this." Stu stood up from the bar, taking his drink and relocating to one of the tables in the back. "You're an asshole," he said.

"Hey, don't shoot the messenger," Ted said, rotating on his

barstool to face Stu. He wore a grin on his face, knowing he had the upper hand. "I just have to say, it brings me peace knowing the school is aware of the situation now. I heard they done the right thing and made you take a leave of absence. I just hope you use the time off and get the help you need. Better late than never."

Stu stopped in his tracks, drink in hand. He had the urge to pitch his glass right at Ted's face.

"You're endangering all of us, Stu," Ted continued. "Just look around. Death is everywhere. You gonna tell Ray? Oh, wait..."

Stu's blood boiled with rage. But he simply put his glass down and headed for the door. He didn't have to put up with this. Reacting would only make things worse. He was leaving.

"You brought evil into Blair, Stu," Ted called after him. "You brought darkness to this town!"

Chapter 49
Jaycie

Jaycie woke up to Mabel gently nudging her shoulder. "Jaycie, wake up—he's outside the window," her friend whispered.

Jaycie was groggy, but she was alert. Her heart fluttered for a moment—this wasn't exactly what she'd pictured when she'd imagined Mabel in her bed. The pillow separating them had been pressed down as Mabel reached over to alert her friend to a sound coming from the window. Jaycie shivered, drenched in a cold sweat, realizing what her friend was trying to tell her.

Jaycie tensed up and looked over at her bedroom window. Mabel was right. There was a rustling sound coming from her window, and a wave of dread washed over her.

"It's Tomas," Mabel said. "He's come for us. I shouldn't have come here." The covers were pulled all the way up to her friend's chin.

"It's okay," Jaycie said. "It might just be the wind." She got out of bed, slowly approached the window, and suddenly stopped. Her friend was right. There was, in fact, a presence, but it wasn't outside the window.

It was *inside* the room with them.

Mabel held the covers tighter. There was someone standing in the corner of the room, concealed by the shadows. Both girls froze in fear. Jaycie stared wide-eyed, unable to move from where she stood next to the bed. She waited for the figure to move. To do something.

To turn her into one of them.

I'm sorry, Jaycie.

A voice spoke from beneath its shroud. Jaycie recognized it.

"Jax?" she said.

She was so relieved she began to rush toward him but quickly stopped in her tracks. There was an immense cold in the room, and it got colder the closer she got to the shadow. She stood in the middle of her bedroom, tilting her head at the anomaly.

"Jax, where the fuck have you been?" She already knew she was not going to like the answer. She knew it would be an irreversible truth that would probably destroy her, but she needed to know. The tears were already welling up in her eyes. She missed her brother so much.

"Can I come in?" Jax asked.

"It's too late for that, dummy," she joked through mounting tears. She slowly approached Jax, but he put a hand up to stop her. Gray moonlight was spilling through the bedroom window. Jax stepped out of the darkness and into the light. He looked pale and dirty. It was as if he were pulling a presence in with him from outside. A presence of death and decay.

Jaycie realized it wasn't her room that was cold—it was Jax. Her brother was bringing in the chill. He *was* the presence.

She pulled up her computer chair and sat. "Tell me where you've been," she demanded.

Jax only shook his head and repeated, "Jaycie, I'm so sorry."

"Stop apologizing and talk to me." She was finding it increasingly difficult to breathe. Jax stepped fully into the light, revealing his face. His ghastly, pale face. Void of any youth her twin brother might have had. Worst of all was the dried blood that circled his mouth and chin.

Jaycie brought her hands up, covered her mouth, and began to sob. "Jax," she choked out. He took another step toward her, and all she could do was shake her head and repeat his name.

"Jax." Her voice was weak and pitiful. She felt her stomach sink to the floor at the sight of her brother. "Jax, tell me what the fuck is going on right now. Mom and Dad have been worried sick. I've been worried sick." She looked at him, but she couldn't see him for him anymore. It was like she was looking into a black cloud instead of at her brother.

"I'm sorry," he repeated. "But I can't come home."

"You're scaring me," she said. "You can always come home. No matter what happened, whatever you did...Mom and Dad love you. I love you. Just come home."

Jax shook his head. "It's not that simple."

"It is," Jaycie said. "It is that simple. We're family, and this is your home. There's nothing that could ever change that."

Jax lowered his head. "Except...it has changed."

"I hate you," Jaycie said. She felt like she was losing him, like he wasn't hearing her. She wanted to reach out and touch him, but he felt far away. He was right there, but it felt as if he was already gone. As if she would never see him again. "I'm your sister, and you can't even be decent enough to tell me what the fuck is going on? What happened?"

"Tell Mom and Dad I'm sorry." He shook his head, turning toward the window to leave. "It was a mistake to come here, I shouldn't have put you in danger."

"No, don't you dare go!" Jaycie got up and grabbed him by the arm. "You can't just go," she said. She hit Jax in the shoulder with a balled-up fist, and it felt like she was striking a solid wall instead of human flesh. It freaked her out, but she looked up at him, demanding answers. "Things get a little hard, and you just fucking give up?"

"I didn't have a choice," he said. "I don't have a grip on things when I'm with Tomas...he has this power to sway people. It's too late now, what's done is done, but I needed you to know."

"I told you, you could always come to me." Jaycie felt a lump in her throat. "I said I would always have your back, but you didn't listen to me."

"I know," Jax said. "You're right. You've always had my back, and it's time I had yours...Tomas says he wants to protect Blair, but that couldn't be farther from the truth. He wants to cause disorder. He wants revenge, and he'll do whatever it takes to burn down the entire community."

Mabel flinched at the mention of Tomas's name.

"I knew it," Jaycie said. "I always had a bad feeling about him, about that house. My gut instinct was right that night, wasn't it? That night of the party?"

Jaycie turned toward Mabel, who she almost forgot was still in her bed. "I was right..."

Mabel nodded. Jaycie thought of her friend's hands. The scars running across her palms. The same scar Jax had done his best to hide since last year.

"You left with me that night," Jaycie said to Jax. "You took this oath before, and you knew what Tomas was going to do, so you made sure that I left."

Jax nodded. "In a moment of weakness, I let fear get the better of me. I took that oath for Tomas. In this last year getting to know him, I learned the truth about the legend we've all heard in Blair, but there's more.

"Jaycie, Tomas...he's a vampire. He died when he was a boy, in 1793. He was very sick. His father was so desperate to save him, he coerced a woman named Grace, Blair's Halfmoon Cave witch, to perform a procedure in an effort to save him. It didn't work. And because of the way Tomas died, because of the forceful way his father treated this woman, they were both condemned."

"Oh my god," Jaycie gasped. "Does that mean—you too?"

Jax pursed his bloodstained lips. "I'm sorry, Jayc—"

"Stop apologizing already," she said. "Just tell me how the fuck we're supposed to stop him."

Chapter 50
Calvin

The speed in which things changed on the beach was remarkable. Everyone stopped what they were doing. The chatter died, the music ceased, and everyone looked east, over Lake Champlain. The extraordinary reaction unfolding in the sky had everyone at a loss, silently watching, mouths agape.

Calvin shielded his eyes from the sudden brightness as the sun reappeared in the night sky. The light, so powerful he could see it through his closed eyelids, swelled at a scary pace, and Calvin regretted his choice to stay on the beach.

The blast of light lasted only a brief moment before the beach resorted to incessant darkness. Calvin removed his hands from his eyes to find that the vibrant colors surrounding Lake Champlain had ceased to exist. The dark purples and greens were gone, as if someone had pulled the plug and turned the entire world gray. A gray so profoundly grim, it was like the sky had never truly been blue. Instead, it was a dusty, melancholic sheen, desolate of all color.

"No fucking way," one boy said, breaking the awe-inspired silence. He held on to his sunglasses as if they'd fly off his face. He stepped forward, his sneakers depressing the sand of the beach. Others followed, watching in wide-eyed amazement.

Calvin, however, did not share in the excitement. He was genuinely afraid. This was not supposed to be.

"Wash out the darkness," someone said in a droning voice. Calvin looked to see that this person had taken off their protective glasses. It was as if they were under a spell, influenced by the dramatic shift in the sky.

"Wash out the darkness," someone repeated.

"Unclean. Wash out the darkness."

Calvin watched as the crowd inched forward, toward the lake. Several people gathered around a Subaru; all stopped and stared. One of them, who had been lying on the vehicle's hood, slid down and stood up, not taking his eyes off the sky for a moment. "Unclean. Wash out the darkness."

One man came out from around the rear of the car. "Wash out the darkness."

He was holding a cannister—gasoline. He tipped the nozzle over his own head and let the liquid pour over his body, dousing himself in gasoline, his expression unchanging. "I have darkness within me. Wash out the darkness."

Calvin stood frozen, watching in horror. The man took out a lighter and flicked the spark wheel, igniting his own sleeve. The flames quickly traveled up his arm, engulfing his entire body. He seemed eerily unfazed as he walked across the gray void of the beach. "Unclean."

It was time to go. Calvin grabbed his skateboard as the atmosphere continued to shift, ebbing and flowing as the two orbs in the sky continued to converge. The gray made way for black as the night grew viscous. As darkness descended over the beach, and Calvin saw he was being watched.

The air felt thinner. Calvin wasn't sure if his surging anxiety was making it harder to breathe, or if the eclipse was having adverse effects on him. But when he locked eyes with Hector, who was standing on the opposite side of the crowd, it almost looked like he was smiling.

Calvin blinked, and Hector started advancing toward him through the gray.

"I said you weren't welcome at school," he said. "What makes you think I'd want to see you around here either?" Hector closed in on Calvin extraordinarily fast. If not for the bizarre circumstances unfolding over the past few minutes, Calvin may have overlooked this detail.

Calvin also noticed the condition Hector was in. Despite the quickness with which he closed the gap between them, Hector was walking as if he had been in a car accident. His crooked limp was pronounced, as if his leg was about to snap like a twig. In addition, his dark shirt looked damp and loose, as if he'd been hit in the stomach with a bowling ball and the impact left a crater.

His face also looked terrible. He somehow looked both pale and jaundiced at the same time. His malnourished face had a hint of yellow, especially around the eyes.

"I wasn't aware you had a monopoly on Blair," Calvin said, sitting back down on his skateboard, showing he wouldn't budge for a bully. Hector tried to kick the skateboard out from underneath him.

Calvin caught himself and was on his feet quickly, his drumsticks held tight in one fist. "Didn't you learn your lesson last time?" Calvin said, standing up to Hector. "Last I checked, you're the one who's not allowed back at Blair High School at all...so I guess it's more my school now than yours, doll."

"*Doll?*" Hector said, growing red with anger. He shoved Calvin as hard as he could. Calvin took a few steps back before gaining his stance in the sand. He could feel several pairs of eyes turn in his direction. Eyes belonging to people who were too submerged in their own zombielike trance to step in and diffuse the situation. Yet the thought occurred to Calvin: the way they looked at him, specifically, like white blood cells trained on an impurity...if they viewed him as such...

"Don't call me 'doll,' got it, punk?" Hector said.

"Do you prefer 'shit-breath'? Because you fucking reek, homie," Calvin spat back, knowing full well the words would blind Hector with rage.

Like a bull who'd seen red, Hector charged at Calvin full speed. Sand kicked up at the feet of the two boys as they both anticipated impact. Hector cocked his fist back, ready to strike as he spit from his mouth an unspeakable slur, one Calvin had never been on the receiving end of before.

Hector would pay for that.

Calvin stomped the ground quickly, right where the edge of his skateboard happened to be in that moment—a detail he'd wisely noted before hurling the last insult. Hector was too enraged to see it.

The other edge of the skateboard flew up and connected with Hector's mouth, right in his teeth. The impact caused his head to whip backward. A spray of blood flew from his mouth as he stumbled, his protective sunglasses flying from his face.

In Hector's moment of vulnerability, Calvin noticed a disturbing detail. The bully's shirt rose up as he stumbled back from the impact, and there was no mistaking the gruesome reality of what Calvin saw. There was blood seeping from a gaping wound in his stomach, running down his pelvis. The wound, visible for only a split second, clearly exposed Hector's pulsing innards. The sight put a temporary hush over Calvin, as he was shocked to his core—he couldn't believe what he saw.

Several glazed-eyed onlookers rushed over to separate the boys. One of them grabbed Calvin by the arms and pulled him away. Others stepped in front of Hector, coming to his aid.

He was the one who started it, yet I'm being restrained.

"You ever come at me with that racist shit again, I'll kill you!" Calvin shouted. Hector wiped his mouth and spat. He paced back and forth behind the wall of spectators, acting like he wanted to charge at Calvin again, but Calvin knew this fight was over. At least for now.

"Alright, kid, you gotta go," an adult said. The man from the fishing store. He tugged Calvin's arm again.

Calvin shrugged. He backed away. When his arm was finally free, he glanced back, knowing he'd won. He wanted Hector to know it, and he gave him a smirk of confidence.

Hector's mouth was bleeding where he'd been smashed with the end of the skateboard. He'd stopped pacing and was now just standing there, watching as Calvin walked off the beach.

As the oppressive grayness of the eclipse grew, he could see Hector smiling through the crowd. It was a soulless smile, punctuated by the blood streaming down his chin. Calvin could see the exact spot where the skateboard had connected with his mouth. A gap resided where his front teeth used to be—until Hector licked the blood away to reveal it wasn't a gap at all. Instead, his front teeth were bookended by sharp, protruding canines. Just like the teeth of a vampire.

* * *

When Calvin was safely back on the main road, he stopped, stood near the fence, and looked back out toward the beach.

The disjointed crowd seemed to conform around Hector. Through his bloodied mouth, he spoke. "An evil has latched on to our town like a parasite," he said.

Chatter rose among the crowd. Calvin watched as their faces seemed to change before his eyes, growing more crazed—bloodthirsty. It was like lost and hungry rats in need of a leader, and Hector had stepped up.

"Only one person has the solution," Hector said. "There is only one way to eliminate the darkness that's rotting our town from the inside. We need to stomp it out."

"How?" someone inquired.

"Tomas Fischer," Hector said. "Come with me. I will take you to him. He will protect us all."

"What about my Martin?" a woman's voice cracked. "Nobody protected him when he needed it. Is he going to bring back my Martin?"

Hector coughed and spat out a wad of blood. "Tomas can do anything. If you come with me, avenging Martin's death will be only the beginning...Martha Brown. Ray Parilla. There are others. Too many. All because we let our guards down. We became complacent. Unaware of the evil around us. In our own homes. Because of this, the sickness must be wiped *out*. Every trace of it must be burned to the ground to start fresh. Destroy. Rebuild."

Calvin could see the crowd listening intently. A few even repeated Hector's words: *Destroy. Rebuild.* Others still chanted, *Unclean. Wash out the darkness.*

"That new boy attacked one of our own," a voice said. "Some new boy. He attacked Hector. Hector who has always been here."

Hector grinned. "I have always been here...yes. Tomas has always been here as well. Among us. Yet who allowed this new boy, this *evil*, into our town? Yes. One of our own. The schoolteacher. He wants to destroy Blair. He's the one who brought evil to our town and allowed it to thrive. Teaching satanic words, infiltrating our school! That's where it starts."

"*UNCLEAN!*" shouted the crowd in unison.

Some began to gather debris, wooden planks to use as weapons.

Calvin could feel the uproar, the mob forming right there on the beach. Like a drop of blood under glass, a wild group mentality spread quickly. Perhaps it was a self-defense mechanism. The town itself releasing pheromones as a defense, turning its inhabitants into bestial-driven beings who aimed only to protect their host.

"Come, follow me," Hector said. "Tomas has our backs, and we must have his. He will guide us to salvation."

Calvin felt his heart leap in his chest. He took a step back, away from the fence. He needed to get far away from this quickly forming mob. He needed to find Jaycie and warn her.

Chapter 51
Stu

When Stu got home from Donoghue's he poured himself a proper drink, since he couldn't finish the one he'd ordered at the bar without getting into an argument. He was desperate to get himself to sleep. The lack of rest was destroying him. He could feel insomnia digging its claws into his sanity.

He took a mild sleeping pill as well, but when he did sleep that night, he awoke often.

The first time he was disturbed out of his slumber, he could hear a scratching sound inside the room. It was subtle enough not to startle him but present enough to draw him out of his sleep. He blinked, looked around the room to find Paula curled up at the foot of the bed, unfazed.

Was the noise in his head? It couldn't be. He could *feel* the scratching coming from the bedposts beneath him. He could feel a presence in the room.

The scratching evolved into a gnawing, crunching sound, as if some creature were hiding under the bed, trying to eat away at the wooden bedframe like a termite.

Stu got out of bed, pulling the sheets and blankets back to peer underneath. There was nothing there. He grinned. He felt silly checking under the bed for monsters, like a child. Paula was still asleep, so the scratching sound was probably a side effect of having mixed the sleeping pill with booze. Although he hadn't had that much to drink and the pills were a low dosage, he supposed he couldn't play with that kind of fire without getting a little bit burned. He ran a hand through his hair, and it came back damp with sweat. It was most certainly the pills.

Stu dried off his hair and face and got back into bed. Luckily, he drifted back into sleep, but when he woke again, it was to a sound far more disturbing than scratching.

The horrific sounds of someone gasping for breath were inside his room. A choking, gurling struggle, as if someone were drowning in their own fluids. Stu tried to move, but his body did not respond. He felt as if he were in some kind of sleep paralysis. He could hear something pattering across the hardwood floor, the moonlight cast a shadow onto the ceiling—and all Stu could see was a dark, humanoid silhouette.

This wasn't some kind of pill-and-booze-fueled hallucination. No, this was too real to be a projection of his imagination. This was really happening. Paula was awake and alert now, her low growl rumbling at the looming shadow.

Paula's growl was followed by an abrupt and high-pitched wail. There was a wet creak of something moving, and Stu could feel the bed shift, but he could only stare helplessly up at the ceiling. He felt his heart sink as the shadow receded and silence took over the room.

Finally able to move again, Stu covered his ears and screamed a bloody, desperate scream. The safety of his bedroom had been compromised. He felt as if he may scream until he passed out, but he was not so lucky.

He reached for his phone, his blood-slicked hands awkwardly dialing 911. He begged for the police to hurry. He knew he sounded manic, but he didn't care.

"Take me instead," he cried. "Paula, no! It should have been me..."

* * *

When the police arrived, Stu opened the door for them. Officer Gary looked at his partner and then looked back at Stu, who was covered in blood.

"Mr. Reinhart, there was a call about a disturbance?"

"My....Paula. Paula...someone broke into my house!" Stu was inconsolable. Tears streamed down his face, and his breaths were sharp, heaving.

"Stuart Reinhart, you are under arrest for the deaths of Fred Brown, Martha Brown, and Martin Welch, as well as animal cruelty. You have the right—"

"What?" Stu gasped. "No, are you not listening to me? Someone broke into my house and killed my dog! It wasn't me! It wasn't—"

"Shut up!" Officer Gary said, jerking Stu's arms behind his back and handcuffing him. "You have the right to remain silent. Anything you say can and will be used against you in a court of law."

"Christ all-fucking-mighty, can I catch a break?" Stu said. "You're not listening to me. Someone broke—"

Officer Gary had had enough. He spun Stu around and landed a punch directly to the mouth. Stu's bottom lip swelled immediately as blood burst forth. He finally stopped talking.

"Stuart Reinhart, they were right about you," Officer Gary said. "You *have* brought a darkness to this town, and now you've been caught in the act. You're going to jail, and maybe this town can finally return to some sort of normalcy."

Stu was shown to the back of the police cruiser and carted off to jail in silence.

Chapter 52
Interlude:1793

They entered Grace's house without knocking—a shameless violation of her privacy. But they were no longer interested in her privacy or what she had to say. They were blood-thirsty. Their minds had been made up; compensation was required. A life for a life.

She froze when she saw them, knowing exactly what was next.

Four men entered her small cottage. Nathaniel Fischer led them, vengeance and guilt painting his face. They grabbed her by the arms and led her outside. They sky was unlike anything she had ever seen before. The sun and moon shared the sky, but they fought for space between the clouds. Everything around her was coated in a dusty gray. There was a congregation gathered together in the town square, all obscured by the strange reaction of this eclipse. This event the *Farmers' Almanac* had predicted.

The steeple of the church loomed high, scraping the darkened clouds. The cross on top looked like a knife stabbing up toward the clouds. Like if it were to pierce them, the sky would rain down black soot on Blair's degenerate people.

They manhandled her until they reached the center of the town square. She recognized most of the faces who solemnly watched as she was dragged around, not one decent enough to intervene.

"The only sickness here is the one infecting your minds!" she vented. "It's made the sky above as black as your rotting hearts."

"Silence," one man said.

Standing erect in the center of the square was a crudely made structure. One which she had seen before, in her travels. She had seen what was done to women like her in New England. Structures like this had one purpose: to take life away in the most painful, malicious way possible.

This particular edifice had been built in haste. It consisted of a wooden ladder positioned in the center of a pile of firewood. Such cruelty was a means to satisfy the bloodthirst of people who were angry and afraid of something they didn't understand. It was meant to divert the shame they felt within themselves and inflict pain upon whoever they deemed to be other.

They tied Grace to the ladder. Rope was fed between the rungs, binding her arms and legs tightly at her sides.

There was silence for a long time. Long enough that Grace had a moment to ponder if any of this was even real. Or if Nathaniel would come to his senses, step forward, and call all of this off. If she would be able to walk away from Blair and—

A man she did not recognize stepped forward. He stood in the space between her and the bloodthirsty residents of Blair.

"The practice in which our neighbors in New England try these kinds of crimes is...ineffective, to say the least," he began. His accent was distinctly English, proper in a way many who lived in Blair weren't. It was clear that this man was from out of town, but that didn't matter to Grace in this moment. She knew there would be no hope of walking away.

"Grace," the man stated, "there is no doubt that you are a witch. Your attempt to use the devil's magic on that sick boy was blasphemous. As a direct result of your irreverence, he suffered a death so heinous, the punishment for it can only be your own death. With the settlement of Blair gathered around as witness, you will be burned at the stake. Upon your death, your heart will be removed, blessed by a priest, and buried. Never again shall such darkness be allowed to flourish on God's soil. Do you acknowledge your fate?"

Grace stayed silent. She would not give these savages the satisfaction of seeing her anguish. She spat on the ground at the man's feet, looking up to find Nathaniel standing among the crowd. They locked eyes briefly before he quickly looked away. In that moment, she could see his insecurity on his face. The guilt of being unfaithful. The sin of forcing her to conjure a cure for something she was ill-equipped to handle. He had ruined her life. He came to her with false promises, telling her she would be part of the community. Accepted. Even loved. All lies to get what he wanted. All of that was on full display on his face. Yet no one would ever see it, because everyone was fixated on her.

The fire was lit, and the crowd watched. The flames sprouted quickly, licking at the soles of her feet. She remained silent, watching the crowd observe her. Some watched blankly. Some were screaming in terror, as none had witnessed such horrors before. Some of the men watched with disgusting looks of accomplishment, as if they had succeeded in flushing evil out of Blair.

They would get theirs—oh yes. As Grace's vision was obscured by the burning pain and the cloud of smoke, her eyes darted around for an anchor. The scent of burning flesh rose into the air as her feet went numb. The last thing she saw before the world went black was the glowing eyes of her one confidant in this horrible town—the goat. Her friend. Her salvation. In her final moment, she was calm, as she knew that, despite all of this, everything was going to be okay.

* * *

The fire was doused.

The charred, barely intact body was taken down and wrapped in cloth. The smell of burnt hair lingered in the air.

Halfmoon Cave sat isolated, south of the settlement of Blair. Deep inside, a naturally formed stone pyre jutted up from the quartz floor of the cave. It would be her permanent resting place.

Finally, they blessed a set of stones they'd burned alongside Grace—the same stones she had used during the boy's bloodletting, which ultimately took his life. The fire cleansed the stones of any darkness they had absorbed during the ritual, and then they were blessed with holy water and arranged around the mouth of the cave, creating a seal that was meant to remain intact.

Her remains were both punishment and reminder. They locked in the evil, reminding those who may try again of the fate that awaited them. A reminder that the people of Blair had come together to thwart off evil and protect their loved ones.

However, a soul could never truly rest—not after its body met a horrific end. In the town of Blair, the concept of a restful burial was destroyed that day. The accusation of an innocent woman, a woman coerced. A woman burned like a witch because of an affair she did not wish to take part in in the first place. And the blood ritual...

Chapter 53

Stu

Officer Gary dragged Stu into one of the cells inside Blair's jailhouse. He removed Stu's handcuffs and then slammed the iron bars shut. The crashing sound echoed through the otherwise lifeless building.

"What about my phone call?" Stu called out as Officer Gary and his partner turned to leave. "I want to speak to a lawyer!" But the officers ignored him.

The Blair jailhouse was a small, two-story brick building. The main floor was a single, open room with two holding cells, both of which were perpetually empty. It also included a nook with a desk and an outdated computer, which, by the looks of it, hadn't been powered up since 2005. The second floor was used mostly for storage. The infrequent use of the jail was a testament to Blair's general lack of crime. Any serious offenses were sent north, to Plattsburgh.

"Are you seriously going to leave me in here overnight?" Stu asked, wrapping his hands around the bars of his cell.

"The district attorney won't be in until Monday," Officer Gary explained. "We've got to hold you until we sort out exactly what's going on. It's for your own safety as much as it is for the safety of everyone else. That make sense?"

"No," Stu said, but he sat down on the cot and looked around. At least the cell was clean. He took a deep breath. He suspected it was going to be a long, lonely night. But he would get out of here. They couldn't do this to him. This was a lawsuit waiting to happen, and he needed to find out who broke into his house. Who killed Paula.

Stu shifted and lay down flat on the cot. He sighed in frustration, as he was certain he wouldn't be able to get comfortable enough to get some sleep. Even if he did, he doubted his mind would stop churning long enough for him to rest.

* * *

Stu awoke to discover two things:

First, he was amazed to find that he'd fallen asleep in this cell after all—albeit not without a knot in his back.

Second, he was no longer alone. There was someone in the cell next to him. He couldn't quite see into the neighboring cell, but he could hear. There was someone in there, half humming, half singing.

Holding rare flowers in a tomb...

Stu felt like he knew the melody, but he was sure he recognized that voice. It was the voice of a familiar young man.

If only he could see into the other holding cell. He was almost certain it had been unoccupied when he arrived earlier in the night, but in the chaos of being dragged into jail, perhaps he could have missed that detail? Or perhaps someone had been brought in while he was asleep? Unlikely, considering how loudly the bars of his own cell had slammed shut behind him.

Stu rubbed his eyes and strained against the knot in his back. He sat upright and craned his neck, trying to get a view from a mirror that hung on the wall across the way. It was hard to see, but from Stu's perspective, the cell looked empty. However, the voice continued to sing.

Down in a hole and they've put all their stones in their place...

Blair was still under the effects of the eclipse. A gray, dim glare spilled in from outside, casting striped shadows onto the floor from the bars of the cell.

Stu stood, wrapping his hands around the bars of his cell door. "Alice in Chains?"

The humming stopped, followed by a low chuckle. "You've heard? Yes. Alice in Chains...they're one of those modern rock groups. Fitting."

Modern? Stu wondered. "Uh, how long have you been in here?" he asked. Although he could not see the man, he tried to strike up a conversation.

I've eaten the sun so my tongue has been burned of the taste...

Stu cleared his throat. "I said how long have you been in here?"

Stu's question was met with dead silence. Unnerving regret settled in. Even the humming had ceased. His neighbor had deliberately disengaged from the conversation. Aware of Stu and intentionally ignoring him.

Stu tensed up. Who was this man in the cell next to him, and what was he doing in there? He continued to glance at the mirror, trying to catch any indication of movement. Any sign that someone was occupying the cell next to him. He needed to know that he wasn't just hearing voices. He needed to know he wasn't losing his mind.

But there was nothing. Not even a breath.

It was as if his neighbor had simply vanished.

Chapter 54
Jaycie

Jaycie woke up to a dozen notifications on her phone—calls and texts from Calvin. She remembered, while she'd left Fall Fest, Calvin had opted to stay behind and wait on the beach for the eclipse to unfold.

"Shit." Her heart skipped a beat as she unlocked her phone.

"We need to talk about FF...Text me when you're up."

Jaycie did, her thumbs typing out a message. "I can be ready in an hour. Let's meet..."

Where?

Jaycie paused for a moment, thinking. According to Jax, they needed to go to back to Halfmoon Cave at precisely the right time: when the eclipse broke after forty-eight hours.

She had woken up with a desire to be alone. Not necessarily avoid the people close to her—just to escape for a while, even if only a moment. The church on Holy Cross Road came to mind, not because she intended to pray, and certainly not because she felt church would bring her answers or even peace. She just knew it would be the last place anyone would look for her.

She typed, "Meet at Holy Cross Church in an hour?"

Jaycie turned and saw that Mabel was still sound asleep. She would let her stay that way. So Jaycie got up and out of bed and quietly got dressed.

A ping sounded from her phone—Calvin responding in the affirmative.

Before leaving, Jaycie turned to look at Mabel one last time. She slept so peacefully; she certainly needed it. A terrifying thought occurred to her—this might be the last time she ever saw Mabel. So much could go wrong as she ventured into Halfmoon Cave, into the unknown. She blinked, taking a mental snapshot of her friend. Her black hair with the purple highlights. Her soft, round lips that parted slightly as she breathed.

Jaycie had to succeed. In the meantime, she knew Mabel would be safe here.

It had been ages since Jaycie stepped foot inside a church. Growing up, the church had been the literal center of town. Going to church was just a nice, family activity people did together. It was nowhere near the obsession it had become recently. Unless, Jaycie wondered, it had always been this way, and now she could see it for the misleading entity it truly was. But there had certainly been an extra emphasis on going to church, it seemed, especially in the last few years. The obsession some of her neighbors had with it was, frankly, a turnoff.

She remembered walking Holy Cross Road with her parents, the street lined with people, the parking lot full of cars. But this cold autumn morning, the streets were eerily empty. Blair's town square a barren husk under a gray spotlight. Perhaps it was because people were avoiding the eclipse. Or maybe it was something else.

The church's steeple, with its cross inverted, was a sign that attention to detail had been left by the wayside. The inversion of the true meaning of the town's faith. Using this place of worship as a cover, an excuse, to push the fear and hatred that lived in the hearts of some of her neighbors.

Even her own parents. When she and Jax were little, their

parents considered themselves churchgoers, but it never felt like something Jaycie *had* to do if she didn't want to. Now, although it wasn't explicitly said, she felt her parents exerting pressure. Small clues like Martin Welch's funeral card on the refrigerator.

Which made Jaycie feel betrayed, in a way. She'd never really felt a strong connection to this place or the messages it pushed. She'd always felt a sort of ick factor when they would try to relate a sermon to life in modern America.

More than once, Jaycie had felt specifically targeted. She felt like she wasn't completely welcome because of who she was fundamentally. They said she was sinful. The rhetoric from political groups, endorsed by the church itself, made her feel condemned. At least, that's how she used to feel. Now, she understood that was not the truth. But it still hurt. It never sat well with her that her parents still went to church despite its stance against people like Jaycie.

The echo of the heavy wooden door's creak sounded through the empty church. Where was everybody?

The church looked a lot smaller inside than she remembered it as a child. The sequence of arches ascended to the steeple that had been damaged from the outside. Yet she couldn't feel bad for it. This place had turned its back on her. She felt like the town of Blair was turning its back on her. Small towns and their fucking insistence on being in everyone's business. Their insistence on being perfect. Well, fuck that. Each one of these judgmental assholes probably had countless demons in their own closets, and then they try to point the finger if you miss one Sunday at this place, playing pretend.

And now Jax was...she still didn't know *what* Jax was now. What his condition was and what it meant. She supposed he was dead. The tales told in those vampire novels...they must have been grounded in some sort of reality. Some fucked-up, real-life experience someone packaged into a story and sold. She supposed all writers did that, to some degree. But this was her brother. Her twin. And now he was...

She couldn't even formulate the truth in her mind. It was difficult to connect the dots of what her eyes had seen when he visited last night. He spoke to her; he was there in the flesh. He blinked, he breathed. Yet he was also dead. Jaycie was brokenhearted, but she was also angry with Jax for feeling like he had nowhere else to go.

She was angry because, although she knew saving the rest of Blair from a similar fate would be the right thing to do, she didn't think they deserved it. She was so fucking angry with every townie who'd given her a side-eye because they knew she was different. They didn't deserve her good graces, her attempts to save this wretched town. But she was going to. At least, she was going to try.

The details Jax had given her were burned into her mind. The unfortunate reality of what she must do. But at least she wouldn't be alone.

Jaycie heard the echo of someone entering the empty church behind her.

"Hey," Calvin said as he sat down next to her. The wooden pew creaked.

"Hey," Jaycie said. Her voice had weight to it, as if it hurt to be around him at this moment. It would have hurt to be around anyone as she steeped in her thoughts, and she dreaded sharing what she knew.

"You okay?" he asked.

Jaycie shook her head. "No. No, I'm not okay. But I will be. You know?"

"Tell me about it," Calvin said. "I've learned more about Blair's dirty laundry in a few weeks than I bargained for. I just wanted a drum set," he laughed. "Instead, I ended up with tuna smashed into my locker and idiots trying to take me down with a chloroform rag. I'd say I've gotten a shitty deal so far."

"I'm glad you're here," Jaycie said.

"Thanks." Calvin shook his head. "That makes one person, at least." He cleared his throat, and the sound carried inside the spacious church. "Listen...I'm terrified about what I saw on the beach last night. Fall Fest got weird after you left. Like, really weird. Some of these people are into some dark shit."

"What happened?"

Calvin took a deep breath. "It's kind of hard to describe. When the eclipse started, it was like watching something supernatural unfold. Like some of the people in this town bent to the will of a force beyond their understanding. As if the eclipse itself triggered some kind of dormant, ritualistic instinct within them. I swear, it was like their brains turned off and their focus became fixated on one thing... But the worst part?" he continued. "They all gathered around Hector. It sounded like they were planning on doing something bad. They mentioned Mr. Reinhart *and* us, like we have targets on our backs for being associated with him."

"We have to tell Mr. Reinhart," Jaycie said.

Calvin nodded. "We need to be discreet about it. From what I saw on that beach, those people are capable of horrific things. They're dangerous and not thinking clearly."

"Speaking of horrific things," Jaycie said. "I spoke to Jax. You're not going to like what we have to do to stop all of this."

"Please don't tell me this gets worse," Calvin said.

"Unfortunately, it gets a lot worse." Jaycie looked up and toward the front of the church. Chills shot up and down her arms at the sight of the giant crucifix at the center of everything. The wooden depiction of Christ on the cross, in all its morbid horror, seemed to be looking down at Jaycie. The ancient execution, cruel and barbaric, a relic of the sadistic punishments humankind conjured up in the past —it seemed so distant. Yet Jaycie knew that although it may have seemed like people had moved on from the terrible actions of their past, they weren't so far removed after all.

"Do you remember that second-to-last mission in *Blood of the Innocent*?" Jaycie asked.

Calvin nodded incredulously.

"Well, we're going to have to replicate that, unfortunately. We need to go inside Halfmoon Cave and pull Grace out into the sunlight the moment the eclipse breaks. That's the only way to end this thing and stop Tomas."

"You just dropped a lot on me, Jace. We have to do *what* now? How do you know all this?"

"Jax told me..." Jaycie paused, taking a shuddering breath.

Calvin raised an eyebrow. "What's wrong?"

"Jax is one of them now...he's a vampire."

Calvin stood up and raised his hands in surrender. "No, nuh-uh, this is officially too much."

"Listen." Jaycie grabbed Calvin's shirt sleeve. "The story of Grace, the witch of Halfmoon Cave—she put a hex on Tomas Fischer's grave centuries ago, during an eclipse just like this one. Tomas's father, Nathaniel Fischer, forced Grace to come up with a cure for Tomas's tuberculosis, but when it didn't work they blamed her for his death—because they always blame the woman. This is the cause of what's happening in Blair. To stop it, we need to pull Grace out of the darkness. Tomas is using her power to turn people in this town against one another. Expose the cracks of the town and destroy it from the inside. He wants revenge for what happened to him, and he won't stop until all of Blair pays for it."

Calvin buried his face in his hands. "Oh my God..."

"We can do this," Jaycie asserted. "We have to do this. There's a reason we were paired up in biology."

"So, we do this and break the hex. What happens to Jax then?"

"I don't want to talk about that," Jaycie said. Jax had confirmed her worst fears—when Grace was freed, it would destroy Tomas Fischer and end the curse over Blair, but it would also destroy anyone else who had turned, including her brother. But Jax convinced her it had to be done. "Right now, my concern is getting this over with so the nightmare can end."

"Understood," Calvin said.

Jaycie nodded. "So, are you with me?"

"I'm with you, lab partner." Calvin stood up. He approached one of the displays holding a miniature wooden cross and wrapped his hand around it. It was slipped into a slot on top of the altar, easy to remove. He lifted it up and turned back toward Jaycie. "If we're dealing with vampires, I suppose a little insurance couldn't hurt."

"Okay good, because in order for us to do what we need to do, we have to make a stop first."

* * *

When they emerged from the church, the pulsing gray darkness in the sky persisted. The town square remained mostly abandoned. With one exception.

Jaycie spotted John Darski at the edge of Main Street. A stack of wooden two-by-fours had been arranged in the middle of the square, along with some rope and other building supplies.

"Jaycie," Calvin said, trying to keep the wooden cross from John Darski's line of vision.

Jaycie turned around and looked up at the wall of the church. The words NO GOD were smeared on the side of the building in dirt. When she looked back, John was looking in their direction.

"Hey!" he shouted. "Did you two do that?"

Jaycie and Calvin looked at each other and reflexively ran for cover, out of John's sight.

"He thinks we wrote that," Calvin said. "It probably doesn't help that I basically stole this." He shook his head, looking down at the cross.

"It's fine," Jaycie said. "If we don't do this, Blair is going to have a lot more to worry about than just a stolen cross."

Chapter 55
Stu

For a long time...

Stu stirred. The knot in his back was getting worse. He had almost certainly dozed off again, as he could have sworn he'd heard the voice of one of his students. He drew back, startled, as he saw a pair of hands hanging nonchalantly between the bars that separated his cell from his neighbor's.

"Did you say something?" Stu asked.

Perhaps his neighbor hadn't vanished?

Perhaps he could come and go as he pleased?

"Indeed. I said, for a long time," the voice said, deeper this time, matter-of-factly. The voice had changed...unless Stu had dreamt about a different voice? *Unless this stranger was masking his voice.*

"What is a long time?"

"You asked me a question, did you not?" his neighbor asked.

Stu paused for a moment, thinking. Yes, he had asked a question, but that was, what? An hour ago? Two? He'd assumed that conversation was long dead.

"I suppose I did," Stu admitted.

"So, to answer your question, I've been in Blair for a long time... does that satisfy your inquiry?"

"I meant how long have you been in the cell next to me," Stu said. He strained his neck again, hoping to get a view of the person in the cell next to him. Still no luck.

"Ah. I suppose I am unsure," the voice answered. "The answer to that question seems a bit hazy."

"Huh," Stu said aloud. "I'm sorry, I don't recognize you at all—I'm pretty familiar with most people in Blair. I thought they might have brought you in for being homeless; that's how people usually end up in here."

"I find it quite rude that you would assume I am homeless," the man said. "I have a home."

"I'm sorry, I didn't mean to presume. It's just...I thought I recognized your voice earlier. I can't see you from here, and I'm just having a hard time placing you."

Silence. Stu exhaled in frustration. His neighbor wasn't the best conversationalist. In fact, he was a bit condescending. Given the lull in conversation, Stu took the moment to sit back down on his cot. He couldn't see his neighbor, and conversation wasn't doing much for him. However, in that moment, Stu caught the sound of rustling coming from within the walls of the jail. A tiny scratching, one that sounded eerily familiar to the gnawing sound he'd heard in his bedroom. The sounds that had begun as gentle rustling and scurrying until they built up to a crescendo, ultimately ending in Paula's death.

He thought he was going mad.

Stu would give anything to unhear those sounds. He would prefer to hear his neighbor humming again. Anything.

"A lot of people expressed apprehension about this eclipse," the voice stated clearly. "Do you know anything about the event, Stu?"

How does he know my name?

"Yes, I know a little bit," Stu said. He shifted uncomfortably on the cot. "From what I read, this specific kind of solar event is far rarer than a typical solar eclipse."

"That's right," the voice confirmed. "Every two hundred and fifty years, to be exact. But who's counting?"

Stu could have sworn he heard a smile behind the voice's *but who's counting?*

Him? Was he counting? Whoever *he* was?

"I don't think I need to explain the difference between this and a standard eclipse, right?" the voice went on. "I anticipate this event to continue through the night. Nearly forty-eight hours of total, grim darkness."

"Two whole days," Stu said in awe.

"Well, yes—forty-eight hours does make out to two days," the voice said condescendingly. Stu didn't appreciate being spoken down to, but he continued to listen.

"And did you know that this anomaly is exclusive to our little community? While our neighbors up in Plattsburgh and over in Burlington experience *some* eclipse characteristics, Blair is ground zero."

"That is interesting," Stu agreed, treading lightly.

"I, for one, have been anticipating this day," the voice said. "Most impressively, the direct effect of this eclipse is something people have failed to document in the history books. I'm sure you've done your research, being a schoolteacher and all. Likely checked books out of the library, read about this panic or that panic, about executions and exhumations. You may have read a thing or two about witches and hexes. You may even be aware of how the very first *Farmers' Almanac* tried to predict this very event over two centuries ago before its coauthor died. But you, like those before you, have failed to recognize the truly incredible nature of what is taking place under these circumstances. People have woken up.

"Our world, under these colorless and grim conditions...it's like we're living in an old black-and-white film. Fascinating. It is said that one should never look directly at an eclipse, that the effects can be damaging to the eyes...I laugh as I see people selling protective eyewear. Fools. No damage can be done during this eclipse. No. The only effect this event will have on Blair is that it will *open* their eyes. Make them see the true evil—each other. Thy neighbor. This is more than an eclipse. It's a reset. A moment in time in which people's deepest, most animalistic instincts kick in. The instinct to defend their homes, to kill if necessary."

Stu looked down to see that he was shaking. "I...I'm trying to wrap my head around all of this. How do you know that's what's happening? Who are you, and why can't I fucking see you?" Stu shook the bars of his cell in frustration.

He received only silence in return.

* * *

Once again, it was hard to gauge just how much time had passed. Stu was getting hungry, but the darkness from the ongoing eclipse made it impossible to tell how long he had been locked in here.

"Has anyone come by since you've been in here?" Stu asked, not certain he would get a response. "Have they fed you?"

A ponderous silence followed. Stu knew his neighbor had heard him, as there was a stirring coming from the cell next door.

"Come to think of it, no," the voice said. "Thankfully, I had a satisfying meal just before I arrived..."

"How long have you been here?" Stu asked again.

"Not long," the voice chuckled sadistically. "However, now that you mention it, I am beginning to feel quite famished. I think I'll go soon. In the meantime, I think I'll help myself."

What followed made Stu lose his appetite altogether.

One of the scurrying, scratching sounds was cut off abruptly. It was followed by a wet crunch. The snapping of bone, like a twig, resonated inside the jail, followed by the sound of slow, deep breathing.

"Hello?" A sharp sting of fear erupted in Stu's nerves. He tried desperately to find an angle and see into the cell next to him. "Sir? What was that?" He needed to know what was happening. The horrific sounds continued, the sounds of a predator feeding on prey. The sound of cracking bone, the separation of muscle from tendons, the deep and frantic breathing. The dripping. Stu could do nothing but listen and hope it would end soon.

And it did.

A projectile came flying from out of his neighbor's cell and landed in the center of the room. A rat. Its stiff, mangled body lay on the concrete floor.

"What the hell was that?" Stu cried out.

"A snack, I suppose," the voice said calmly. "It will do for now. But, admittedly, it was not as quenching as the pup."

Although he still could not see into the next cell over, Stu could hear the sadistic grin forming on the man's face. The room filled with the sound of his breathing as it grew erratic. The room began to spin.

"Who are you?" Stu asked, his voice trembling.

"The answer is simple." The voice shifted in pitch, went an octave higher. It sounded younger. Was it the same voice from his dream? Then, in the darkness in front of Stu's cell, a shape took form. A figure, as if walking out of a thick fog, materialized before Stu's eyes. It was someone he recognized.

Tomas Fischer, from Blair High School.

"You son of a bitch!" Stu shouted, hands grasped tightly around the metal bars.

"Not many people were around the last time an eclipse like this occurred in Blair. The population was so small at the time—there were perhaps one hundred and thirty people living here in 1793. Now, not many people will remember what's going to happen, because when all is said and done, there will be nobody left to tell the story."

"You killed my dog?" Stu was so consumed with anger that he barely registered the fact that Tomas had seemingly transported himself out of his cell and into the middle of the room, as if carried by a gust of wind. "I ought to fucking kill you!"

"Now, now," Tomas said. "You just hang tight. There will be no killing—at least, not yet. Your neighbors will take care of that. Be patient, Mr. Reinhart."

Stu watched as Tomas turned and made his way to the jail's front door.

"Get back here!" Stu called out after him. "Fuck," he muttered.

Chapter 56
Jaycie

They moved quickly and quietly in the darkness, sneaking onto the roped-off property. Fred Brown's farm felt like a cold clone of the haven it used to be. Just a day earlier, during Fall Fest, it was vibrant, the way Jaycie remembered it from when she was young. Now, it was a crime scene.

It broke her heart knowing what had to be done next.

Thanks to Jax's instructions and *Blood of the Innocent*, she was prepared. As demented as their plan was, it was their last option. Their only chance to stop chaos from unfolding in Blair.

According to Jax, a sacrifice had to be made before they entered the cave. It was for their protection. Jaycie wasn't entirely sure it was going to work, but she knew they had to try. She was willing to do anything for this nightmare to end.

Jaycie wasn't sure if Calvin was putting on a front, but he seemed slightly more optimistic. "So much for missing out on the dissection project," he commented. Jaycie knew his sarcasm was a cover, blocking his true feelings about what they had to do. It seemed like the most tragic joke of all—of all the classes they'd assumed they wouldn't need in real life, the lesson on dissection was near the top of that list.

Maybe he was faking optimism so they could just do it, get it over with before they had a chance to back out. Like if they hesitated for a single moment, they'd lose their nerve.

At least they weren't targeting a human child, like in the game. Descending fully into that kind of darkness was not something Jaycie wanted to do.

Blood of the Innocent.

She was growing to resent that game now.

She hated that one of Fred Brown's goats would have to serve their purpose. It was a cruel and barbaric conclusion. Yet all of this was cruel and barbaric. This all began with the blood of the innocent being spilled when Martin Welch was killed. It seemed tragically poetic that it would have to end the same way, with one of the goats.

The farm was mostly quiet, except for the melancholic bleating of the goats. It was as if they were fully aware of the tragedy that had drowned their home in recent days, as if they were aware they had become orphans. Aware that the fate of Blair now rested on the assumption that sacrificing one of them meant saving the rest.

They found the goats and pinpointed the smallest one. Calvin's hand shook as he produced the blade from his jacket pocket. Now Jaycie knew for certain he was only pretending to be ready for this. He was clearly just as rattled by the task at hand as she was.

The box cutter looked fake in the gray darkness. Calvin explained that it had been the easiest thing to get his hands on at home that would get the job done. At least he hoped it would be quick and accurate.

"Do you want me to do it?" Jaycie asked. She saw Calvin's hand shuddering uncontrollably. She didn't want to do it, but she didn't want it to be any more difficult than it needed to be either.

"No, I got it," he said, and then he proceeded. The blade went in smoothly, running across the animal's skin with ease. Jaycie positioned a pan underneath the wound, allowing it to fill with blood. She hoped it would be enough. If they went through all of this and ended up vulnerable when they entered Halfmoon Cave, it would all be for nothing.

When it was finished, they took the blood and began to cover themselves. An unholy baptism. They let the blood drip down from their heads and shoulders, slow and sticky, like crimson honey.

Jaycie watched as the goat's blood ran down Calvin's face in streaks. She thought she was going to be sick at how heavy the coating felt on her skin. It felt wrong.

"We need to hurry," she said, trying to distract herself from the feeling. "We need to get to the cave right before the eclipse breaks." *Easier said than done*, she thought to herself. They only had so much time before the cloak of darkness lifted, and that time was quickly approaching.

Chapter 57
Donoghue's

Darkness encroached on the town of Blair, disrupting the town's sense of day and night. In a way, it was both at once. The air felt warm, as if the afternoon sun were at its peak, but the darkness permeated everything. This phenomenon, in a way, brought some together. For others, the prolonged darkness stoked the flames of confusion.

The gathering place for those trying to find their composure during the inexplicable darkness was Donoghue's Tavern. People hid from the darkness brought on by the eclipse, but also the ominous shadow that death had cast over the town. The bar had become the de facto center for those who were trying to find their way, to hold on to the last shred of community and what it meant. If it ever had any meaning at all.

An eerie silence filled the dark tavern. Henry Donoghue was parsing out drinks from behind the bar, and the sound of glasses clinking together dominated the space entirely.

Except for the presence, however, something among the regular patrons who occupied the bar—an omnipresence, an idea. It was felt but not seen. At least, not at first.

Henry Donoghue, like some of his neighbors, felt the shift in the atmosphere long before he saw the eclipse. Perhaps it was around the time of Martin Welch's death, but the feeling was irrevocable—something had changed. And tonight, it felt as if that something was incarnating right here inside the bar.

Someone who looked like he could have gone to Blair High School emerged from the bathroom. He was dressed entirely in black, exceedingly tall with a face as pale as the moon. Henry felt a sort of inherent unease toward this person's appearance. A built-in human instinct. The reflex one has when choking, for example, when their hands go instinctively to their throat. Henry didn't remember this man entering the bar at any point during the night (or day), but it was possible he'd simply missed him. The bar was busier than it normally was.

Still, this man—or boy?—had a presence that Henry couldn't imagine overlooking. The longer Henry looked, the younger this individual seemed, but it was the eyes that made it difficult to pinpoint his age. His eyes held a dark, ancient wisdom few people in Blair possessed. His features felt wrong, like they didn't belong together.

He took a seat at the bar in an attempt to blend in with the crowd. However, his mismatched features made blending in impossible. He made eye contact with Henry, summoning him forward so he could order a drink.

Henry paused in front of the man, eyeing him down. This stranger was surely too young to be in the bar. "Evening, sir. Can I see some ID please?" Henry had a thought. The lines blurred between day and night, young and old...

"ID..." He rolled the word on his tongue, as if offended by the very concept. "Henry, it's me, Tomas. Tomas Fischer. We graduated Blair High School together. Class of '75, remember?" Tomas looked deep into Henry's eyes, persuasion burning in his black irises.

Henry searched his own memory, and realization washed over his face. Yes, it did *seem* to be true. He must have attended high school with the gentleman sitting in front of him.

How could he be so senseless?

"Tomas." Henry frowned. "My mistake. It seems time has been kinder to you than it has to me. What can I get for ya?"

"That's quite alright." Tomas licked his lips as he looked up at the bar, studying the selection. "I've been away for a while, but I'm back…I think I'll have a whiskey, neat. Gristmill, please."

Donoghue turned and reached for the bottle of Gristmill stashed away on the top shelf, his arm like a mechanical crane grabbing a prize. He poured the drink and placed it in front of the man who claimed to be his former classmate.

Tomas looked down upon the amber liquid and smiled. It was a strange smile, both longingly nostalgic and quietly sinister. Like he was feeling joy while also containing the desire to do great evil, like a mischievous child ready to burn ants with a magnifying glass.

"This is one of the oldest whiskies in the country," he said. "Did you know this company started when George Washington himself started a distillery? Opened in 1797—the same year Blair was incorporated into the union." He lifted the glass and rotated it in front of him, watching intently as the liquid crawled up the side of the glass.

"That so?" Donoghue said, staring.

"Indeed, it is so," he said. "In fact, that wasn't the only event of significance to happen in Blair that decade." He placed the glass down, whiskey undrunk. He looked deep into Donoghue's eyes, as if his meaning was more in his eyes than in his words.

"The people of Blair did a very brave and noble thing just four years earlier. I'd argue that if they hadn't, this town wouldn't exist as it does today. They saved their community from descending into an uninvited darkness. Do you know how?"

Donoghue shook his head, but he leaned forward.

"They killed a witch," Tomas said, finally taking a drink of his whiskey. "Who knows the kind of depravity and evil they spared future generations from."

Henry was enthralled. He was curious how Tomas knew so much about Blair's history. Had they learned this in high school?

"This town was allowed to thrive because the men before us made a hard decision. It seems as if Blair has indeed thrived...until now."

Several other people at the bar had turned to listen to Tomas. His voice hadn't risen above a casual murmur, so they gravitated toward the man and his story, toward his charisma.

"I have the impression that the very darkness which plagued Blair in its infancy has returned somehow. It has returned, like mold, a single spore left behind undetected, now growing in the underbelly of our home."

"Yeah," someone said. "He's right! There sure is a darkness hanging over our town lately."

"The question is," Tomas said, "what are *we* going to do about it?"

Donoghue sighed. "I'd do just about anything for life to get back to normal around here. I think everyone here shares that sentiment." People nodded, sipping their drinks in agreement.

"Interesting," Tomas said thoughtfully. "Even if it meant burning Blair to the ground to start over? A sort of destroy-and-rebuild scenario? To ensure that not even a single spore of evil was left behind, to prevent it from growing and spreading all over again?"

The front door of the pub creaked, and several more people filed in. Henry turned to look, recognizing the familiar faces. "Hey, no minors in here," he said when he recognized Hector Stroud.

"It's fine, he's with me," Tomas said. "We're all in this together now."

"What about my Martin?" the boy's mother reiterated; her voice cracked. She and her husband had entered the pub with Hector. "Nobody protected him when he needed it. We were told you can fix that."

Tomas paused for a moment, as if letting the woman's words absorb into the rest of the crowd. Letting the notion that death was lingering over the town really sink in. Letting them believe they could change the town's current trajectory.

"Martin Welch." Tomas pivoted on the barstool to face the rest of the crowd. "Such innocence. Taken from us, and why? Because this town has been subjected to evil, that's why. The door has been opened for atrocities to come into our community. Our homes."

Tomas stood. "I'm truly sorry for your loss. If I could, I would have stopped it. I would have stopped the deaths of all of our beloved neighbors. Fred and Martha Brown, Ray Parilla...who else? Who's next? None of them deserved the ending they faced. But had I known, had *any* of us known what was among us, I don't believe we would have let our guards down.

"Damage has been done, yes, but that doesn't mean we can't stop the bleeding. This evil must be wiped *out*. Every last trace of it must be burned to the ground to start fresh. Destroy. Rebuild."

Unclean...

Wash out the darkness...

Tomas looked in the direction of the monotone utterance. "Yes, that's right."

"We just came from the beach," said Hector as he approached.

"There was a boy there," another said. "He attacked one of us. One of our own."

"Yes, some new boy, someone who doesn't belong."

"That's right," Tomas said. "Someone new...and who let this happen? I'll tell you who—it began in the school. A single spore of evil. Dark ideas spawned from the mouth of one of the teachers, is that correct? Yes, the one in the prison right now. He sought to spread an evil lie to the youth of this town. To use their innocence in his favor, for his agenda. He even ignored the recent instruction to document the books he included in his lessons. What is he hiding?

"It's a sickness...and now, that sickness has spread. This Stuart Reinhart is the one who opened the door, who allowed the evil inside. And now it has latched itself onto two more."

"Unclean!" the crowded bar shouted in unison, growing into an uproar.

"However, Stuart Reinhart was not always this way, correct?"

Tomas asked. "He was corrupted somehow. Exposed to whatever darkness had been left over from the inception of Blair itself. I suppose when one digs deep enough, they're apt to find all kinds of evil from the past. Or perhaps it found him. Latched onto him and made him a vessel. And as a result, this dormant evil has been woken up."

"Grace..." someone said. "She's real?"

Tomas's lips curled into that nostalgically sinister smile once again. "Well, Grace *was* real. Her spirit lives on inside the teacher. We burn the teacher, we burn the spirit of Grace..."

"So, this Grace has power over Reinhart?" Donoghue asked, leaning over the bar. "What does she do?"

"The witch convinces people to kill," Tomas said. "Although 'convince' implies some kind of back-and-forth conversation. Negotiation. It is more one-sided than that. She *moves* people to do terrible things. To kill themselves. To kill each other. Even their own loved ones," Tomas lied. "She is speaking through Reinhart, but she also moved him to kill his own dog, is that right? I believe he's responsible for convincing Fred Brown to kill Martha. He's the one who sent a wild animal to kill Martin Welch. If he isn't stopped, you could be next."

"I was there," Officer Gary said from a table. "He was covered in blood. He wasn't right. No one who wasn't cursed would do such a thing."

"We must burn the teacher!" someone shouted. The anger was rising in the room.

"Punishment is the only way!" Tomas said, stoking the growing sentiment. "This town is unclean, and the darkness must be washed out."

"Unclean," several voices said in unison.

"Follow me," Tomas said. "All of you. We must act, now."

* * *

Something had birthed into the air like a pathogen. It infected everyone in the town of Blair. The desperate thirst for revenge was contagious.

The crowd gathered in the town square, where they found John Darski already working. The cross atop the church spire bent downward, a reminder of the town's corruption. A reminder that a fox had entered the henhouse, pulling strings and making the townsfolk do things they would have never thought to do otherwise. However, they were too blinded by fear to realize that the fox they feared was the one directing them to do things. To turn into bloodthirsty monsters themselves. Infiltrating Blair from the inside.

They worked through the night, erecting a structure in the center of the town square with great efficiency. A crude, medieval framework designed to inflict pain.

Tomas directed them in its construction. Several people, including Donoghue, wondered how this highschooler was calling the shots, explaining how to build this device. Still, it was all coming together smoothly. The manner in which Tomas spoke was strong and conclusive, so they complied without question.

It was as if the town of Blair had released some kind of poisonous pheromones in a final act of self-defense, turning its inhabitants into parasites whose only reason for being was to protect their host. All toxins must be flushed out.

Chapter 58
Interlude: 1793

She had warned Nathaniel. He knew the risks involved. Still, the uncoiling of his relationship with this woman had been the most uncivilized. Deep down, Nathaniel knew he was the one responsible for bringing darkness to Blair. That he was the one responsible for his son's death.

He'd brought in evil when he let his pride move into temptation. And then his temptation led to fear, and he lost his grip on the town, on his family. Things were falling apart at the seams, and the only option he'd conceived was to cruelly use this unknown woman, this outsider, as the scapegoat to his sins.

And now Tomas was dead. Overcome by consumption, an unknown disease in a terrifying new world. There would never be peace in the place called Blair ever again.

Yet Nathaniel could never confess to his actions. He would take them to his grave. He didn't feel guilt. He felt shame for being unfaithful to his family. For allowing consumption to cross Blair's borders and infiltrate his quiet oasis.

He returned to Halfmoon Cave the day after they killed Grace. The smell of burning flesh still lingered in the air. Or maybe the scent was burned into his senses, and he was cursed to forever smell that hideous aftermath.

Nathaniel stood in front of the mouth of the cave, reflecting on where things had gone so wrong. This land had once been peaceful—on the surface. However, now, as he stood outside of Halfmoon Cave, the effects of the bizarre eclipse still lingered, same as the scent of death. The patch of grass under his feet appeared gray in the dull, muted sunlight. The calm Winooski River flowing behind him now made his heart ache instead of bringing him solace.

He saw the stones arranged at the mouth of the cave. They had been blessed by a priest, and they meant to act as a barrier to contain the darkness within. But Nathaniel knew it was all a fraud. The stones, like the town of Blair itself, were now cursed. The apparatus that was death had moved into this world and taken his son away from him, and the corpse inside the cave was the navigator, the witch who guided evil's way. But all of that was a lie. He'd brought the darkness to Blair. Not the woman who now slept her restless sleep. Any evil that lay within the cave was a product of his own doing.

The gentle breeze swayed the tree branches above Nathaniel's head, the canopy shielding him from the ugly sky of the eclipse. There was a voice in that breeze.

Nathaniel turned around to find his goat, Midnight, had joined him here, in this cursed resting place. He thought perhaps he had forgotten to latch the enclosure, and Midnight had found his way out of the goat pen and followed him here. Poor thing must have felt as lost and alone as he did. Goats were smart animals; he could probably sense the grief.

"You had a bond with Tomas, did you not?" Nathaniel asked the goat. He approached it quietly, remembering having seen his son talking to the animal. The vision of his son's hand on the goat's brow resonated.

Nathaniel repeated the gesture, resting his hand on the goat's brow. He could feel something within the goat, an awareness he had never picked up on before. Not from this animal or any other.

Then he pulled his hand back in shock.

"She spoke to you..." Nathaniel said. "What did she tell you?"

He watched the goat for a long time, as if foolishly expecting an answer. It watched him. It almost felt as if the animal were judging him.

"What did *you* tell her?"

Nathaniel placed his hand back on the animal's head, and what he saw opened a pit inside of him. He saw his son, Tomas, for a brief moment. And then he saw his own sanity spiraling out of control. There was nothing but madness inside. No—it couldn't be. He saw an endless darkness inside the animal as it stared back at him, unblinking. Judging.

Thousands of voices screaming into an endless void of suffering. Faces writhing in torment, twisting into inhuman displays. Tomas was among them, the condemned. Nathaniel's worst fear realized. His boy, cast into everlasting fire, by his own doing.

The vision began to encircle him, and soon he was being pulled into the hellscape in front of him. He could feel his mind being pulled from his body, breaking in a lunatic flash. He pulled his hand back from the goat, and the darkness ceased, but the pain endured all the same.

The lingering pain was unbearable. Nathaniel looked up to the trees, their branches hanging low over the mouth of Halfmoon Cave.

The twine-spun daisy wheel was nailed into the trunk of the tree. The spot where Grace had turned her curse upon Blair into a tangible relic. It also revealed to Nathaniel a place to climb. Thick branches, accessible from the ground, reached higher, to the place above, where limbs extended from the tree, welcoming him in a noose's embrace.

Your son is dead...because of you...

Blair is in darkness...because of you...

Oh, this goat knew things. It knew... It had guided her, and now it was guiding him. Nathaniel could feel it.

He listened.

Nathaniel, in his final moments, followed the goat's instructions. He lifted himself up into the branches of the tree. Fixed himself in the rounded-off branches and took a final look out toward Lake Champlain.

This ground would be forever cursed. The town of Blair would forever be steeped in darkness. And it was all...his...fault.

Nathaniel let gravity take him, and the branches creaked as they held his weight, suspended above the cave.

Chapter 59
Stu

This was all a huge mistake. Surely it was only a matter of time, Stu thought, until someone came by the jail to help him. He didn't deserve to be here, locked away like a criminal. All of the pain Blair had endured recently had been unloaded onto him. Someone needed to come by and right this wrong. *Someone* needed to realize who was truly behind the events for which he was being charged.

Stu's life had spun radically out of control.

He lay on the cot inside his cell, soaked in the darkness of the eclipse. It felt like a weight pressing down on his body, like he was the only one in town who knew the truth.

He heard echoes of footsteps through the gloom. There were so many, all treading in Stu's direction. They were accompanied by voices. Angry voices. Voices starved for vengeance.

Stu's heart sank as realization settled in—whoever had come for him was not here to help.

"Stuart Reinhart," a voice echoed from within the gloom. Stu got up from the cot, approached the cell door, and tightened his fists around the bars. He watched as Gary White, the officer who'd arrested him, entered. He was accompanied by the familiar faces of Henry Donoghue and John Darski. Behind them followed one of his students, Hector Stroud.

"It's my duty to inform you of the severity of your transgressions," Officer Gary continued. "Your arrest for animal cruelty and murder is only the beginning. In fact, the community of Blair is trying you for crimes far more serious. Crimes against the town—for putting all of your neighbors and colleagues in grave danger. You are guilty of opening the door for evil forces to enter our town. For introducing witchcraft and black magic and forcing these ideas onto the children of Blair. Thankfully, very few have subscribed to your extreme ideas, but your followers are out there. You are to give us the whereabouts of these two other wretched souls; otherwise, you will be tried as a witch yourself. Do you understand?"

"What the fuck are you talking about?" Stu said, backing away from the bars of his cell. "This is insane. I'm not a witch. I'm a school-teacher!"

"Open it up," Henry Donoghue ordered. "I want to look him in the eye." Officer Gary complied and unlocked the bars that separated Stu from the outside world.

Henry entered the cell. The vitriolic look on his face was confusing to Stu, as this was not the face of his friend. The big man struck Stu in the stomach, knocking the wind out of him. Stu doubled over in pain. When he looked up, through blurred vision, the looks he got in return were filled with an animalistic hunger for vengeance.

They wanted justice, and they didn't care how it came. Stu understood the terrible things that had fallen upon this town recently. He knew the collective temperature among his neighbors was high. The people of Blair were dead set on compensation for the pain and fear they'd experienced, and they weren't going to stop until they got it.

Stu was yanked out of the jail cell with so much force, he thought they were going to dislocate his shoulder. They led him out of the jail, through the dark abyss of the eclipse, and into the town square. His picturesque town had changed dramatically beneath the gray. Two fires had been built in the center of the town square, their glowing light muted by the gloom. Yet they'd also put a spotlight on something in the middle of the street.

A structure glowed white in the light. Two wooden pillars had been erected in the town square like twin skyscrapers, devised to support a makeshift pulley system. It was clear this had been thrown together overnight, under the gloom of the eclipse. But what was more painfully obvious was the core of the whole thing. The dark centerpiece of the morbid punishment device cooked up by Stu's bloodthirsty neighbors.

A wooden cross lay flat at the base of the structure. Ropes threaded up through the wood and looped back to the top of each pillar by way of metal attachments. Stu choked as realization dawned on him.

They intended to crucify him.

The craftsmanship that must have gone into erecting such a structure in the time Stu had been in that jail cell was astonishing. He thought of the noises he'd heard in the distance through the night, or day—as if it mattered anymore—and came to realize his neighbors had been building this...for him. They intended to hurt him, and they'd been planning to for a long time.

Stu tried to resist as they led him toward the ominous structure. It towered over the gathering crowd, casting two long, dark shadows onto the dirt of the town square like the outline of a crime scene. In the center of the black rectangles was another shadow, that of the upside-down cross still hanging from the church's spire. It hung there ominously, as if tracing an outline, telling the bloodthirsty residents of Blair—X marks the spot.

Put your cross of punishment here...

Stu was hungry and weak. His ability to fight back was lacking at best. He was spun around and forced down onto the flat surface of the cross. Someone pulled his arms and lined them up straight along the wood, and he could feel rope tightening around his wrists and arms. Someone else pulled his legs straight, and a length of rope was quickly fastened around his legs and ankles, far too tightly—he could feel his skin ripping beneath his clothes as the rope tightened around his limbs.

He'd never felt so uncomfortable in his life. The imperfect construction pulled his limbs in painful and unnatural angles. It was made to be uncomfortable...but for how long would he have to endure it?

He felt a shuddering bang as something beneath him slammed into place. Then he felt his stomach in his chest as the cross moved. It was thrust upward, lifting Stu above the crowd. He felt as if he were as high in the air as the church's spire itself, casting its long, ungodly shadow.

To his dismay, the cross kept moving. Before he knew it, Stu was facing downward, feeling gravity pull his body toward the ground. The only thing holding him up were the ropes, tied tightly and squeezing his wrists and ankles against the unforgiving wood. He glanced up at the crowd as he was turned upside down, rotated like a pig on a spit. He saw eyes on him, staring.

He felt the blood rush to his head, and he was addled and dizzy as he floated above the town square. The cool night air grazed his face, and he suddenly gagged, but it wasn't from being hung upside down. It was the smell of something rotten wafting into his face.

"What is that?" Stu struggled, the ropes pulling tight against his skin. There was a heavy silence among those gathered. Only the dead stares of people he'd called his neighbors, his friends. Far below, he could see the stares of Henry Donoghue, John Darski, his friends Cliff and Ted, and even some of his colleagues from Blair High School. Logical, sensible folks who'd assembled to partake in turning the clock back to 1793—turning it all the way back to a time steeped in witch panic.

He saw Principal Holden and recalled being told to take some time off. He regretted not backing off; continuing to dig for answers. Yet part of him knew that nothing would have changed his fate. He saw Mr. and Mrs. Welch among the crowd and thought...

Oh God...

"Please," Stu said. "You're all making a huge mistake. Think about what you're doing."

The crowd only stood by, as if awaiting instructions. They looked angry, confused, and, worst of all, ravenous. Like hungry dogs waiting for a command.

They just watched, as if Stu's words didn't register at all. As if the glowing light undulating on their faces had them in a kind of sanguinary trance.

"Henry," Stu coughed, the word dry, caught in his throat. "Henry, please."

"Don't give me *Henry, please*," Henry mocked. "You are to tell us where the Brogdon girl went. Tell us where she went with that boy... that outsider."

"I don't know where they went," Stu said, thinking that even if he did, he wouldn't say.

"They were students of yours," Henry said. "And we know they bought into the corrupt lessons you taught in that classroom. They're of your ilk—therefore, they must be eliminated. Otherwise, Blair will never be clean! You know where they are." His words lingered in the smoke-stained air.

"I don't know where they—ah!" Stu cried out in pain. Something pulled from the side of the structure, and the ropes tightened. It felt like if they pulled any tighter, the pressure would tear his arms clean off. He could feel his muscles stretching to the max. He didn't know how much more of this pain he could endure.

"Tell us where they are and what they plan to do," John demanded from below. His hands were still on the lever that controlled the network of ropes that kept the cross inverted. His eyes burned with hatred. They seemed distant, almost empty. "If you turn them in, if you tell us everything, we will let you down. You will be spared from punishment."

"I'm telling you," Stu gasped, his throat as dry as sandpaper. It was growing more and more difficult to breathe upside down. And the smell...the horrific scent lingering in the air seemed to be getting closer. "I don't know where—ah! I don't know where they are!"

"You don't seem to understand," Henry said. The flames of the bonfires bounced behind him, throwing shadows all around the town square. The silhouettes of people looked like rats forming a circle around their king. Someone walked up behind Henry and dipped a torch into one of the raging fires.

Stu recognized in that moment—the crucifix, the structure he was affixed to, was meant to be ignited. All wood. Perhaps it would be quick.

"If you don't give us the information we require...we will burn it out of you. And then we will burn Brogdon and Roberts."

This is it, Stu thought. His fate would mirror that of Grace [Last Name Redacted]. He wondered if they were going to slice his heart out of his body as well...bury him inside the cave and—

That smell...

"This isn't normal," Stu choked. "I have rights! This is murder!"

It was as if time stopped at the utterance of that word. *Murder*. It sounded surreal rolling off his tongue. Like an echo.

"Did you really find my boy?" Mrs. Welch's voice cracked as she stepped forward from the crowd. Her gentle, good-hearted voice was distinct to Stu's ears. He remembered how soothing her voice had been the first time he sat down with the Welches during parent-teacher conferences a year ago. Martin had always been one of his standout students, and it was clear he got all of his best qualities from his parents. However, there was no mercy in her voice tonight. Instead, there was an accusatory sting in her words as she looked up at Stu. There would be no shred of calm for Stu as he hung suspended in the Blair town square.

"Or did you do it?" she asked. "You didn't find my boy that day... you killed him. Didn't you?"

No, Stu wanted to say, but he felt his throat closing. The angle from which his body hung made it difficult to breathe. He couldn't tell if it was his vision failing him, or if the effects of the eclipse were waning, but the gray seemed to give way, slightly, to a darker black, a more natural-looking night sky.

I didn't do this.

"Stu, you claimed to have found Martin Welch near Owl's Head Park," Henry said, holding his hand out to keep John from torching the structure. At least for now. "You claimed to have happened upon the aftermath. Why should we believe *you* didn't kill Martin? Didn't rip his throat right out with your teeth? Why should we believe *you* didn't kill Martha Brown, Ray Parilla? We found you covered in your own dog's blood. You refused to disclose the books you teach in your classroom. Ultimately, *you*, Stuart Reinhart, have done this to Blair. You unleashed evil against your own community."

Stu wanted to tell them how sorry he was for what happened to Martin. He wanted to beg, to plead for them to let him down. He wanted to talk about this, to work together with his neighbors. They had to know this wasn't the way—that he was innocent.

Stu could feel movement below him. It felt like the structure was swaying in the wind, except there wasn't a breeze.

He could feel hands gripping the narrow, bottom edge of the inverted crucifix. Something had crawled up one of the towers of the structure and leaned across to meet him in the middle, suspended in the air. Stu felt fingers close around his legs. Whatever it was balanced itself above Stu's body. It was a person...someone who didn't belong up here. And whoever it was brought that smell with them, causing Stu to retch.

Stu blinked rapidly, scanning the crowd below—above—him, to see if anyone was seeing what he was seeing. Something was crawling on him, like an insect caught on a net. But all the eyes below were blank and lacking—except for one pair. He saw Tomas Fischer among the crowd, watching with sadistic awareness, a terrible grin on his face as his plan to drive the town of Blair into chaos unfolded.

It was all him...

The thought occurred to Stu as his personal space disappeared. It was Tomas Fischer who killed Martin Welch. Tomas who was responsible for all of this. The vengeance-seeking townspeople had gathered together to punish whoever was tearing their town apart, yet they stood with him instead, watching as an innocent person suffered. The ultimate scapegoat.

The thing lowered itself down—up—Stu's body, digging sharp fingernails into the flesh of his thighs. It ascended until it was face-to-face with him—suspended in the air. Stu slowly opened his eyes to see the dead, half-rotted face of Martin Welch staring back at him.

As Stu looked into the open, cavernous dark of Martin's gaping mouth, his mind collapsed. Martin was dead. Stu had found him torn to pieces. This wasn't possible. None of this was possible. This was nothing but a horrible nightmare. His mind and body had been flipped upside down. Reality seemed to cave in on itself at the very moment Martin dug his teeth into Stu's jugular.

John Darski finally lowered the flaming torch beneath the structure. A brilliant flame ignited, glowing in the white light under the shadows of the eclipse.

Stu felt the blast of heat on his scalp and his ears, even burning the back of his neck. The blood pouring from his throat spilled down, coating the sides of his face. It felt like boiling lava on an open wound. Martin fed ravenously. Mindlessly. Stu's eyes rolled back, and the last thing he saw was the shadow of the inverted cross in the dirt.

Chapter 60
Jaycie and Calvin

When Jaycie and Calvin reached the mouth of Halfmoon Cave, the strength of the eclipse was already beginning to wane. They stood at the cave's entrance, covered in blood and afraid. The intense gray reflection of the sky was deteriorating. There wasn't much time left.

Jaycie had doubts. She worried that their sacrifice of that innocent goat might be for nothing, but she had to trust Jax, and it was too late to second-guess. She had to get Grace into the sunlight. Then this would all be over.

Jax had told her everything. What he learned from being around Tomas Fischer, being under his supernatural hold. Tomas had told him what it was like to live in 1793, what it felt like to have his blood drained from his mortal body, and what it was like to die. He explained how the legend of the Halfmoon Cave witch was true, yet Grace was not always a witch. No, she had turned to the magic of the dark lord, forced onto that path by Nathaniel Fischer.

Jax told her that Tomas had tried to get close to Grace before, that the only way to protect yourself from her posthumous powers was to cover yourself in pure blood. The blood of the innocent. And most importantly, he'd learned that this once-in-a-lifetime eclipse acted as a window, the time in which those who had taken Tomas's oath would permanently join him as one of his own. The event was also the one time in which Grace could be set free from her own oath to the dark magic that had doomed her as a witch.

This had to work. It was too late to turn back now, and she was determined not to fail.

They entered the cave as quietly as possible. Their hands began to tremble, shaking from the fear of what lay ahead and the shock of being covered in blood. Their panting breaths and unsteady nerves took over as the blackness of the cave swallowed them. The darkness within the cave was immeasurable compared to the gloom in the sky cast by the waning eclipse. They were tiny vessels diving deep into the unknown. Specks floating out to space, careening into an endless void. And worst of all, they had no safety vest. No escape route if things went bad.

The incessant stillness of the dark was home to a gnawing sound. A disgusting warbling that sounded as if hundreds of creatures were surrounding them on their descent into the cave. The walls were alive with the sounds of scratching and feeding. It made their skin crawl. Despite the sounds, there was in fact only a single presence deep within the oppressive recesses of the cave. Their end game.

It was a complex thing, Jaycie thought as they progressed inward. Grace was thought by many to be an entity consumed by pure evil. A vessel in and of itself, fully engrossed in whatever cosmic evil she had let in all those years ago, consumed until Grace, whoever she had been before, was now less human—less of herself than she had been when she was alive. And if this thing inside the cave was still alive, as some theorized, it certainly did not resemble the victim who'd died in vain all those years ago. She had become a myth, molded by the secondhand accounts of those responsible for her end.

Jaycie could hear Calvin breathing next to her. He was afraid, and she was too, but they stood together.

She blinked, adjusting her eyes to the darkness. She could see it—

see *her*, what they'd come for. An otherworldly being inside the cave. Something from a different time and world—a world that no longer existed. A remnant from a time in human history that was (Jaycie couldn't fathom it) more barbaric than the present. The entity that occupied Halfmoon Cave was older than Blair itself, and the evil that resided *inside* her had sunk its dark roots into the town and held on. Until now.

To Jaycie's shock, the figure was sitting upright. It was as if Grace had been waiting for their arrival as her body decomposed within the cave. The fabric that covered her remains had withered greatly, exposing the extent of her flesh's putrefaction.

The fact that the body had only partially decomposed after centuries of being hidden away inside Halfmoon Cave was astonishing. Perhaps it was some sort of mummification post-burning that had preserved the body. Or maybe the body had been writhing with so much evil that it remained unnaturally intact for all these years. Regardless, the stench was unbearable.

The skin that remained was covered by burns and scarred over. The charred black and gray no longer resembled human flesh. Her face looked as if it had been frozen in time, the vengeful grimace of an old folk legend. Her mutilated legs hung off of the stone pyre like a child's legs dangling from a doctor's exam table.

The figure did not move upon their arrival; however, Jaycie could feel its gaze. It did not have to move for her to know it was aware of them, and it was watching.

To break her hold, she must be set free. To break her hold, she must see the sun.

Get her into the sunlight, Jaycie recalled. *Just get her into the sunlight and this will all be over soon.*

Jaycie stepped forward, her hand shaking. She offered the Devil's Spiral flower to the witch, unsure if it was even a good idea to do so. The original purple flower from the mantel of the Fischer House.

The cave was dead silent save for their gasping, panicked breaths. Calvin looked back and forth from the body to the cave entrance. It was only a matter of time before Tomas and Hector arrived, and he wasn't sure he and Jaycie could handle a witch *and* two vampires. And if the angry mob descended on them, what would their fate be then?

Suddenly, Grace took a breath. A long and corroded inhale, like the creaking of a floorboard. To their surprise and horror, in a jarring display of impossible logic, the witch stood up, her ragged and charred legs holding up the rest of her body in a morbid display of strength. She stood there staring at the pair who dared to step into her den.

Horror washed over Jaycie like a tsunami, but she moved closer, holding the flower up.

Please just take it. We're not here to hurt you.

Grace took it, sucking the flower into her mouth like a piece of debris. She hummed a sound of nostalgic pleasure, shooting a revolting chill through Jaycie's bones.

"Now what?" Calvin whispered. "How are we supposed to move her out of here?"

Jaycie thought for a moment. The eclipse was ending, that much she knew. It was as if the sky over Blair knew it was time. The darkness was slowly making way for light, inviting them outside.

There was no turning back. It had to be done now, and Jaycie knew they would have to physically guide Grace out of the cave. She took a breath and nodded at Calvin as daylight began to sliver into the cave.

"I'm going to take her hand," Jaycie said. "Let's go."

She reached out to touch the hand of the witch when suddenly, the brimming light from the mouth of the cave darkened once again.

Two silhouetted figures stood between them and the outside world.

"Shit," Calvin breathed.

At the cave's entrance, Tomas and Hector stood waiting. And certainly not far behind was the rest of Blair, those who'd heeded the call to action on the beach. They were out for blood.

Hector still had blood coating his mouth from where Calvin had caught him earlier with the skateboard. His disheveled appearance gave Calvin a slight boost of confidence, which he desperately needed in this moment. He had bested Hector once before; he could do it again. They had come so far. The hard part was over—it *had* to be over. They hadn't made it this far only to be stopped now. The goat sacrifice would not be for nothing—in fact, he realized their plan was working. They had not been immediately annihilated upon entering the cave; therefore, Jaycie's theory was right. Which meant Jax was right...

I can do this, Calvin thought. They needed to get Grace outside. He could simply grab her and rush the entrance of the cave. One quick motion toward the light. Tomas and Hector wouldn't be expecting it. It would be like punching in a touchdown from the one-yard line. Let them try and stop him.

Jaycie's fingers twitched in a reflexive attempt to will Calvin to stop, but it was too late. He was already in motion. Unfortunately, Jaycie was not the only one who saw his plan for what it was. In a split second, Tomas was inside the cave and on top of Calvin.

Grace crumbled to the ground like a falling house of cards. Jaycie screamed as she watched Calvin's body go stiff underneath Tomas.

"Don't move," Tomas growled, looking up at her with a sadistic grin on his face, sharp canines protruding from his sickly gums. She watched as his form changed before her eyes, his face shedding the veil of youth to show his true form—a pale, beastly face, alien in nature. His fingers elongated, stretching over Calvin's face, creating a sort of cocoon around her friend's head. His oblong fingernails sharpened at the ends like paring knives. Jaycie watched in horror as Tomas's index finger bent and twisted, hovering outside the entrance of Calvin's ear.

"If you move," he said, still grinning up at her, "I will skull-fuck your friend here until he forgets his own name."

Jaycie felt nauseous at the sight of that finger, bent and rotten like a dead tree branch. She began to sweat; she could still hear the gnawing sound nearby. Grace had stood up and was now facing the wall, her back exposed. Insects crawled on her scorched flesh, some diving in and out of open, gaping pores.

Hector limped over to Tomas. "This is why you should have committed to our movement when we asked you to," he chimed in. "Did you think it was smart to come here and try to kill a witch? Do you have any idea how powerful she is? Are you two out of your fucking minds? You feel her behind you, don't you? The torment she can put into your mind is far greater than anything *we* can do to you."

"That's right," Tomas snarled, still pinning Calvin to the ground. His finger wriggled around the entrance of his ear like a worm. "But we're going to give you one last chance to join us. To make good on your mistake."

The crucifix had been knocked from Calvin's hand, and Hector bent down and picked it up off the ground. "This only works in the movies, doll," he said, snapping the cross in half. "Besides," he continued, "you know as well as I do that there is no god."

"What?" Jaycie said, shaking. She remembered the words NO GOD smeared in dirt on the side of the church, and a chill crept down her spine.

"You're the one who wrote that silly little message, aren't you?" Tomas laughed. "Pathetic cry for help. Nobody cares...what, did you think someone was going to see that and *do something*? Pitiful fools. But I'll have you know, you got it half right. You see, there is an afterlife. I've seen it. I exist in it. And I can tell you, it is every bit as cold and lonely as the life you're living. If you're lucky, you'll only experience the blank darkness of nothing when you die. However, if you end up like me—like Jax—you'll continue on, existing with no purpose. Doomed to chase an insatiable hunger. To wander an empty existence with only spite to look forward to."

"We didn't write those words," Jaycie said, tears rolling down her cheeks. She could hear the witch gnawing behind her, getting closer as Grace inched her way along the cave's wall.

"We didn't write those words," Tomas mocked, the tip of his nail now beginning to penetrate Calvin's ear.

"Yeah, don't be stupid," Hector added. "Are you joining us or what? I recommend you do. I promise you, death is far lonelier if you go by yourself."

"And you stand no chance against a witch, especially alone," Tomas said.

"That's where you're wrong," Jaycie said. "We didn't come here to kill her...we came here to free her."

Tomas's grin contorted into a scowl. "This is what happens when you get involved in things that don't concern you." His jaw came unhinged, his blackened teeth exposed, hovering just above Calvin's face.

In that moment, another shadow entered the cave, moving quickly. Tomas sensed it, whipped around to intercept it, but the shadow was too fast. It took Hector down in one swift motion, a splatter of blood exploding from his destroyed abdomen.

Jaycie locked eyes with Jax. She stood frozen, overjoyed that he was actually here. However, Tomas was on him quickly. He leapt through the air, sinking his teeth into Jax's shoulder. The two rolled, tangled together like animals fighting.

"Go!" Jax grunted, powering his way on top of Tomas. He grabbed for the broken pieces of the crucifix and stabbed them into Tomas's gut. Tomas let out a monstrous scream but continued fighting, slashing at Jax's face with his razor-sharp nails. He wasn't going to stop, not until...

Jaycie turned toward Grace, the old scent of burnt flesh wafting in her face. She grabbed both arms and, with all her might, began to move toward the mouth of the cave. The sunlight was already shifting, spilling through the gloom. She moved as quickly as she could, lungs burning and legs throbbing.

Tomas saw this and swiped at Jaycie's legs as she passed, but Jax kept him busy, plunging his teeth into Tomas's arm. Then she passed by Hector, who was split in half at the waist yet still animated. He, too, swiped at Jaycie, scratching her calf. She endured the pain and pushed through—there was no time to stop and wince at a scratch. No, this was it.

She pulled Grace out of the cave and into the light as the eclipse broke.

Jaycie squinted as sunlight hit her face. Although it had been only two days of total darkness, it felt like forever. She let go of the witch as they both spilled to the ground. As the sunlight hit the witch's burnt flesh, the old corpse let out a piercing shriek that rang out over Lake Champlain. The scream echoed on into a thousand voices, releasing centuries' worth of suffering—centuries' worth of buried secrets finally seeing the light.

Jaycie closed her eyes and threw her hands up to her ears to block the devastating sound. It only lasted a moment, because when she opened her eyes again, the scene in front of her was peaceful. The figure she had tumbled out of the cave with was now looking at her, not as an old witch, but as the young woman she had been before Blair made her into a monster. The moment was fleeting as licks of sunlight danced on her unblemished, glistening skin. The woman's red hair was brilliant in the morning sun.

Jaycie watched in relief and awe as Grace absorbed the sun, melting away until what was left became a whirlwind of ash in the air. The breeze gently carried away the spiral of dust, and the Half-moon Cave witch was finally free.

All was not quiet, though. Not yet. Jaycie looked in time to find Tomas and Hector writhing on the cave floor, still drenched in darkness. They howled in pain, seething at their failure. Jaycie knelt down and looked at Tomas at eye level. She wanted to make sure he knew that she was the one who had stopped him.

As she watched them die, Jax approached, stopping right before the line of light inside the cave, as if it were an invisible barrier. He looked at his sister, who had achieved what she set out to do, and he was proud of her.

"Jax." Her voice cracked.

The sound of a whirling siren could be heard nearby, but to Jaycie it sounded far off and dreamy. She didn't want to waste this inevitably last moment with Jax, but he was direct with his next words.

"You have to go."

"I'm sorry," she said.

"Stop apologizing." Jax smiled. His time left was short, yet he needed for Jaycie to be okay. "This isn't over...Henry Donoghue is still in the town square with an angry mob, and they're dangerous. I don't think they're going to stop."

"But I can't leave you here," she said.

Calvin stepped out of the cave, joining Jaycie's side.

"Go to the lake house," Jax said. "Blair isn't safe. Just go."

Jax sat down on the ground as Calvin pulled Jaycie away. "Come on," he said. "It's time."

As they escaped around the edge of the woods, the scent of burning wood filled the air. There was something heavy in the atmosphere following the break of the eclipse. Although the light had returned and all appeared normal, there was still a sense of danger in the air. There was a nagging question in Jaycie's stomach: Why would people want to hurt them? She took Jax's word and wouldn't stay to find out. They began their trek toward the Adirondack Mountains and out of Blair.

Chapter 61
Jaycie and Calvin

The sun was shining brightly in the sky. It was intense compared to the blanket of darkness they'd drowned in for the past two days. But Jaycie and Calvin moved in between the trees, staying hidden until they reached Jaycie's house.

Jaycie could feel hatred lingering in the air. It circled the drain in the aftermath of the eclipse, leaving some of the residents of Blair in a state of bloodthirst. It couldn't last forever, but for now, it wasn't safe.

"You know how to drive, right?" Jaycie asked as she picked up the keys from the kitchen counter. She stopped for a moment, worried where her parents and Mabel were. Where they part of the mob in the town square Jax had warned her about? Were they targets of that mob? Jaycie felt a pit in her stomach at the thought, but she pushed it down, for now.

They needed to avoid being seen until they reached Route 3. That would take them out of Blair and into Lake Placid, but they needed to be discreet. The smell of burning was getting stronger, but there was dead silence.

"I have my learner's permit, but that's it," Calvin said. "I haven't practiced since I lived in the city."

"Good enough." Jaycie handed him the keys. "I'll tell you which way to go."

They got into the car, backed out of the driveway, and slowly rolled onto State Route 3. Jaycie always paid close attention on their family trips. She would look out the window on the way up to their cabin in Lake Placid, watching the trees go by. The image of the mountains coming into view on the horizon was etched into her mind. Those mountains always signaled that vacation fun was just ahead, a weekend of campfire and games. Now, that same view of the Adirondacks signaled safety. Jaycie peered into the rearview mirror, seeing a pillar of smoke rise above people's homes in Blair.

The Brogdon family cabin always felt like a safe haven for Jaycie, even as a little girl. So if there was ever a place to escape to, this was it.

It took an hour of careful, slow coasting, but they made it to the end of Route 3. Jaycie pointed, and Calvin turned the wheel, following her instruction. When her family's cabin came into view, she felt relief wash over her. It was exactly as she remembered, in all of its quaint charm. A black, two-story A-frame house with windows that stretched from the ground level all the way up to the roof. The cabin boasted a porch in the back with a breathtaking view of the Adirondack landscape. An uninterrupted view with nothing but the sky, the mountains, and Lake Placid. The majesty of the view made Jaycie tear up a little, like something so beautiful had no business existing in a world with such ugliness.

Jaycie had a catalog's worth of memories of sitting and watching the sunset with her family. She got choked up when she saw three camping chairs sitting vacantly, knowing she'd never be able to share this view with Jax or Martin again.

Jaycie punched the code into to the front door. It had been a grueling journey to this point. After everything that had unfolded in Blair, and without a moment to recover, they entered the cabin in silence. They were mentally and physically exhausted, still covered in goat's blood, but they made it. They were alive, and they were safe.

"There are two guest rooms downstairs," Jaycie said. "You can settle in and wash up down there if you want. There should be towels and extra clothes in the closet. We always kept vacation clothes out here." She took a breath, feeling heavy with melancholy for being here without her family. Knowing that Calvin would wear her brother's clothes...

Calvin nodded and thanked her. It would be good to get out of their bloodstained clothes and splash water on their faces.

Jaycie made her way into the first-floor bedroom, the room she'd shared with Jax. Two twin-sized beds were arranged on the right side of the room, each with a nightstand and a lamp. A pair of closet doors ran flat along the opposite wall, and there was a third door for a private bathroom in the middle.

Jaycie got into the shower and let the heaviness go. Steam gathered into a cloud on the ceiling. The blood of the innocent and wicked alike, that which had stained her skin, melted off of her body. It washed down the drain, but the invisible scars would remain forever.

She got out of the shower, wrapped herself in a towel, and sat down on the bed. She let out a sigh, still not believing what she had just gone through. In this moment of solitude, the weight of it all finally crashed down on her.

The cabin was quiet except for the sound of running water coming from Calvin's shower. Yet...

One of the closet doors stood ajar.

Someone was standing inside the closet.

Jaycie jumped up from the bed and screamed. "Who's there?"

A figure was standing just beyond the half-open door, an apparition obscured by the darkness, but Jaycie would recognize her brother's blonde hair anywhere.

"Jax?" she trembled.

Jaycie stood frozen as her brother's eyes watched her from inside the closet. It couldn't be. This had to be a hallucination. She'd watched her brother die in Halfmoon Cave. Hadn't she? Did he manage to escape somehow?

"Jax is that—" She couldn't get out a complete thought. Overwhelmed with emotion, she began to cry.

A knock came at the bedroom door, and Jaycie put a hand over her mouth, stifling her cry.

"Hey, are you okay?" Calvin asked, peering in.

A lump caught in Jaycie's throat, and she nodded. "I'm okay, thank you."

"I get it," Calvin said. He looked around the room briefly, and his glance became fixed on the closet door. It was closed. Yet his eyes locked there for a second, as if acknowledging something, a wan smile on his face. "The sun is setting," he said. "It's kind of pretty. Thought you might want to go watch it. Kind of forget about things for a minute."

Jaycie's breath caught in her throat. What had Calvin seen? Why did he pause? More importantly, what had *she* seen? Yet she quietly nodded. She stood up, got dressed and followed Calvin outside. He was right, the sunset was beautiful. She looked out at the colors blending over the mountain range in the distance, and then she said. "I don't want to forget."

Calvin looked at her. He knew exactly what she was getting at, and he didn't need to say anything in return. She had deep roots in Blair. He didn't. Perhaps it would be easier for him to leave behind the last couple of weeks. To forget. While he was already thinking of what was next, after Blair, it wasn't so simple for Jaycie.

"Thank you for being a friend," he said.

"Ditto."

They looked back out over the horizon and noticed a plume of smoke in the distance, rising above the mountains.

"Is that north?" Calvin asked.

Jaycie nodded. "I think so."

"Do you think that's coming from Blair?"

"It's possible," she sighed. "Although we're about forty miles away. It might be hard to see smoke from that distance, even if we are up in the mountains."

"I wonder what's going on there right now," Calvin said.

Jaycie shook her head. "Nothing good, I'd imagine."

The gray smoke swelled and dissolved into the evening twilight until it blended into the sky above. It made Jaycie wonder what was happening back home. Was this Blair's fate? If a pillar of smoke could easily blend into the clouds above until it was invisible, could the same be said of Martin? Of her brother? Herself? If a community, a whole town, could let fear fester inside them to the point of rot—to the point they destroyed their neighbors, themselves—would it be better to burn and be forgotten? Perhaps, from the beginning, it was always meant to burn. Always meant to go up in smoke and fade into the clouds until forgotten. Perhaps the good times always do come to an end.

Acknowledgements

This is the part where I do my best to thank all of those who have continued to support me on this journey. Writing a book is a (mostly) solitary process which doesn't really work without the right support system.

First and foremost, to my wife, Carly. Thank you for helping me make it through this difficult year. Your support and patience have been a big part in making my obsessive passion for writing actually work. I love you.

To my editor, Caroline Knecht — I try to look at each book as an opportunity to become a better writer. Not only in terms of skill and storytelling ability, but also to be able to view things from a different perspective. You've been a key part of that process.

When went to my first book/horror convention, I didn't know anybody. I need to give a shoutout to those absolute gems who have taken me in and made me feel like I belong in this community. Thank you all for being a friend as well as an inspiration to me. It means more to me than you can all know. Clay McLeod Chapman, Vaughn A. Jackson, Stephanie Pierre, L.C. Marino, Corey Farrenkopf, Angela Sylvanie, Hilary Wilson, Jenny Kiefer, Christopher Michael

Blake, Garrett Boatman – thank you all for giving me a place to call home.

A big part of being in this book community thing are the people who bring a positive spin and help you discover some of the best books which aren't typically talked about. The folks from BookTok and beyond who I consider good friends! Anny Wilkes, C.P. Bearden, JB McLaurin, Jess Dotson, Veronica, Jim Groves, Crys Evans, Mickey Tompkins, Tristan Zelden, Jon Wesley Huff, Aeron, Nita, Deathly Rose and so many more!

Finally, my longtime friends and family who have continued to support me through the years. If you didn't give up on me after reading my first book in 2019, you're a real one. Josh Kline, Jazz Khalid, Fatimah, Nia, Kelvin Canda, Hilary Kaufman, Becca Perry, Shawn O'Donnell, Mark Thigpen, John Pallicar, Dan Maragni.

Finally, a special thanks to you, reader. You gave this book a chance and that means the world to me. If you don't mind giving this book a quick review online (whether you liked or disliked the book - every review counts), that would be greatly appreciated.

Tunes

15 songs to pair with reading of In The Shadow of a Broken Spire:

Korn - Thoughtless
YOB - Beauty in Falling Leaves
All Shall Perish - The Past Will Haunt Us Both
Rancid - Liberty and Freedom
Woods of Desolation - Like Falling Leaves
Soundgarden - Fell on Black Days
Alice in Chains - Down in a Hole
Abigail Williams - Into The Sleep
Dragged Into Sunlight - I, Aurora
Disentomb - Your Prayers Echo into Nothingness
Immolation - Illumination
Black Dahlia Murder - Moonlight Equilibrium
Gaza - Mostly Hair and Bone Now
Decapitated - A View From a Hole
Cattle Decapitation - Time's Cruel Curtain

About the Author

Ed Flora is a Brooklyn, New York native currently living in Westchester with his wife and their dog. He is an author, musician and self-proclaimed, semi-professional, amateur home-chef. His previous novel, The Triangle Forest, and more are available on gravesendbooks.com.